VIENNA SUMMER

Nancy Buckingham

St. Martin's Press, New York

Library of Congress Cataloging in Publication Data

Buckingham, Nancy.
  Veinna summer.

  I. Title.
PZ4.B923Vi 1979   [PR6052.U26]   823'.9'14   79-4895
ISBN 0-312-84579-0

1

May 1897

Men were much bolder here than in England. Victoria tried not to notice that every man who strolled past their park bench in the sunny Volksgarten gave them a glance of unhurried appraisal.

It was her stepmother who caught their attention, of course. Whether army officers resplendent in their uniforms of sky blue and scarlet or dark blue and white, with cascades of gold braid and swords swinging at the belt; or grave, bearded gentlemen in dusty frock coats, who looked like professors; or argumentative young fellows in floppy hats and flapping cloaks, who might well have been their students, men of all types and men of all ages turned their heads to admire Franziska.

But Franziska herself seemed blithely unaware of them. She leaned back with closed eyes, her face protected from the sun's harmful rays by her silk-fringed parasol. There was an air of suppressed excitement about her, though; a tension that had been growing more evident all day, despite her attempts to hide it. It must be thrilling for her, Victoria realized, to be back in her native Vienna after . . . how many years would it be? Everything here was so different from Birmingham; even from London, which Victoria had visited on two occasions. It was all so exotically foreign, so *theatrical*, her father would have described it delightedly.

'Why did you never persuade Papa to come to Vienna for a visit, Franziska?' she asked. 'He would have loved it.'

Her stepmother, jolted out of her reverie, tilted the parasol aside and gave her a reproving frown.

'Don't speak English, Vicky, keep to German now. The only way to become really fluent in a language is to use it constantly.'

'Sorry!' Victoria repeated the question in German, and there was a momentary hesitation before Franziska replied.

'Can you imagine your father sparing enough time away from his theatre? I used to have difficulty persuading him to take a few days' holiday each summer so we could all go to the seaside. Besides, I was happy to remain in England while dear James was alive. It was only afterwards that I felt this longing to return.'

They fell into silence once more. A small boy in blue petticoats came bowling his hoop along the path at a great pace, pursued by an anxious young nursemaid. Three nuns walked past sedately, whispering among themselves. A heavenly scent of hyacinths drifted toward them from the massed flowerbeds, and from somewhere beyond the trees Victoria could hear the throbbing beat of a military band. Relaxed by the languid warmth of the late spring afternoon, she had to stifle a yawn.

It had been a short night for them, following a tiring journey. The channel crossing, Victoria's first sea voyage, had been rather rough, and the Orient Express had been delayed for several hours at Munich while a faulty locomotive was replaced. They had not arrived at Vienna's Westbahnhof until past midnight. By the time a cab had conveyed them through the dark wet streets to their pension accommodation in the Spiegelgasse and they had taken some refreshment, it was well into the early hours.

Franziska stirred and consulted the silver pendant watch at her breast. It was the second time she had done so within ten minutes.

'It's time for *Jause*, Vicky.'

'*Jause?* What's that?'

'It is like tea in England, only in Vienna we drink coffee. And the pastries are the most delicious in the world, I promise you.' Franziska rose to her feet in a graceful movement. 'Come, child, and we'll find a suitable café.'

'I wish you'd stop calling me child,' Victoria objected. 'I'm eighteen now.'

'That is no age at all.'

'Yet you've told me often enough that you were earning your own living by the time you were fourteen. Anyway, it was only yesterday that you asked me to call you Franziska instead of Stepmama.'

'Can you wonder at it? I've always felt it put years on me, having you use that term.' She nodded impatiently. 'Oh, very well, I'll try to

6

remember. But I do wish you wouldn't be so argumentative, Vicky. It's very tiresome.'

They left the Volksgarten by the gates opposite the Burg Theater, a splendid edifice in the Renaissance style. Looking across the width of the Ringstrasse, the great boulevard that encircled the inner city, Victoria saw that the military band was performing to a large audience in a sunny open space between two leaping fountains in front of the gothic-spired Rathaus. But Franziska turned the other way into narrower streets hemmed in by tall buildings.

Before leaving England they had ordered new clothes, and Franziska had decreed that they should drop their strict mourning now for something less severe. Victoria's dress was a pale lavender poplin, while Franziska wore a skirt and jacket of dove-grey taffeta with a deep jabot of white lace. Her fine, rich chestnut hair was untouched by grey and her figure was lithe and graceful, matching a complexion kept youthful by the skilful use of artifices. Most people would have judged her no more than about thirty-seven, but her stepdaughter suspected she was several years older than this. Latterly, since being widowed, Franziska had talked a good deal about her past life before she had come to England and met and married James Wayland; but, as always, she was sublimely vague about details.

That her father had been instantly captivated by this beautiful woman of Vienna had been obvious to Victoria from the moment he had first set eyes on her. She was a member of a German operetta company on tour in England, and before the end of their fortnight at his theatre he had proposed to Franziska and been accepted. Victoria had needed to keep a tight rein on her instinctive feelings of jealousy. After three years as the central figure in her father's life, following her mother's sudden death from a burst appendix when she was only nine, it would have been easy to hate the intruder. But she was too honest not to admit it had been a successful marriage. Franziska had made her father happy and brought laughter and gaiety into their lives again, and for this Victoria was grateful. She had never been able to feel real affection for her stepmother, any more than she received it in return, but it was tacitly agreed that they should put on a show of mutual fondness; and if Franziska was more skilful at this than Victoria, it could be attributed to her stage experience.

They came to a busy but narrow thoroughfare called the Herren-gasse. On the way they had walked past an attractive-looking café with tables set out on the pavement and cheerful music coming from within, so Victoria was disappointed when her stepmother paused at a dark, quite uninviting entrance with a swinging sign that announced it to be the Café Radetsky.

'I remember this place from the old days,' she said. 'It had quite a reputation for being popular with literary and stage personalities.'

Inside it was as gloomy as the exterior had promised, with a preponderance of dark woodwork and a low, stone-vaulted ceiling. There were only two other women present but quite a number of men, many of whom were lounging round a huge circular table, perusing newspapers on bamboo frames or arguing amicably with each other. The whole place seemed to Victoria to have the aura of a gentlemen's club, as if most of those present were habitués.

Franziska chose a small table near the entrance. A short, plump waiter in a long white apron bustled up, and she ordered *café mélange* and pastries.

'But first, Herr Ober, bring us something to read.'

'Certainly, madame. The *Neue Freie Presse*, the *Wiener Zeitung*, the *Neues Wiener Journal?*'

She gave a little trill of protesting laughter. 'Goodness, it is so long since I was in Vienna that I am quite at a loss. I had better come with you and select something for myself. I will only be a moment, Vicky.'

The waiter led her to the newspaper rack and they fell into conversation. Like every male Franziska encountered, regardless of status, he had fallen instantly under her spell. Her choice made, he bore the two illustrated magazines back to their table and, as Franziska resumed her seat, he laid them before her with a reverential air before scurrying off to fetch their order.

'It is such a civilized habit, to sit as long as one pleases over a cup of coffee and a selection of journals,' Franziska said with a contented sigh. 'So unlike England, where one is expected to make haste and depart.'

It was excellent coffee, Victoria found, and the pastry was a melting concoction of apricots and cherries and thick whipped cream. Franziska seemed to have little desire to read, after all; she merely leafed through the pages, giving the illustrations no more than a passing glance. The suppressed excitement Victoria had noted about her stepmother earlier was more marked now, and she had the oddest feeling that Franziska was waiting for something to happen.

Minutes went by with conversation droning on in the background, punctuated by an occasional burst of laughter. Curls of blue cigar smoke hazed the air. The waiter flicked a marble tabletop with his napkin, straightened one or two chairs. Then the doors swung open to admit a tall, well-dressed man of about twenty-six or twenty-seven. For a fleeting moment his eyes lingered upon Victoria and her step-mother with the appreciative look of a connoisseur of women, before he glanced away and lifted a hand in greeting to two friends at a table across the room. The waiter had sprung into action, hurrying forward to take his gloves and cane and tall silk hat.

Victoria suddenly felt breathless, swept back to the occasion four years ago when she had lost her heart in a single second to the famous actor Mr Johnston Forbes-Robertson. Spellbound by the magic of his performances, she had watched him every night of the two weeks he had played to packed houses in her father's theatre. The first time had been from her usual opening-night seat in the orchestra stalls, but afterwards she had observed from whatever corner she could squeeze herself into – in the wings among the confusion of props and scenery, or high above the stage on the forbidden catwalks when she could slip up there unseen. And this man instantly evoked the image that had lain precious in her mind ever since, having the same compelling personality as the actor, the same lean vitality. His features too were set in the classical mould, with a broad forehead and strong nose and chin – manly, rather than handsome – and dark eyes that smiled on the surface yet seemed to conceal in their depths a certain weariness with the world he knew.

The waiter was greeting him in tones that could be heard distinctly. '*Guten Abend*, Baron von Kaunitz. I trust that your excellency is in good health?'

'Thank you, yes, Karl. And that lad of yours, is he now fully recovered from the scarlet fever?' His voice was deeply modulated with rich overtones – exactly the voice Victoria had expected and hoped for.

He was moving away when, astonishingly, her stepmother repeated the name.

'Baron von Kaunitz!' Franziska spoke it softly, but in a carrying tone, hardly as a question, nor yet to call his attention. Rather as if musing to herself.

The man turned and gave a tiny, formal bow. '*Gnädige Frau*, you wish to speak to me?'

Franziska laid her fingertips against her cheeks in consternation.

'Oh, my dear sir, how abominably rude you must think me. But I was so taken by surprise at hearing the waiter mention your name.'

'It is one you know?'

'It is one I used to know, many years ago. Baron Heinrich von Kaunitz.'

'My uncle. I am Lorenz von Kaunitz, the son of his twin brother, Gustav.'

'Well, well, who would have believed it.' She inclined her head and surveyed him smilingly. 'Yes, I think I can detect a family resemblance. You cannot imagine how delighted I am to meet you, my dear Baron von Kaunitz.'

His responding smile was charming, but faintly guarded. 'The pleasure is equally mine, I assure you. But you have the advantage of me, *gnädige Frau.*'

'I am Mrs Wayland, and this is my stepdaughter, Miss Victoria Wayland.'

He bowed, murmuring, '*Küss die Hand.*' Indicating the vacant chair at their table, he asked, 'Might I perhaps join you for a few minutes?'

Franziska glanced to the table across the room, where the two men were watching events with interest. 'If you are sure that we should not be keeping you from joining your friends.'

'They'll have to wait.' He seated himself and turned to Victoria, who felt a tremor of excitement as his eyes met hers – eyes that were a smoky dark grey. 'Am I to take it that you are from England, Miss Wayland?'

It was curiously difficult to summon her voice. 'Yes . . . in fact we only arrived here yesterday. But my stepmother is Austrian, of course.'

'Viennese!' Franziska corrected. '*Eine echte Wienerin!* There is a difference, eh, Herr Baron?'

'Indeed there is a difference! We Viennese claim it as our birthright to assume ourselves superior in every respect to those unfortunate enough to be born in other parts of the Austro–Hungarian empire – or anywhere else, for that matter.' They were smiling at each other again, and Victoria was aware of the subtle man-woman interplay, unmistakably there despite the gulf in their ages. Then suddenly his attention was upon her once more. 'You speak German very well, Miss Wayland, with a most charming accent.'

'Thank you.' She was immoderately pleased by the compliment.

'I've had a fair amount of practice because my father could speak the language, and when he and my stepmother were married they used it quite often.'

'I see! And your father?'

'He passed away just before Christmas,' Franziska told him. 'Poor James had always been a very fit man, but he was struck down by an attack of enteric fever and died within a fortnight.'

There was a respectful moment of silence. 'So you used to know my uncle, Mrs Wayland?'

'It was a long while ago, of course, but once upon a time we were very good friends. How is dear Heinrich these days?'

'He is well, thank you.' Lorenz von Kaunitz surveyed Franziska with frank admiration. 'It would be only truthful to add that he has permitted the passing years to leave their mark – unlike yourself, *herrliche gnädige Frau*.'

'Flatterer! He had a small daughter, I remember.' Franziska daintily pursed her lips. 'I seem to recall that her name was Brigitte.'

'Your memory is excellent. My cousin Brigitte is married with a family of her own now, and Uncle Heinrich has a son and another daughter, besides.'

'How nice! And what about you, Herr Baron, are you a family man yet?'

'I have a son.'

'He would be just a baby, I imagine?'

'Emil is a little over four.'

'A charming age! I expect he is a source of great delight to your wife and yourself?'

He nodded non-committally. 'And may I inquire, Mrs Wayland, if you are in Vienna just for a visit, or do you plan to settle here?'

'As to that, who knows what the future holds? We came because I longed to see my beloved Vienna again, and where better for Victoria to study music?'

'Where indeed? Which particular branch of music is your speciality, Miss Wayland?'

His sudden question threw Victoria into a flurry of nerves. She was still brooding over the fact that he had turned out to be a married man with a child, when for some reason she had not envisaged this.

'Oh ... the piano. I've been having tuition for several years and I was intending to study at the School of Music. But my stepmother pointed out that I could equally well do so at the Conservatoire here. Of course,' she added hastily, 'I may not be accepted as a student.'

'If not, it will be their loss. But I am convinced that so charming and, without doubt, so talented a young lady need have no fear of a refusal.'

Franziska released a soft sigh. 'Where else in the world are men so *galant*, my dear?'

Victoria had believed herself immune to flowery compliments. With her father the manager of the Birmingham Alhambra she had been brought up in a world of artificial gallantry, so why did her heartbeat quicken in this ridiculous way when Lorenz von Kaunitz addressed her in such extravagant terms? If only she could display the same cool composure as Franziska.

A few minutes later the baron rose to take his leave of them.

'Do please remember me to your uncle,' Franziska commissioned him.

'I shall make a point of it, *gnädige Frau*. But you were not Mrs Wayland then, so you must tell me the name by which he would have known you.'

Franziska's laugh was a melodious contralto. 'Alas, it is a name that a man of your years will not recall. Such an age has passed since it graced the billboards of the Theater an der Wien.'

'So you were on the stage? I should have guessed.'

'How, pray?'

There was a spark of challenge in his dark eyes. 'Only a lady of the theatre could achieve such perfect poise and such natural charm. What was the name, if you please?'

'Scholtz, Franziska Scholtz. You will not forget it?'

'Have no fear of that! Mrs Wayland, Miss Wayland, I bid you *adieu*. Doubtless our paths will cross again before long. Where are you staying, by the way?'

As Franziska did not reply at once Victoria started to tell him, but her stepmother cut across her.

'For the time being we have taken rooms at the Hotel Maria Theresia. I expect you know it?'

'In the Kärntnerstrasse?'

'Yes. It will suit us for the moment. Later we will lease an apartment, or perhaps a villa somewhere on the outskirts.'

'The Maria Theresia is well spoken of, I'm sure you will be comfortable there.' He bowed to them. '*Auf wiedersehen*, ladies.'

'Why did you pretend that we were staying at an hotel?' Victoria demanded in a whisper, when he had left them to join his friends.

Franziska flicked a speck from her gloves where they lay on the table. 'Would you expect me to parade our poverty before a well-to-do man like him? There are times, Vicky, when a small fib is preferable to the sordid truth.'

'But there's nothing sordid about the Pension Anna. It's a perfectly nice place – quite clean and comfortable.'

'And cheap! That was its main merit in our eyes. Its only merit.'

'Well, I suppose it doesn't particularly matter,' Victoria said with a shrug. 'Baron von Kaunitz isn't likely to find out that you weren't telling the truth.'

'I shall make very sure that he does not! We will call at the Maria Theresia and arrange to move there before we go to the theatre this evening. I remember it as a good-class place. I dined there occasionally in the old days.'

Victoria gasped. 'You can't be serious? This hotel will cost us far more than we're paying at present – it's bound to.'

Her stepmother eyed her with cold reproof. 'I shall be the judge of what we can afford, Vicky. Your father very properly left the little he had to leave in my hands, remember, and I shall do with it what I consider to be in the best interests of us both.'

Victoria was stabbed again by the familiar pain and resentment at the terms of her father's will, made in haste just a few days before his death. If only poor Papa had thought to bequeath her a specified portion of his estate, perhaps through some sort of trust fund, rather than leaving her entirely dependent upon her stepmother's whims. Not that she feared Franziska would deliberately abuse his faith in her, but this was not the first time she had showed signs of acting impetuously. It was part of Franziska's temperament to make grand gestures without reckoning the cost.

'Who are these von Kaunitzes, anyway?' Victoria asked through tight lips. 'Why is it so important to impress them?'

'Baron Heinrich was an admirer of mine in the old days.' Franziska tilted her head, revealing the lovely curve of her throat, the still-youthful bloom of her skin. 'I had a host of admirers when I played at the Theater an der Wien, but Heinrich was special. He became a close friend, a much valued friend. So naturally I want him to think well of me now. You can hardly blame me for concealing the fact that our financial situation is vastly different from his.'

Victoria had a flash of insight. She suddenly felt convinced that there had been nothing accidental about this encounter with Lorenz von Kaunitz.

'You knew Baron von Kaunitz would be coming here this afternoon, didn't you?' she said accusingly. 'I thought it was very odd that you chose this café instead of that more attractive one we passed on the way. But now I understand.'

Franziska looked outraged, her amber eyes narrowing to pinpoints. 'Don't be absurd! I merely wanted you to sample a typical Viennese café. And how, pray, could I possibly have come by the information you suggest when we have only been in Vienna a few hours? Why, I didn't even know of the young man's existence.'

To Victoria her stepmother's protests seemed surprisingly emphatic if the meeting was as innocent as she pretended. Victoria recalled that when she had woken up that morning, rather late, Franziska had not been in her room next door, and was nowhere to be found. She had reappeared a few minutes later in her outdoor things, explaining that the lovely morning had enticed her out for a short stroll through the Graben to St Stephen's Cathedral. Was it then that her stepmother had gleaned information about this von Kaunitz family?

She said defiantly, 'You must admit that it seems a strange coincidence.'

'My dear girl, life is full of coincidences. Come, we will go at once and arrange about the hotel.'

She signalled the waiter and dipped into her purse for a coin, which he received with profuse thanks. Across the room Baron von Kaunitz saw them leaving and rose to make a small bow, to which Franziska responded with a smiling inclination of the head.

'Wasn't that a five-crown piece you gave the waiter?' Victoria asked, as they emerged onto the pavement. 'Surely it is far too much for just coffee and pastries?'

'Five crowns!' Franziska raised her delicately-arched eyebrows. 'Whatever next? It was only a gulden.'

Victoria could not be certain of what she had seen, but her suspicions were reinforced. The waiter, she guessed, had been handsomely tipped for his assistance in the 'chance' meeting with Lorenz von Kaunitz – an arrangement Franziska must have made with the man while she had been talking to him by the newspaper rack.

They took a cab, driving past the massive domed gateway of the Hofburg, through the arcade by the Winter Riding School and across

Josefsplatz. Already, from their sightseeing this morning, Victoria was beginning to recognize some of the main landmarks of the inner city.

It was a relief to discover that the Hotel Maria Theresia, though clearly in a very different category from the modest Pension Anna, was not quite so grand as she had feared. Stifling the objections on the tip of her tongue, she went meekly with Franziska as they were escorted up to the second floor in an electrically operated lift and shown into a pair of adjoining rooms. Her stepmother surveyed the accommodation in her most imperious manner, testing the springiness of the beds with her hand and flinging wide the wardrobe doors.

'Yes, I think this should suit us well enough,' she conceded at last. 'Don't you agree, Vicky?'

There might still have been a chance to voice an objection, but at that instant Victoria noticed that the tall windows gave a fine, unimpeded view of the State Opera House, which to her epitomized the glory of Vienna, this golden city of music. Her anxieties about spending too much money were swamped by a sudden flurry of excitement.

'Oh yes, it's lovely!' she exclaimed delightedly. 'It couldn't be better.'

Her stepmother frowned at such immoderate enthusiasm before the *maître d'hôtel* and informed him with a cool nod that they would take the rooms.

'She is not his wife, of course,' said Franziska, in a voice of conviction.

From their seats in the *parterre* Victoria glanced up again, this time covertly, at the first-tier box from which Lorenz von Kaunitz had made them a salutation. He was in evening clothes now and the woman with him wore a shimmering gown of yellow satin. She was extremely beautiful, small-boned and delicately made, with a head borne high on a slender neck, the rich copper tones of her hair gleaming in contrast with the creamy whiteness of her bare shoulders.

'How can you be so certain she isn't his wife?'

'My dear, one can always tell. A man who has been married long enough to have a four-year-old son is not so attentive to his wife, nor so thoroughly lost in admiration.'

'I don't think he looks particularly lost in admiration,' Victoria objected, uncomfortably aware of the quiver in her voice. 'More . . . well, pretending to be, I would have said.'

Franziska laughed understandingly. 'He is very handsome, is he not? Very attractive.'

'In a way, I suppose.' Victoria fidgeted with her Chinese fan, splaying it open and snapping it shut. 'I thought it was very embarrassing in the café this afternoon when he kept paying outrageous compliments. It seemed so artificial.'

'Where would women be without gentlemen's compliments?'

'But when it's just empty flattery, not sincerely meant.'

'The time to be concerned, my dear Vicky, is when no man feels compelled to flatter one. Until then, it is sensible to accept what is offered and be grateful. Now . . . the overture is about to begin.'

Even when the curtain had risen it was quite some time before the familiar magic of the theatre began to work its charm on Victoria. She was too intently aware of the man in the box above them, who might perhaps at this moment be looking down upon her as she sat illuminated by the brilliant light spilling from the stage. But why, she argued despairingly, should he have spared her more than a fleeting thought when he spotted them a few minutes ago? Doubtless by now, with the music of *Die Fledermaus* ringing in his ears and a cool, slender hand lying within his clasp, he had forgotten that Victoria Wayland existed.

During each of the two intervals she noted that Lorenz von Kaunitz and his companion left their box as soon as the curtain fell. But she saw nothing of them in the lounges and vestibules, even though Franziska wanted to peer and pry everywhere, with fond reminiscences of what the Theater an der Wien had been like in *her* day. Nor was there any sign of the couple at the end of the performance when she and Franziska had to scramble for a cab in the mêlée outside.

A spatter of summer rain was beginning to fall and the driver climbed down to raise the folding hood to protect his passengers. Then as the cab started off for the Hotel Maria Theresia, lurching and slipping on the wet cobbles of the Magdalenenstrasse, they fell to discussing the performance they had just seen, Franziska critically, Victoria abstractedly. Baron Lorenz von Kaunitz was not once mentioned by either of them.

2

Victoria had cause to be grateful, next morning, for her stepmother's impetuous nature and forceful charm. Most people would have set about the matter of securing an enrolment at the Conservatoire by trying to persuade someone influential to act as sponsor for the prospective candidate. But not Franziska. She preferred to storm the barricades.

It was a fine and sunny morning after the overnight rain, with the air clean-washed and silken soft. Franziska suggested that instead of taking a cab they should walk to the headquarters of the Musikverein in Karlsplatz.

'This section of the Ringstrasse had been built before I left Vienna,' she told her stepdaughter. 'The linden trees are grown much bigger now, though. I remember the opening of the Opera House . . . I went to the first performance there.'

'When was that?' asked Victoria, thinking artfully that a date might provide more information about her stepmother's past.

There was a tiny pause. 'Oh, I don't recall, but it was about this time of year, at the end of the spring. They did *Don Giovanni*, and everyone who was anyone attended the gala opening – except for the Empress, which caused quite a scandal. The first night had been postponed a whole week on her account, to allow her to get back from her hunting estate in Hungary. But even then she didn't turn up. The Emperor must have been furious – and in those days the poor man didn't have Katharina Schratt as a consolation for the dance his wife leads him.'

'Who is Katharina Schratt?'

'A star actress at the Burg Theater.' Franziska gave her a sidelong glance. 'Some say she and the Emperor are no more than close friends, others are not so charitable . . . They are known to breakfast together frequently. And to think it was the Empress Elizabeth herself who arranged this curious *ménage à trois*. Such a thing could only happen in Vienna. I used to know *Die Schratt* slightly. I was introduced to her once at the Concordia Ball, and afterwards we saw one another around from time to time.'

It seemed to Victoria an ideal opportunity to put the question she had always hesitated to ask before. 'What made you decide to leave Vienna? I've often wondered. I mean, when you had been born and brought up here.'

There was a longer pause this time, then, 'When one is an actress, one's career must come first. I was offered a contract in Berlin, and after that I toured several German cities. You know how it is, one engagement leads to another.'

'Did you have no family here, no parents?'

Franziska shook her head. 'There was nobody. And somehow I never did return here – until now. Oh, it's good to be back, Vicky. I'm sure you will come to love Vienna as much as I do. Just look around you . . . can you smell that heavenly lilac blossom? Nowhere in the whole world is there another city so beautiful as my Vienna.' She began to sing softly to herself. '*Wien, Wien, nur du allein* . . . the city where my dreams come true.'

At the Musikverein, Franziska dealt with each obstacle in turn. The first, a commissionaire in a splendid gold-braided uniform, she swept aside without effort. Reaching an outer office, they encountered a grizzled clerk who seemed to carry the accumulated dust of years on his frail shoulders. He insisted fussily that protocol must be observed; a letter requesting an appointment would receive due consideration. However, he was eventually prevailed upon to refer the matter to his immediate superior, and this individual turned out to be a younger man and more malleable. He would see what he could do, he readily agreed when Franziska appealed to him with a dazzling smile. He undertook to use his utmost endeavour on the ladies' behalf. Inviting them to be seated, he departed at speed, and after only the briefest wait they were escorted upstairs and ushered into a room where an elderly, bearded gentleman in an old-fashioned frock coat listened with polite attention as Franziska persuasively argued Victoria's case.

'It would give me the greatest pleasure to help your stepdaughter, *gnädige Frau*,' he said, removing his pince-nez to polish them, 'if only I—'

'You are too kind! Shall you hear her play now?'

'Well . . .'

Franziska gestured a slim gloved hand toward the piano. 'What will you perform for the Herr Professor, Vicky? That Chopin mazurka, perhaps? The one I like so much.'

Victoria saw the startled look in his red-rimmed eyes before he rose and nodded courteously by way of invitation. Her cheeks warm with embarrassment, she went to the piano and raised the lid. Not for the world would she be so pushful on her own account, but neither could she let slip a golden chance like this.

'I've had no opportunity to practise for the past few days,' she murmured, as she seated herself on the stool and arranged her skirts. 'I beg you to be good enough to make allowance for that, Herr Professor.'

'*Aber natürlich*. Pray take your time and flex your fingers with a few scales before you commence.'

Although she made a bad start with the B flat mazurka by striking two false notes, she quickly gathered confidence and rose to the challenge, playing with all the skill at her command. The professor listened gravely, stroking his grey beard. When she had done he made no immediate comment but began to question her about the tuition she had so far received, and to what she aspired in music.

'Of course my greatest ambition, my dream,' she confessed, 'is eventually to become a concert artiste. But I know the chances of that are slender. I hope, though, that I may attain a sufficiently high standard to earn my living from the pianoforte – perhaps as a *lieder* accompanist.'

The professor gave an approving nod to this. 'I must tell you at once, Fräulein Wayland, that I do not detect in your playing that spark of genius which could turn you into a concert pianist. You are very wise not to set your sights beyond your abilities – as alas so many of our students are inclined to do. Whether or not you can succeed in a pianistic career remains to be seen. You possess a technical competence, with good clarity of tone, and there is a pleasing tenderness in your playing. In my opinion you would respond well to the tuition we can give here.' He went on to say that he could promise nothing, but that he would recommend her acceptance for piano classes when the Conservatoire reopened in September for the new term. They could rely on hearing from him.

'I must confess,' said Franziska as they came away, 'that I had no idea it would cost so much. One must expect to pay highly for the very best tuition, I suppose, but how we are to manage the fees I really do not know.'

It was like a dash of icy water on Victoria's bubbling enthusiasm. 'Oh please – this is terribly important to me. I long to study music more than anything else in the world. And the Herr Professor did say that I would respond to tuition.'

Franziska asked the commissionaire to summon a cab. 'Don't fret, Vicky, I expect we shall manage somehow.'

'The Herr Professor suggested it might be possible for me to miss out the preparatory classes and go directly into secondary study. That would reduce the cost, wouldn't it? And perhaps I could find some pupils of my own, even at this stage . . . children who are just beginning at the piano.'

'We will have to see – but it may not prove necessary. There is usually an answer to every problem.'

Back at the Hotel Maria Theresia the youthful clerk at the reception desk, his eyes swimming with adoration, informed Franziska that a gentleman awaited her.

'Really! I wonder who it can be?'

'He left a card for *madame*.' As this was presented Victoria noticed that it was engraved with a coat of arms.

'Oh, Vicky darling, you will never guess!' exclaimed Franziska delightedly. 'It is dear Heinrich . . . Baron von Kaunitz.'

Mention of the name von Kaunitz brought colour surging to Victoria's cheeks. 'Why has the baron come here?' she asked faintly.

'Why? Because he heard from his nephew that I was in Vienna. Heinrich has wasted no time, I must say.' Franziska's eyes were sparkling as she turned back to the clerk. 'Well, young man, where is the Herr Baron?'

'In the palm lounge, *madame*. I will despatch a page to inform his excellency that you have returned to the hotel.'

But before he could strike the polished brass bell on the counter, Franziska halted him with a raised hand.

'No, I think we will surprise the baron, eh, Vicky? Come . . .'

Victoria was curious to see Lorenz von Kaunitz's uncle. There was a certain resemblance in their features, but it was not marked. He was, perhaps, more conventionally handsome than his nephew, though inclined to fleshiness, particularly around the jowls. His iron-grey hair, which he wore quite long, was brushed back behind his ears, and a thick moustache of a darker grey covered his upper lip. As he came forward to meet them, screwing a monocle into his right eye-socket, Victoria found it difficult to interpret his expression.

'My dear Heinrich, how splendid to see you again.' Franziska's voice was joyful as she swept up to him with her hand outstretched. 'I should have known you in an instant, even passing in the street, you are so little changed.'

He took her hand and kissed it. 'You are too kind, Mrs Wayland.'

'What is this – Mrs Wayland? I am Franziska to you, my dear. I always was and I hope I always shall be. Come now, I want you to meet my young stepdaughter, Victoria. Vicky dear, this is my esteemed old friend, Baron Heinrich von Kaunitz.'

He murmured a token, *'Küss die Hand, gnädiges Fräulein,'* and returned his attention to Franziska. It was obvious that he was intently aware of her, all his senses alert, but not in the way men customarily responded to her stepmother. There was a wariness in this man's attitude, even – was it possible? – a veiled hostility.

'My nephew gave me your message,' he said, in an even tone.

Franziska's delicate eyebrows arched higher. 'Did I give him a message for you?'

'Lorenz said that you asked particularly to be remembered to me.'

'Well, naturally!' She laughed and put a hand impulsively on his forearm. 'I was overjoyed when I heard the waiter at the Café Radetsky utter the name von Kaunitz. That was explained to you, I presume?'

'Indeed, yes.'

'In that instant, Heinrich, everything came flooding back, things I almost believed I had forgotten. And your nephew was so charming, so very attentive. A real breaker of hearts, I fear. Already, I may as well tell you, he has enraptured poor Vicky.'

'Franziska, please!' she protested, feeling the colour rushing to her cheeks.

'So I am not permitted to speak the truth? Ah well, it is unkind to tease you, I suppose. I think, Heinrich, it is just as well that the young man is already married, or half the girls in Vienna would be out to snare him.'

Victoria was in an agony of embarrassment now, and longed to flee upstairs to her room. Yet equally she wanted to remain and hear what transpired. Franziska suggested that they should all sit down, and they moved to a small bamboo table screened by drooping fronds of a potted palm and far enough removed from the string quartet which was spiritedly rendering a selection from *Traviata*. The baron raised his finger for a waiter and ordered a bottle of wine.

'So you married an Englishman, Franziska?'

'Yes, dear Vicky's father. Poor James passed away last December. So tragic!'

Baron von Kaunitz offered no sympathy but merely waited for her to continue, his frock coat undone and two fingers dug into the watch pocket of his watered-silk waistcoat.

'We were heartbroken, Vicky and I, and in the end we decided to move right away from Birmingham, which could only hold sad memories for us both. Vienna seemed the obvious place. After my long absence I yearned to see my beloved city once more, and meet again the friends I had known. Alas, I fear not many are left now, so my joy was all the greater to learn that you, my dear Heinrich, were fit and well.'

To this the baron inclined his head in the smallest acknowledgement that could be made without discourtesy.

Franziska chattered on, 'And then, Vienna seemed ideal for Vicky, too. You see, she is very musically inclined and shows great promise at the piano. But what did Birmingham have to offer such a talented girl? Already, this very morning, I believe we have stormed the ramparts of the Conservatoire. From what the Herr Professor said, I am confident that dear Vicky will gain admission when the new semester commences in September. Is that not splendid?'

The baron appeared far from overjoyed by this news. 'So you intend to take up residence in Vienna?'

'Where better, Heinrich?'

The waiter arrived with the wine. When the three glasses were filled, Franziska was the first to raise hers to her lips.

'Let us drink a toast to Vicky . . . success in her musical studies. And to ourselves, dear Heinrich, may today mark a new flowering of our friendship. Come, do not hesitate, or I shall begin to think you are not glad to see me.'

He raised his glass, bowed his head gravely toward Victoria, and took a small sip of wine before replacing his glass on the table with pointed deliberation.

'It was all a very long time ago, Franziska. A great deal of water has flowed under the Danube bridges since then.'

She nodded, pensive. 'Ah yes, the world moves on! But some things remain forever unchanged. As one grows older, one tends to live in the past more and more. Do you find that, Heinrich?'

'On the contrary, I try to put the past behind me, and concentrate instead on the present and the future.'

Franziska gave a sigh. 'But you see, my dear, you are a man and men have so many interests to occupy them. I have nothing but my memories . . . memories of the happy days gone by.'

It was an absurd remark from a woman who looked in the very prime of her life, a picture of glowing health. Here in the hotel lounge, with Venetian blinds filtering the harshness out of the morning sunlight, it was impossible to detect the network of tiny lines that had lately begun to appear around Franziska's mouth and eyes, while her complexion looked as soft as the bloom on a peach. The baron, however, was slow to respond to this challenge to gallantry, seeming distracted by his thoughts. But as Victoria watched, his lips curved into a reluctant smile and his eyes kindled with admiration.

'Don't try and pretend you are in your dotage, my dear Franziska. I'll be damned if I've seen a finer woman in many a long day. By God, young Lorenz was right in what he said.'

'And what did he say?' she demanded archly.

'Oh, never you mind about that.'

Franziska's laugh rang out as pure as a silver bell. 'What a tease you are, Heinrich, and always were! Vicky darling, you will only be bored by the two of us reminiscing about the old days, so why don't you run along and get some of your letters written? I will join you shortly.'

'But there is no great hurry about my letters.'

'I can see that I must act as your mentor. Your friends in Birmingham will think you have forgotten them if you do not write soon.'

Victoria rose reluctantly and the baron rose too. As he made her a formal bow, she perceived the strength and toughness of the man behind his smooth mask of courtesy.

'*Gnädiges Fräulein*, I bid you farewell,' he said.

'Oh Heinrich, do not speak of farewell,' protested Franziska, 'only *wiedersehen!* You will be meeting Vicky again. Often, I hope.'

At the doorway Victoria glanced back and saw the baron edging his chair closer to Franziska's. Already they had forgotten her.

Upstairs in her room she found she could not settle to letter writing and gave herself up to conjecture, gazing through the window at the great Opera House just across the way. The fact that those two had surely been lovers at one time did not shock Victoria as it might have shocked other girls of her age. In the theatrical world in which she had been brought up, such liaisons were not uncommon, and she knew that a woman like Franziska must undoubtedly have had several romantic attachments in the years before she had come to England and met and married James Wayland. But the thought that her stepmother might be hoping for a renewal of intimacy with a former lover, especially so soon after her husband's death, was very distasteful to Victoria. She could not escape it, however.

The baron's attitude puzzled her. Despite his obvious admiration for Franziska, he had seemed uneasy, almost hostile. Was that because he feared his wife might somehow discover the truth about himself and Franziska all those years ago? But would such a possibility disturb him, a suave and sophisticated man of Vienna? It clearly did not disturb his nephew. Lorenz von Kaunitz was also married, yet he could openly flaunt his mistress in a box at one of the city's most fashionable theatres.

When Franziska came upstairs almost an hour later Victoria was seated at the writing table, a pen hovering over a blank sheet of hotel notepaper. Again she was aware of the suppressed excitement in her stepmother. Franziska left open the communicating door between their rooms, and talked gaily while she changed her clothes for their outing to the Kahlenberg heights after luncheon.

'I have been having such an interesting chat with dear Heinrich. He was telling me about their country estate out at Eisenbad. It is a resort town scarcely more than half an hour from Vienna by train, and he made it sound so attractive that I am quite persuaded to take a villa somewhere near for the summer. Heinrich assures me that there are always a number of delightful little places available for letting, and I am determined to go there without delay and make inquiries. All the best people get out of town during the hot months.'

Victoria was bewildered by yet another abrupt change of plan after only a single night at the Maria Theresia. She said unhappily, 'I wish I could understand what this is all about.'

'What what is all about?'

'Your sudden interest in Baron von Kaunitz.'

'It is not a sudden interest. I told you, he was a very dear friend of mine in the old days.'

'Yet he didn't look all that pleased to see you this morning,' Victoria ventured to point out.

'What nonsense! Why, he couldn't wait to come and renew our friendship. You must not be misled by his manner, Vicky. Dear Heinrich was always inclined to be reserved. But he is quite delighted that I am here, and you and I have a most pressing invitation to call upon his family when we are settled in our summer home.'

Victoria was astonished. 'Call on his family? But surely . . . his wife . . .'

Franziska, fastening the high lace neckband of her mauve silk dress, paused and gave her stepdaughter a sharp look through the doorway.

'What are you hinting at? You cannot imagine that I have any thoughts about Heinrich von Kaunitz beyond pure friendship? Heavens above, I am still mourning your dear father! Or had you forgotten that?'

Shamefaced, Victoria mumbled an apology. A moment later Franziska came right through from the other room, twitching straight her tight sleeves with a little tug at each cuff. She stood before her stepdaughter and laid a gentle hand on her shoulder.

'My dear Vicky, do not let us be at odds. You must understand the situation. We are two women alone in the world. Whether in England or Austria, Birmingham or Vienna, our position is extremely vulnerable. The friendship of a man of influence such as Baron Heinrich von Kaunitz could be very valuable to us.'

3

The search for the right summer villa took several days. Victoria and her stepmother went to Eisenbad by train each morning, and hired one of the station flys to take them around. It was not an easy time, for they constantly disagreed. Franziska was always attracted to the more showy of the places that were to let but, not unnaturally, these were also the most expensive. Victoria would have been happy with something a good deal humbler, but she needed to have a piano for her daily practice – which had to be resumed without delay if she were not to fall hopelessly behind.

Eventually they settled on a reasonable compromise. The cottage – it was hardly more – possessed a certain quiet charm. Low and white-walled with a terracotta roof and latticed windows, it stood in a small neat garden. It was somewhat dark inside, though, being overshadowed by the surrounding woodlands of the Wienerwald. Franziska, glancing round for something else that would wholly condemn it, questioned whether the forlorn-looking baby-grand of dubious make could possibly be good enough. But Victoria ran her fingers lightly over the yellowed keys and discovered to her relief that it produced a passably good tone. She insisted that a visit from a tuner would put it to rights.

In the evening of the day on which the lease was signed they celebrated by going to the opera. Disappointingly, though, the performance of *Lohengrin* was not to be conducted by the new man Gustav Mahler everyone was talking about, who was reputedly ill.

'Never mind,' said Franziska, as they made their way up the impressive staircase adorned with the statues of the nine Muses, 'the main thing is coming to the Opera House. One gets such a sense of occasion here.'

The following evening the two of them sat on little gilt chairs in the rococo ballroom of a princely palace near the Freyung, and heard a young Russian pianist with wild eyes and a shaggy black beard give a passionate new interpretation of the works of Mendelssohn and Liszt. Another time, they listened in the balmy twilight to an open-air concert in the leafy Stadtpark, the orchestra in the vine-entwined bandstand playing waltzes and marches by the Strausses and Lanner. Victoria wondered how she would ever tear herself away from this glorious city of music for the months they would be living in Eisenbad.

On the morning of their move to the country it turned dull, with a hint of rain in the air. Nevertheless, after luncheon, when they were unpacked and Franziska had retired upstairs to rest, Victoria set out on an exploratory stroll. Their villa was situated on the slope of a wooded valley a little above the red-roofed township, and she chose a bridle path that climbed higher still.

Presently the newly-leafing oaks and beeches thinned, and she came to some gilt-tipped railings through which she had a distant glimpse of a stately baroque mansion set in spreading parkland. Huge stone caryatids supported the imposing front portal, and a series of arched pediments were each crested with a sculpted figure. The walls had been painted a pale chrome yellow and the shutters at the many windows were olive green, the same colouring as the Imperial summer palace at Schönbrunn. There was a lake, too, looking now like a stretch of grey silk under the leaden sky. As she watched, a flight of ducks rose in a flurry from the water's smooth surface, pivoted, then flew in her direction, passing directly overhead with a loud whirring of wings.

Victoria would have liked to linger but it was starting to rain, so she turned back and hurried for home. At the front door she removed her damp cloak and took it to the kitchen to be dried before the range. Gerda, the woman who with her husband looked after the villa and went with the lease, was making *Apfelstrudel*, and Victoria inquired about the big house.

'Why, that's the Schloss Kaunitz. It's the family home – where they live during the summer.'

'The von Kaunitz family?'

'*Ja.*'

Pretending no more than a passing interest, Victoria managed to elicit a few details about the schloss's occupants. The head of the household was clearly Baron Heinrich.

'You've met him already, so I heard your stepmother say. And his wife is Baroness Mathilde.' Gerda prodded her steel-rimmed spectacles higher up her stubby nose. 'Their elder daughter is married now and lives over by Melk somewhere, but young Baroness Liesl is still at home. And then there's their son, Lieutenant Baron Otto, whenever he's on leave. He's an officer in the cavalry, and a proper bright spark – a real one for the ladies that young fellow is, and no mistake!'

Victoria remarked with weighty casualness, 'We met Baron Lorenz von Kaunitz in Vienna. Does he live at the schloss, too?'

'*Ja*. He's Baron Gustav's son. Baron Gustav is the brother of Baron Heinrich – his twin brother. He's a widower, poor man – his wife died many years since.'

'Baron Lorenz is married, is he not? With a small son?'

'That's right. A dear little chap, Emil is. No wonder he's the apple of the old gentleman's eye.'

'You mean his grandfather, Baron Gustav?'

'*Nein, nein*, not that the Herr Baron isn't fond enough of the child. But I meant old Herr Czernin.'

'Herr Czernin? Who is he?'

Gerda began rolling out the pastry to wafer thinness on a floured cloth.

'Let me see now. He'd be Baron Gustav's father-in-law, Baron Lorenz's grandfather. So that would make the old gentleman little Emil's great-grandfather. That's it! Over eighty, he must be now, and ailing and expected to pass away at any moment for as long as I can remember, and that's going back a bit! He fair dotes on that grandson of his, too, I've heard tell, and why not, pray? Every blessed thing will go to Baron Lorenz when the old fellow dies. Everything!'

The awed tone in which Gerda had pronounced *alles* made Victoria prompt, 'Everything?'

'All his money and the foundry and all. Herr Czernin started it up from nothing, you know, when he came from Bohemia as a young chap. They make machinery for farms and suchlike. He must be one of the richest men in Austria, I shouldn't wonder.'

So Lorenz von Kaunitz would one day be immensely wealthy. Somehow the thought was depressing to Victoria, as though it had suddenly swept him beyond her reach. But this was absurd, because he had never been within her reach. And neither would she wish him to be, not a married man. Worse still, she added fiercely in her mind, the sort of married man who flaunted his mistress in public.

In the days that followed Victoria revisited several times the spot where she could look through the railings. Once she saw a small boy in a sailor suit playing a game of ball with a nursemaid. And another time she glimpsed a flash of bright scarlet on the terrace and guessed it must be the young cavalry officer. But there was never a sign of Lorenz.

She did not mention these secret excursions to Franziska. And certainly not to Baron Heinrich, who unaccountably had already called upon them three times, seeming to grow a little more jovial and at ease on each occasion. On his next visit, he had promised, he would bring his brother with him.

The two men were due now, at any minute. Victoria stood at a small window which overlooked the front gate, concealed from view by the tulle curtains, keeping watch for their arrival. Franziska was still titivating herself upstairs in her room.

They were not, in fact, identical twins as Victoria had for some reason expected. When they came into view she saw that Baron Gustav was a couple of inches shorter than his brother, and less trim of figure. Both wore soft panama hats and carried tan gloves and malacca canes; a pair of elegant middle-aged gentlemen dressed casually for the country.

Victoria hurried to the foot of the stairs and called softly, 'Franziska, they are here!'

A serene voice floated down to her. 'I shall not be long. Keep them entertained for me.'

She guessed that the number of minutes her stepmother would keep the two barons waiting would be calculated to a nicety. Franziska would make her appearance when their anticipation had reached its peak, and just short of the onset of irritation. Lacking any such feminine guile, Victoria did not even wait for Gerda to answer the jangling bell, but went to open the front door herself.

'*Guten Morgen*, Herr Baron,' she greeted Heinrich. 'Do please come in. My stepmother will be down in a few moments.'

He smiled upon her benignly. 'May I present my brother, Baron Gustav von Kaunitz. Gustav, this is Miss Wayland.'

'I am charmed, *gnädiges Fräulein*.' But his face remained impassive as he bent in a token gesture of kissing her hand, and his eyes, when he straightened again, were watchful.

Leading the way to their small parlour, Victoria felt acutely nervous. She made a few trite remarks about the weather having improved, and noted that it was only Heinrich who responded. She wondered why Baron Gustav had ever agreed to call at the villa when, quite clearly, he expected so little pleasure from his visit.

The men declined to sit down, but stood at the French window which opened onto a trellised veranda where virginia creeper trailed. Beyond the small oval of lawn a shrubbery blazed gold and orange and bright flame red.

'You have remarkably fine azaleas there,' Heinrich observed, grasping a fresh line of conversation.

'Yes, indeed. One can catch their perfume from here.'

Gustav said nothing. And he continued to say nothing when Heinrich volunteered that, according to the foreman gardener at the schloss, it was going to be a good year for roses due to sufficient rainfall at the appropriate time. Victoria began to wish desperately that Franziska would come to her rescue, but there was still no sound on the stairs.

Searching for something that would draw the reluctant Baron Gustav into conversation, she faltered, 'I ... my stepmother and I happened to meet your son in Vienna, Herr Baron.'

Gustav stared at her as though she were a little unbalanced in stating a fact he already knew, but Heinrich said smoothly, 'Remarkable, was it not, that you should have run into one of our family so soon after your arrival in Vienna? My nephew was most taken with you both. But then, Lorenz has an eye for a pretty woman.'

'A veritable *galant*, that son of yours, Baron Gustav.'

The two men spun round and Victoria turned thankfully to see her stepmother standing on the threshold, a picture of elegance in a flowing white muslin dress with trimmings of pale mauve lace. It was a stage entrance, and quite stunningly effective.

Heinrich performed the introductions. 'You two never met in the old days, did you? But my brother was most anxious to remedy the matter without delay, Franziska. Isn't that so, Gustav?'

Reluctant admiration shone in Baron Gustav's eyes, but still he remained unsmiling. 'It is indeed a great pleasure to meet you, *gnädige Frau*.'

'Let us sit outside,' Franziska suggested. 'What refreshment may we offer you, gentlemen? A glass of wine, or coffee, or perhaps a nice cool Pils? I have some bottles ready in an ice-pail.'

The men chose beer, and Franziska signalled with her eyes for Victoria to go and tell Gerda. When she returned, they were seated in basket chairs on the veranda. Franziska had been careful to select a shaded spot for herself.

'I was explaining to Baron Gustav that this little place was the best we could find at this time of year. The nicest summer villas had all been snapped up earlier. Still, it will suit us well enough. The surroundings are very pleasant, and what is more to the point, we have good friends almost on our doorstep.'

'Doubtless we shall all be seeing a good deal of each other,' Heinrich observed.

'I am counting on it,' she replied roguishly.

The men stayed for nearly an hour and the atmosphere grew more relaxed each minute. Baron Gustav cast aside his taciturn mood and slowly became more animated. On parting, Victoria noticed, he held Franziska's hand much longer than necessary before raising it to his lips.

'I hope you will permit me to call upon you again, *gnädige Frau*,' he murmured, and clearly he meant without his brother.

'You will be most welcome, Herr Baron. Any time you care to honour us with a visit, Victoria and I will be delighted to see you.'

'Then I shall make a point of coming. Very soon.'

The two men walked in silence until they were safely out of hearing. Then Heinrich said, 'Well, Gustav?'

'She is certainly a fine looking woman,' he acknowledged.

'As I kept telling you. The Franziska Scholtz I used to know was but a pale shadow of this woman. You're a damnably lucky fellow.'

'Can you be sure she will agree?'

'Why the devil not?' Heinrich demanded irritably. 'Naturally you'll have to go through the motions and do the thing in style. She'd expect that. But she'll agree, by jove!'

'I suppose you're right.'

Heinrich smiled complacently. 'When have I ever been wrong? I suggest you don't delay matters. Take my word for it, Franziska won't object to being swept off her feet.'

The letter from the Conservatoire requesting Victoria to attend for an audition gave her only a single day's notice. It had been addressed to the Hotel Maria Theresia by mistake, and sent on from there.

'How careless of them!' said Franziska. 'It's impossible, of course. We have Gustav coming tomorrow.'

'Oh please, Franziska, can't we put Baron Gustav off for once? I'm sure he would understand.'

'There's no need for that, Vicky. We'll just telephone or send a wire, asking for an audition at a later date.'

'Oh, no!' she cried, alarmed. 'I don't think we should do that.' There was too much at stake to take any risk, however slight.

'But it's their fault,' her stepmother pointed out. 'And you need time to prepare yourself.'

'I'm as ready as I shall ever be, and this way there'll be less time to worry myself into a state of nerves.' Franziska seemed not to understand how important this was to her, and she went on a little wildly, 'There's really no need for you to come with me. I know where to go, and I could manage perfectly well alone.' Victoria expected a battle of wills, but surprisingly her stepmother merely looked thoughtful. She quickly threw in more ammunition. 'You never used to worry about me going around by myself in Birmingham. I'd be perfectly safe in Vienna. I could take a cab each way to and from the station.'

'And you'd have to be sure to sit in the ladies' coupé on the train.'

'Yes, of course I would.'

Franziska hesitated only a moment longer. 'Well then, I suppose if you're really so set on it . . .'

Victoria found herself hugging her stepmother in a rush of gratitude, kissing the petal-soft cheek.

'Goodness, you can be so impetuous at times!' said Franziska, laughing breathlessly. 'Now, as to plans. We must think what you will wear to make the right impression, and later on we'll stroll down to the station and find the best train for you to take.' She was suddenly in high good humour, and hummed to herself as she sat mending a tear in the hem of a petticoat.

They walked to the station in the cool of early evening, crossing the river by an old stone bridge, then through the pretty Stadtpark where magnolias were bursting into flower under the honey-coloured walls of the Kurhaus. Already Mrs Wayland and her stepdaughter were known to some of the townspeople, and they paused now and then to exchange a few friendly words.

Just across from the main square the little railway station slumbered in the amber glow of sunlight. The horses of the Posthof hotel omnibus sleepily scraped the cobbles of the forecourt, and waiting cab drivers lounged against the paling fence holding a desultory conversation.

In the booking-hall, Victoria and her stepmother consulted a time-table on the wall and selected a train which fitted in nicely with her appointment at four o'clock. They were at the pigeonhole buying a ticket, to save the need tomorrow, when a train from Vienna drew in. There was a hiss of steam and the station was suddenly bustling with life. People hurried past them, jostling one another to be first to the waiting cabs.

'Good evening, ladies.' The deep, rich voice, first heard days and days ago and then for such a brief time, was instantly, achingly familiar. Victoria spun round and met the dark, amused eyes of Lorenz von Kaunitz. 'I wondered how long it would be before we chanced to meet again. I gather you have taken a villa here for the summer.'

Franziska awarded him a sparkling smile. *'Guten Abend*, Herr Baron. How delightful to see you! So Heinrich told you about our move? We are quite close neighbours now.'

'Most convenient! But it wasn't my uncle who mentioned the fact . . . one hears these things. I understand that my father, too, has called upon you.'

'Yes, a most charming man. As I might have expected from having met his son.'

'You are too kind.'

Victoria became aware that although he spoke to Franziska, he was looking at *her*. He appeared to be studying her intently, and she hastily glanced away. Colour crept to her cheeks, then flooded even more strongly at the humiliating thought that he could see the effect he was having upon her.

As the three of them moved toward the exit, Franziska explained what had brought them to the station. By now there were no cabs left in the forecourt, and Lorenz asked if they would wait for one. 'It will only be a few minutes, I expect.'

'Thank you,' Franziska replied, 'but Vicky and I are planning to walk home, as we came. It's very pleasant at this time of day.'

Lorenz von Kaunitz smiled. 'That's what I think, too. It's a welcome relief to have a stroll through the woods after spending all day in Vienna. May I perhaps accompany you?'

'How nice – but is it not out of your way?'

'Scarcely at all.'

They strolled through the town together, crossed the bridge and took the lane toward the villa. Lorenz wore his double-breasted frock coat open, showing a sprigged blue waistcoat, and he carried a black morocco portfolio tucked casually under his arm. In answer to Franziska's inquiries he explained that he went each day to the agriculture equipment foundry in the Ottakring district, which he managed for his grandfather.

Unexpectedly, Victoria found she was being asked a question.

'Do you feel confident about the audition tomorrow, Miss Wayland?'

She would have liked to appear cool and detached, but finding no convincing answer to that effect, she was trapped into simple candour.

'I'm a bundle of nerves at the prospect.'

'Understandably.' He sounded genuinely sympathetic. 'But I'm sure it won't prove too much of an ordeal. Anticipation is generally worse than the thing itself.'

Franziska said, 'I would naturally have gone with Vicky, but I have another engagement.' She paused an instant, and added with a pretty smile, 'Your father has promised to honour me with a visit.'

'But you have only to suggest another day. He would understand.'

Franziska shook her head quite decidedly. 'There's no need to put him to the trouble of changing his plans.'

'No need at all,' Victoria confirmed. 'I'm perfectly capable of looking after myself.'

They had to step aside onto the celandine-starred verge to allow room for a returning station fly. It whirled by at a rapid pace, the driver touching his whip to his brown bowler hat in salutation.

As they walked on, Lorenz said, 'If you intend to return at about this time tomorrow, Miss Wayland, then may I suggest we meet in the city and travel back together?'

Victoria stared at him dumbly, her wits scattering to the four winds. Franziska answered for her. 'What a delightful idea! It is very good of you to offer, Herr Baron. Most kind!'

'The pleasure will be mine! I'll come to the Conservatoire, Miss Wayland, to collect you when you are finished.'

They were strolling without hurry, yet they came to the villa all too soon. At the white wicket gate Lorenz paused and raised his hat to them. 'Until tomorrow then, Miss Wayland.'

She tried to smile back at him with a sophistication to equal Franziska's, as though the arrangement seemed in no way

34

extraordinary to her. Inwardly, though, she was far from calm and her heart was thudding with a painfully erratic beat.

'Perhaps one day soon, Herr Baron,' said Franziska, 'you too will call upon us. Pray do not stand upon ceremony. Vicky and I will be most happy to see you at any time.'

'So kind of you, Mrs Wayland.'

As he turned and walked back the way they had come, moving with long, swift, easy strides, Victoria lingered by the gate and watched him, pretending she was admiring some spikes of blue lupin. It astonished her to recall that on their first meeting she had likened him in her mind to Mr Johnston Forbes-Robertson, for she saw now that Lorenz von Kaunitz was not made in the pattern of any other man. He was uniquely himself.

'Don't stand there staring,' Franziska called, under her breath. Then, when Victoria guiltily joined her at the front door, she added with a teasing glance, 'It never does, you know, to allow a man to see that one is so interested in him.'

4

An orchestra was at rehearsal in the concert hall of the Musikverein when Victoria emerged from her audition, and the soaring strains of the grand march from *Aida* sounded like a paean of triumph in her especial honour.

At the foot of the main stairway a porter in a gold-braided uniform informed her that His Excellency Baron von Kaunitz was waiting in an ante-room. Too excited now to be nervous, she burst in upon him breathlessly.

'Just think, they have promised me a place in September! Isn't it almost too good to be true?'

Lorenz responded by coming forward and taking her two hands in his. 'I am so happy for you, Victoria. This is what you have longed for, and I am sure you will be a great success in your musical career.'

'Thank you, Herr Baron, you are very kind.'

'Please don't be so formal with me,' he said. 'My uncle is Heinrich to your stepmother, so cannot I be Lorenz to you?'

'But...'

'At least when we are alone together,' he urged.

Yesterday the idea would have shocked her, seeming a grossly over-familiar way of addressing a married man she scarcely knew. But somehow today, intoxicated with her success, none of the normal conventions seemed to apply. Lifting her chin, she gave him the sort of mannered look she had often seen Franziska bestow upon a man. 'Perhaps. We shall see.'

He regarded her with half-closed eyes, his mouth puckered in amusement. 'You are teasing me, Victoria.'

'Teasing you, Herr Baron ...?'

He raised a finger. 'Lorenz!'

She bit her lip, then laughed, pretending the slip had been deliberate. 'Very well then . . . Lorenz.'

'That's better. Come, we may as well be on our way.'

They walked through the ornate foyer and emerged onto the *platz* opposite the great domed Karlskirche flanked by its monumental twin pillars. The early evening sunshine poured in shafts of fluid gold from a gentle blue sky skeined with tiny twists of cloud. The beauty of Vienna with its stately buildings and gracious trees caught at her throat and made her feel breathless. She was committed to living here for several years at least, and she felt nothing but delight at the prospect. Already England and her childhood belonged to the past.

'There is no need for us to hurry back to Eisenbad,' Lorenz said. 'I thought perhaps I could show you one or two places of interest, and then we'll dine somewhere to celebrate your success.'

'Oh, but Franziska will be expecting me on the ten past six train, and she'll be worried if I'm late.'

Victoria's protest was instinctive, but she felt shaken and a little afraid to realize how dearly she would have liked to fall in with his suggestion. Never before had she dined alone with any man but her father, and the thought of dining with *this* man was at once rapturous and terrifying.

'No really,' she added in a voice that was less than firm, 'I'm afraid it isn't possible.'

He regarded her again in that faintly quizzical way with his eyes narrowed, though perhaps this time it was only against the slanting sunlight.

'I was expecting you to raise an objection, which is why I sent a telegram to your stepmother explaining that we shall be returning rather later than planned.'

'But you had no right to do that without asking me first,' she flared. Then more quietly, 'Franziska will be annoyed that you should take her permission for granted.'

'Do you really suppose she will mind?' he asked blandly.

Considering the matter, Victoria doubted if Franziska would take exception to her spending an extra hour or so in Lorenz's company, unchaperoned, when she herself had so eagerly espoused his suggestion of escorting her home from Vienna. Her stepmother was never a woman to be hidebound by the conventions.

'No, I don't suppose Franziska will mind very much,' she admitted.

'More to the point, do *you* mind?'

Victoria skirted a direct answer. 'We must not be *too* late, though.'

'Of course not. I thought we might go first to the Prater. The Riesenrad is just opened, you know, and everyone is talking about it. If the crowd is not too great we could take a ride.'

Victoria had seen the spider-web structure of the great wheel from several vantage points about the city. From the tower of St Stephen's Cathedral, when they had triumphantly climbed its five hundred and thirty-three steps, and from the wooded heights of Kahlenberg, the day they had gone there by rack railway after their first visit to the Conservatoire. The Ferris wheel had again been clearly visible from the terraced gardens of the Belvedere Palace, the official residence of Archduke Franz Ferdinand who was now heir to the throne following the death at Mayerling, in a suicide pact with his mistress, of the Emperor's son Crown Prinz Rudolf – a scandalous event which, as a child, Victoria had secretly read about in the *Birmingham Post*.

The idea of riding on the giant wheel, floating high and clear above the ground, brought an added flush of excitement to her cheeks. 'It is something I have been longing to do,' she admitted to Lorenz, 'but Franziska insisted it would make her giddy.'

He nodded, smiling, and signalled across the *platz* to a rank of waiting *fiacres*, one of which promptly wheeled over to them. She and her stepmother had always used the cheaper *einspänner*, and it seemed very grand to be riding in a two-horse carriage, the folding hood down for the fine evening. Victoria was intensely aware of the man beside her and kept taking sideways glances at him, though she needed no reminding of that profile with the strongly marked classical lines.

They drove by way of the Ringstrasse, crossing the Danube Canal by a chain bridge onto the wide Praterstrasse. As they went Lorenz questioned her about the audition, and Victoria explained how she had been received by three professors; the one she had seen before, and two colleagues. Firstly, she was required to name the notes of several intricate chords, then to play the opening theme of Beethoven's Fifth Symphony, and afterwards transpose it into another tonality. Finally, she had been asked to perform a piece of her own choosing.

'What did you play for them?' Lorenz inquired.

'Mozart – the A minor rondo.'

'And were you very nervous?'

'Dreadfully! When I found that my hands were actually trembling I was terrified I would muff my notes, and that only made me more anxious still.'

She could not admit to Lorenz that, even so, she had never before played with greater sensitivity, with greater tenderness – and in some curious way *he* was responsible. She had been wishing, almost, that the encounter at the railway station yesterday had never happened. For when she should have been using every precious moment to practise at the piano and otherwise ready herself for this afternoon, she kept finding his image intruding into her mind. She had scolded herself sternly, reminding herself that there was nothing about Lorenz von Kaunitz to deserve her admiration . . . a married man who publicly paraded a mistress! But it was no use, he coloured her every thought and emotion. Somehow, she knew, it was *because* of him that today she felt a new sense of maturity; saw everything with new eyes, listened with new ears, colours and sounds all seeming more vivid than ever before.

With a sudden rush of panic Victoria realized that she was in danger of falling in love. But this was not how she wanted it to be, her heart cried angrily. Not with this man!

'You are really dedicated to your music, aren't you?' he said.

She forced a little laugh. 'You seem surprised. Why should I not be?'

'You come from a family of musicians, perhaps?'

'Not particularly. My mother used to play the piano quite well, and it was she who first taught me when I was little. But we met a number of professional musicians through my father's theatrical connections, and when I showed a keen interest in a musical career he arranged for me to study the piano seriously.'

Lorenz inquired, 'Your father was on the stage, like your step-mother?'

'Oh no, Papa wasn't an actor. He was the manager of the Alhambra Theatre in Birmingham. That's how he came to meet Franziska. She was with a German touring company he had engaged for a season of operetta, and they were married within six weeks of setting eyes on one another.'

'So she swept your father off his feet. But then she is that sort of woman, is she not?'

'I'm not certain what you mean,' Victoria said with a frown. Had there been an undertow of criticism in his voice?

'I mean,' he explained, 'that she is a very striking woman with a compelling, dramatic quality to her beauty. And she knows to perfection how to make herself attractive to a man.'

Victoria said quickly, defensively, 'I'll have you know that I am very fond of Franziska.'

'As one would expect. You have so much in common.'

'What have we in common?'

His eyes sparkled with amusement. 'Come, Victoria, you are casting for compliments. Apply my description of your stepmother to yourself.'

She is a very striking woman with a compelling, dramatic quality to her beauty. And she knows to perfection how to make herself attractive to a man.

Victoria said faintly, 'That's nonsense, I am not in the least like Franziska.'

'No? You are still very young, but in a few years' time, when you have acquired the poise and style your stepmother possesses, I think you will be more than her equal. Quite *formidable*,' he added softly, saying the word in the French manner.

She felt . . . what did she feel? Flattered? Or was there irony behind his words? She was not sure. If only she could counter his remarks as tellingly as Franziska would have done.

He said, 'We are almost there. Do you see the big wheel?'

'Have you ridden on it before?' Victoria asked eagerly.

'Yes, once.'

With whom, she wondered. The woman in the theatre box? Perhaps he could read her thoughts, for he added, 'I took my small son.'

'I expect he was very excited,' Victoria said, smiling again.

Lorenz nodded, and an oddly pensive look came into his face. 'I like to see as much of Emil as I can. I think it is good for a growing boy to be with his father. Besides . . .'

Her curiosity was not to be satisfied, for the *fiacre* pulled up at that moment at the Praterstern. Lorenz alighted and offered her his hand to assist her down. He paid off the driver and as they threaded their way through the fairground crowds he did not return to the subject of his son.

At the Ferris wheel, which near-to seemed bigger than she had ever imagined, towering above them like a monster cage of latticed metalwork, they joined the throng of people pushing toward the turnstile. So many were eager for this exciting new experience that it required several cabins to complete the circle and disgorge their complement of

40

passengers before at last it was the turn of Victoria and Lorenz to step aboard. Securely locked in with a score of others they were carried upward in silence, almost imperceptibly, halting at intervals to allow other cabins to empty and refill, then gliding on once more. She stood beside Lorenz at the viewing window and gazed out at an ever-widening panorama of Vienna; the domes and spires of the churches and public buildings, the splendid horseshoe of the Ringstrasse, with the distand wooded slopes of the Wienerwald a dramatic backcloth. As they rose higher into the deepening blueness of the sky they seemed to float in space, cut off from any contact with the earth below them.

'From up here,' she said in wonderment, 'there seems no solid substance in anything down there, no reality. It's like a fairytale world.'

'A more apt comment than you realize.' His voice contained a kernel of bitterness, and she turned her head to look at him.

'What are you saying?'

He shrugged. 'It all looks very admirable on the surface, this capital city of the great Habsburg empire. But scratch away the glitter and what do you find? That which is genuinely old is falling into decay, and the new is a hotch-potch of vulgar fakery.'

Vienna was *his* city, yet she was the one to defend it. 'You mean, I suppose, because the new buildings are a mixing of past architectural styles ... classical, renaissance, and gothic? But surely that doesn't matter, when the overall effect is so splendid? The Ringstrasse must be the most magnificent thoroughfare anywhere in the world.'

'The rottenness goes deeper than just the architecture, Victoria. An era of history is spinning to an end, and we are too blind to see it.' His mouth tightened in a small, humourless smile as he went on, 'But I am being serious, and that's a punishable offence in Vienna. For the Viennese, life is an endless comedy in which nothing can be more important than the pursuit of pleasure.'

Victoria was so astonished, so shocked, that she could think of no answer to give him. They had reached the highest point now and Lorenz took her elbow and drew her to the other side of the cabin for the descent. From here their view was away from the city, looking right across the River Danube to the flatlands beyond, which stretched to the distant wilderness of Asia. It was from out of the mists of these vast plains, she recalled with an awed sense of history, that invading armies had attacked over the centuries, to be flung back by the brave defenders or sometimes quietly absorbed, their alien cultures helping to make Vienna the magnificent metropolis it was now.

But Lorenz von Kaunitz was trying to deny Vienna's greatness. She asked in a wondering voice, 'Are you not proud of your native city?'

'I am proud of what it *has* been, and what it *could be*. I'm proud of Vienna's leadership in science and medicine and so many branches of the arts. I love my city, Victoria, but should love blind me to its shortcomings?'

With a slight judder their cabin reached the ground platform, and they stepped out. All around them the crowds weaved excitedly, their voices adding to the clamour of the fairground touts, the carousel steam organs and the café orchestras.

Lorenz became lighthearted once more. 'It's far too early to dine yet, so shall we enjoy the fun of the fair?' Sensing her hesitation, he added, 'You needn't worry, it's never a rough crowd here. In the Wurstel Prater everyone mixes together and social barriers are forgotten.'

'Well ... for a little while, then.'

'Good! We'll start off on the scenic railway, and then I'll show off quite shamelessly at the shooting gallery and win a prize for you. After that some dancing. For a few kreuzers one may step into the arena for a waltz or a polka, and it's much gayer than any smart ballroom.'

Eagerly, she gave herself up to the pleasure of this evening with Lorenz: the pleasure of sitting beside him in the semi-darkness of the box-like 'railway' compartment, while exotic painted scenes of Japan and Switzerland and the Rocky Mountains of America were wound past the window; of proudly watching him score four bullseyes with six shots and win a tin locket with gaudy stones of coloured glass; of being held, blissfully, in his arms as they whirled to the strains of a Johann Strauss waltz. Afterwards, breathless and laughing, they sat at a crowded round table and drank cool white wine drawn from a great barrel set on trestles, wine that tasted clean and crisp and refreshing. When a flower woman with a huge wicker basket came past, Lorenz bought Victoria a little posy of lilies-of-the-valley, and a red carnation for his buttonhole.

'And now,' he said softly into her ear, 'it is time we dined.'

They travelled by *fiacre* once more, back toward the inner city, the last of the summer daylight hazing gently into a languid violet dusk. After they had recrossed the Danube Canal she lost all sense of direction, but it hardly mattered. The carriage seemed to glide as if the cobbled streets were strewn with feathers, and when Lorenz took her hand in his she felt only the thrilling warmth of his touch, and had no stirrings of alarm. The situation was highly unconventional, of course, but was not this Vienna? And was not Lorenz a family friend, to whose care she had been entrusted by Franziska herself?

'We must not be too late getting home,' she murmured.

'Leave everything to me.'

When they drew up, light spilled out from an impressive entrance, and a commissionaire in a cockaded top hat hurried forward to hold the carriage door. With her hand on Lorenz's arm, Victoria drifted into a foyer where crystal chandeliers glittered and the floor was a sea of dark red carpeting. They mounted a flight of shallow stairs and were led along an upper gallery by a deferential waiter. He flicked back a curtain and threw open a door, and stood aside for them to enter.

'Is this satisfactory, *Exzellenz*?'

Lorenz swept a glance around. 'Thank you, yes. We will dine at once, if you please, Herr Ober.'

As the man bowed out, Victoria drew off her gloves and surveyed the room dreamily. A small oval table was laid for two with white napery and sparkling silver, and red roses in a porcelain bowl subtly scented the air. The window drapes were drawn across, and silk shades on the wall sconces softened the light to a rosy glow. Standing in a curtained alcove was a scrolled sofa, deep-buttoned and covered in crimson velvet. Faintly, as if from some distance off, she could hear an orchestra striking up a waltz tune.

'Are we to dine here alone?' she asked Lorenz in surprise.

'I thought you might prefer to be quiet. The food in this place is superb. I have ordered already, and I am sure you will approve my choice.'

Victoria considered this gravely. She had imagined a large crowded restaurant, a fashionable one, that went without saying. But perhaps he was right, perhaps it would be more relaxing and less demanding after the excitements of this special day to dine here quietly with him.

A discreet tap on the door announced a waiter with wine in an ice-bucket. He drew the cork, poured a little, and stood awaiting Lorenz's verdict.

'Thank you, I will see to it myself.'

43

The man withdrew and Lorenz filled two crystal goblets, holding one out to her.

'I have already taken a couple of glasses of wine this evening,' Victoria reminded him hesitantly.

'This wine is from the Wachau, it is very light and harmless,' he assured her. 'Taste it and you will see.' He touched her glass with his and she sipped a little. The wine was dry to the palate, with an elusive nutty flavour. Quite delicious.

Lorenz suggested she might be more comfortable without her hat, and she crossed to the gilt-framed mirror above the mantel to take it off, removing the long tortoiseshell pin. He came to stand behind her and she could see his reflection. There was a look of admiration in his dark eyes which gave her a quiver of pleasure.

'I've never seen you before without a hat,' he said. 'You have very beautiful hair, like the colour of ripe corn rippling in the sunlight.'

'I wish you wouldn't always pay such extravagant compliments,' she protested, feeling that the moment was spoiled.

Lorenz raised his hand to a tress of hair at the nape of her neck, running it slowly through his fingers. 'You are a rare creature, Victoria. A woman who objects to a man's compliments.' In the looking-glass their glances met, and his eyes held a question she did not understand.

'But they sound so artificial, so insincerely meant,' she stammered.

'Is it insincere to wish to give a woman pleasure?'

She had no answer to give him, and the waiter's tap at the door saved her the need. He wheeled in a laden trolley and prepared to wait on them, but Lorenz said, dismissing him, 'That will be all until I ring.'

'Let us eat at once,' he suggested, when the man had left. 'I shall serve you myself.'

Victoria scarcely noted what it was they ate, except that it was all quite superb – a cold *consommé*, a *soufflé*, some kind of meat in a rich sauce, and a gâteau with thick whipped cream. She let Lorenz refill her glass and she felt relaxed and very happy as they laughed and talked together. The rose-shaded lights seemed to merge into a single warm enveloping glow and she was only vaguely aware of his fingers on her wrist, probing beneath the cuff to caress the soft skin of her forearm. Then to her feet and his arms were around her, drawing her close to him, and his lips were on her hair, her temples, brushing her cheeks with little fleeting kisses until his warm mouth met hers in a long sweet embrace. Instinctively she clung to him in a blissful dream, and his kiss became more passionate and demanding.

'Come,' he murmured. 'You are so very desirable, and I am impatient.'

It was only then, as he drew her even closer and tried to lead her toward the sofa in the alcove, that the mist in her brain suddenly cleared. Shocked, she pulled herself free and cried in a strangled whisper, 'No, you must not . . .'

'You have nothing to fear. No one will interrupt us.' He pulled her toward him again, one hand moving up from the level of her slender waist to cup the soft round curve of her breast. 'You are so lovely.'

Victoria wrenched herself free from his grasp. Sick with misery she glanced around this intimate private room, so rich and sumptuous with its silk and plush, but seeming to her now cheap and tawdry and unutterably vulgar.

'This was your objective from the start, wasn't it?' she cried accusingly. 'This was your one purpose in suggesting you should meet me at the Conservatoire this afternoon!' Her voice broke on a sob. 'And I was naïve enough to believe you were sincere in offering to escort me home.'

'As I was. I shall escort you home at the proper time.'

'No, I am leaving now! This very instant, and without you.'

Hastily she gathered up her belongings, trying to retain a small degree of dignity. She pressed her hat on her head and stabbed in the pin, not caring that it was slightly askew. All she wanted to do was to get out of the room, away from him, away from the nightmare.

'Why this performance of injured innocence?' Lorenz sounded ruffled himself. 'I apologize if I went too far too quickly. No doubt in England such matters are conducted differently, but you are in Vienna now.'

Incredibly, he was suggesting that *she* was the one at fault. Victoria was appalled, and felt she could not leave without trying to defend herself, without hitting back at him.

'I realize,' she said shakily, 'that I should never have agreed to spend the evening with you. That was a foolish mistake, I can see it now. But I took you for a gentleman, and I thought you were merely being kind. I have never given you the smallest reason to think . . . to believe that I . . .'

'Have you not?' he scoffed. 'Why, you and your stepmother

virtually accosted me at the Café Radetsky that day. You cannot deny it.'

'I do deny it! Of course I deny it.' She was trying hard to blot out her own unhappy suspicions about the incident at the café. 'The explanation is very simple, as Franziska told you herself. She knew your uncle many years ago, and when she heard the waiter mention your family name it came as a surprise. Was it so very remiss of her to repeat the name in your hearing?'

'It was very clever of her. The stratagem worked beautifully.'

'What stratagem?'

'Your stepmother had offered the waiter a bribe to greet me by name and in loud clear tones so that she could identify me when I arrived.'

A shapeless fear clutched at Victoria's heart, but still she conceded no ground. 'All this is pure invention on your part,' she began bravely, but her words died as she saw the chilling look of triumph in his eyes.

'I'm afraid I have it from Karl himself. When I questioned him he was very apologetic, fearing that I would be annoyed. But I can't blame the man. After all, my name is not a secret. I presume your stepmother had somehow discovered that it is my habit to spend an hour or so with my friends at the Café Radetsky every Wednesday afternoon.'

'But ... but this is absurd,' Victoria faltered helplessly. 'What possible motive could she have for wanting you indentified?'

'It is obvious to me that she wished to renew contact with my uncle, but was anxious to make it appear to have happened through a chance encounter. Her ultimate motive I can only guess at.'

Victoria stared at him in bleak dismay, conscious that her lower lip was quivering. She still sought desperately for an answer to his accusation, but her vivid recollection of that afternoon was like a gag against her tongue. She had no doubt at all now that Franziska had deliberately chosen the gloomy Café Radetsky in preference to a more attractive place; that going across to the newspaper rack with the waiter to choose some journals to read had merely been a ploy to speak privately to the man; and that the money she had paid him when they left had indeed been a five-crown piece, and not the single gulden that Franziska had pretended.

She was aware that Lorenz was watching her intently, trying to read her mind. Feeling trapped, she voiced a stray thought without considering where it might lead her.

46

'Franziska and your uncle were very close friends at one time. She told me that they first met when she was appearing at the Theater an der Wien—'

'In various minor roles,' he interjected. 'I took the trouble to investigate. She was a mere *vedette*.'

'You make even that sound like a crime,' Victoria said hotly. 'Franziska has never claimed to have been one of the leading artistes.'

All at once Lorenz was contrite. 'You're right, it was an unfair point to make.'

Her bristling defences collapsed before the sudden softening of his attitude. She felt bitter tears pressing against her eyelids which would not be stifled. They brimmed over and trickled down both cheeks as she stammered out wretchedly, 'You seem to regard my stepmother as some kind of . . . of adventuress.'

'I was merely proving to you that our meeting at the Café Radetsky was not the chance encounter it was meant to seem – as I suspected from the very first.'

'And you believe that I was involved, too,' she whispered, unaware that she was conceding her own belief in his charge against Franziska.

Lorenz gave her a strange, long look, his eyes searching. 'Victoria, please forgive me. All my instincts told me that whatever your stepmother was contriving, you were not a party to it. I strenuously resisted my instincts, though, because I feared they were making a fool of me. And yet, your demeanour, your whole attitude to life and your serious desire to study music – none of these things indicated a young woman who was . . .' He baulked at the description, and pleaded again, 'Do say that you forgive me.'

'But I don't understand. If you believed well of me – or at least, if you wished to believe well of me – then why did you . . . why did you bring me to such a place as this?'

'I viewed it, I think, as a kind of test. If in truth you were trying to use me, then I could play the same game. Can you blame me? Could any man be blamed for seizing the chance to make love to you, if that was the bait being offered?' He raised his hands in a small, helpless gesture. 'You make me despise myself, Victoria.'

Her tears had dried on her cheeks. She felt consumed by a sense of despair, adrift in an alien, adult world she could not understand. 'I had better leave now,' she murmured. 'Will . . . will you please have someone call a cab for me.'

'In a few minutes. And I shall come with you. But first, I must try to dispel the harsh thoughts you are harbouring about me.'

'Does it matter? You and your family can wish for no further association with my stepmother and me, not now.'

'It matters very much, Victoria. I hope most earnestly that what has happened this evening will not bring our acquaintanceship to an end. You must believe that,' he insisted, and she could not doubt the sincerity in his dark eyes. 'As for my uncle and my father, I confess that their attitude puzzles me. I have told them of my suspicions concerning your stepmother, but they only seemed amused, and assured me I had no cause for concern.'

Victoria said on a whispered breath, 'I think – it is an inescapable thought to me – that Franziska and your uncle must have had some sort of romantic liaison in the past.'

'That would scarcely be surprising! In her younger days she must have been outstandingly lovely.'

'But your uncle was already married,' Victoria said, artlessly.

'It is not uncommon, you know, for a married man's eyes to stray. And now, of course, in the middle years Uncle Heinrich is even more susceptible to a beautiful woman who flings herself across his path.'

'But Franziska wouldn't ... she couldn't! As she reminded me herself, she is still mourning my father.'

'So you've already questioned her on the subject? You had your own suspicions?'

Victoria's rising colour answered him. She said hurriedly, 'Franziska is not a bad woman, you must not think too harshly of her. She is vain, I know, and she always likes to have her own way and be the centre of attention. But at heart she is kindly and well-meaning. She was a good wife to my father and ... we are not close, I know, but she has always been a good stepmother to me.'

'Perhaps,' Lorenz reflected, 'it is merely that she hopes my uncle, a man of influence and standing, can help to smooth her path now that she has returned to Vienna.'

Gratefully, Victoria seized upon this suggestion. 'I'm sure you are right. In fact, Franziska made the point herself that two women such as we, two women alone in the world, are in a vulnerable situation.'

Lorenz frowned. 'Forgive me, but what is your financial position? Is it insecure?'

'It is less secure than I would like,' she confessed after a moment's hesitation. 'Papa left sufficient for our needs, but ...'

'But you fear it is not being wisely used?' When she did not reply, he persisted, 'Your stepmother is too extravagant, perhaps?'

'Franziska does not see it as extravagance,' Victoria said defensively. 'It is just ... well, it is her nature to act impetuously, and sometimes this involves us in additional expense. Like deciding to move to the Hotel Maria Theresia although the pension we were originally staying at was quite adequate for our needs.'

'You moved to the Maria Theresia *after* meeting me at the café?'

'Yes,' Victoria admitted, realizing that again she had betrayed more than she had intended.

'Your stepmother is an astute woman capable of quick decisions,' Lorenz said thoughtfully, 'but that does not of necessity make her dangerous. We must try, you and I, to discover exactly what it is she has in mind.'

His suggestion that they should act to the same purpose, as though allies, brought a new quickening of her pulses. With one finger he lightly traced a line down her cheek where the tears had dried and she shivered under his touch, aware of the tenderness he was expressing. She felt a sudden flame of longing, and it made her afraid.

Lorenz said, his voice husky, 'We had better go now, I think. While you get yourself ready, I will order a cab.'

In the *fiacre*, he said, 'You must not take this amiss, Victoria, but if you are ever concerned about finding the fees for your studies at the Conservatoire, I may have a solution to offer.'

She felt dismayed that, after all, he had understood nothing and was still intent upon seducing her.

'Thank you,' she replied in a stiff voice, 'but Franziska says we shall be able to manage.'

'But if, as you fear, she spends money incautiously, what then?'

What then indeed! A vision of her father's all too modest legacy dwindling to nothing sent fear flickering down her spine. Were they truly in a position to manage her tuition fees at the Conservatoire, which would amount to so much more than the cost of studying music in England? Guilt followed swiftly, too. For although she was in no way a party to her stepmother's mysterious plans, Victoria could not avoid the thought that she was in some way responsible for them nevertheless. That *her* present needs, *her* future security, were to some extent what Franziska was scheming for.

'We shall be able to manage,' she reiterated stubbornly.

'I was merely going to point out that if you find yourself in difficulties there are such things as scholarships. My grandfather, through his farm machinery business, sponsors several students at the Conservatoire. I am sure I could persuade him of your merits.'

'I ... I could not allow that.'

'You would permit your pride to stand in the way of your studies?'

She thought for a moment. 'No, not pride.'

'What, then?'

'It's impossible, you must see that.'

'It is by no means impossible. I shall keep it in mind, should the need ever arise.'

At the Südbahnhof, they found that the next train to Eisenbad was about to leave. As they hastened onto the platform Lorenz hailed a porter who held the door for them, and they climbed aboard just as the guard's whistle shrilled. They had a compartment to themselves and Lorenz drew the yellow curtains across the window, enclosing them and shutting out the night.

They sat facing one another on the buttoned leather seats. His closeness, the intensity of his gaze, embarrassed Victoria, but there was nowhere else to look. For something to do she unpinned the posy of lilies-of-the-valley he had bought for her at the Prater, and inhaled their pure, sweet fragrance. She felt very tired, drained of anger, drained of all emotion. She was thankful, as the train rattled on through the darkness, that Lorenz made no attempt to talk.

5

In the days that elapsed between their evening together in Vienna and the bombshell that was soon to come, Victoria saw Lorenz on two occasions.

The first time she was walking through the Stadtpark one Sunday afternoon on her way to the post office in the square. Families were out enjoying the warm July sunshine, and their shouts and laughter drifted across the grass to the seat-lined promenade between the rose beds. She paused to study the bronze statue of Johann Strauss *père*, then as she strolled on she heard her name called from behind.

'Hallo!' Lorenz said when she spun round. 'I spotted you from the café over there. Where are you off to?'

'To post these.' Victoria held up the little batch of letters to show him, and Lorenz fell into step beside her. She was delighted to see him again, but she felt an odd restraint upon her – a restraint that he seemed to share. Their conversation was not easy and they spoke only of innocuous, impersonal matters, such as the fine warm weather and the various entertainments and other activities arranged in Eisenbad for the summer season. When Lorenz referred to Queen Victoria's diamond jubilee celebrations that had just taken place in England, she seized upon this eagerly.

'When we left home everyone was getting very excited about the jubilee,' she told him. 'People were making red, white and blue bunting to drape out of their windows, and all sorts of parades and street parties were being organized for the great day. I was sorry we should be missing it all, but Franziska was impatient to get to Vienna once she had made up her mind to come.'

'Ah well, there'll be similar excitement here next year when the

Emperor celebrates his *golden* jubilee. Though Franz Josef has little cause for celebration, I'd have thought,' he added dryly.

'Oh, but surely . . . so long upon the throne. They have so much in common, our Queen and your Emperor.'

'Perhaps. I suspect, though, that the British monarchy will survive a great deal longer than ours.'

A child's rubber ball bounced across the path, and Lorenz retrieved it and tossed it back. Victoria suddenly became impatient with herself for avoiding the one subject that haunted her thoughts. Swinging round to Lorenz, she burst out, 'Have you spoken to your uncle again about Franziska?'

He nodded. 'More to the point, I have spoken to my father, too. You are aware, I expect, that he and your stepmother spent the evening together while we were in Vienna. And they have met more than once since.'

Victoria glanced away from him. It was indeed Lorenz's father's association with Franziska which now troubled her even more than his uncle's. She could not avoid a feeling of shame, even though Lorenz knew she was not a partner in her stepmother's contrivances.

'What did your father have to say?' she asked anxiously.

'Very little, apart from telling me not to concern myself about his affairs.' Lorenz shrugged. 'I suppose he can safely be left to look after himself if he wants to lose his head over a woman. Though I still have an uneasy suspicion that there could be more in this than appears on the surface.'

'But what can there be? I have tried to talk to Franziska, but she only scoffs at me. She did admit frankly, though, that she considered the friendship of the two Barons von Kaunitz of inestimable value, and something which no woman on her own could be expected to forgo when it is proffered.'

'Then I expect there is no more than that involved,' he said. But Victoria detected a thread of doubt in his voice.

A couple of days later Lorenz called upon them at the villa.

'You insisted that I was not to stand upon ceremony, Mrs Wayland,' he said, when Gerda showed him into the parlour. 'So I have taken you at your word.'

'Come in, come in,' Franziska invited gaily. 'Is it not delightful, Vicky, to have friends who feel sufficiently at home to dispense with the formalities?'

'*Guten Tag*, Herr Baron,' Victoria said nervously.

His smile reproved her. 'Now who is being formal?'

Franziska glanced from one to the other of them, amused. 'You have my permission, Vicky, to address this young man by his given name, though I strongly suspect that you have already taken that liberty.'

'Hardly a liberty,' Lorenz suggested, 'when our two families are rapidly achieving such a friendly relationship.'

Franziska's smile was complacent. 'Do come and sit down – here beside me on the sofa. Have you not been to your foundry today?'

'I left earlier than usual, in order to pay this visit.'

Franziska clapped her palms together in an expression of rapture, the jet mourning rings on her slender fingers glittering in a beam of sunlight that pierced the French window.

'We are flattered, are we not, Vicky? You will take some refreshment, Lorenz?'

'I am refreshed already by such charming company.'

'Then let a glass of wine add to your pleasure.'

He stayed for nearly an hour, and for most of the time Victoria stayed silent. She was consumed with embarrassment over Franziska's flirtatious manner, and she hated Lorenz for responding to it. He seemed to have little attention to spare for her, and when he did occasionally glance in her direction she studiously looked away.

When he had gone, Franziska said, 'He is a real charmer, is he not? You realize, I suppose, that his eyes were all for you.' Her smile faded and she became thoughtful. 'It is sad that he should already be married – and not at all happily, I gather. But there it is! You must take the greatest care, Vicky, not to lose your heart to him.'

Victoria wondered uneasily how much her stepmother had guessed about her feelings for Lorenz. She had counted herself fortunate that on the occasion she had returned late from the evening with him in Vienna, Franziska had been so full of the delightful hours spent in Baron Gustav's company that the catechism Victoria dreaded was postponed till next day, by which time she felt calm enough to parry her stepmother's questions into harmless channels. Since then, she had been at pains to give no hint of her interest in Lorenz, scarcely even mentioning his name.

'You've no cause for concern on my account,' she said stiffly. 'After all, you were the one he was flirting with ... to such an extent that I felt quite embarrassed.'

Her stepmother flicked her wrist in a small dismissive gesture. 'Pouf! That sort of thing means nothing. It's just a pleasant little game between the sexes we Viennese like to play.'

Victoria did not hear the carriage draw up outside. She had dined alone this evening and now, with the lamps in the parlour lit and the green curtains drawn across the window, she was back yet again at the piano when the door from the hall burst open and Franziska swept in, still wearing her black evening cape.

'Vicky, darling, you will never guess!'

Absorbed in a difficult fingering exercise of leaps in dotted rhythms, Victoria merely glanced over her shoulder. 'Guess what? Where is Baron Gustav?'

'He is not coming in this evening, I asked him not to. I wanted to be alone when I broke my news to you.' Franziska paused, then as if unable to resist the dramatic gesture, she ran swiftly forward and flung both arms round Victoria's neck. 'Dearest, is it not too wonderful? Gustav has done me the honour of asking me to be his wife.'

Victoria's two hands crashed down upon the keys in horrid discord. 'I don't understand. It ... it's not possible.'

'But it is true! I knew you would be astonished – as I was myself, I must confess. After we had dined, Gustav suggested that we stroll in the Kurhaus gardens ... so romantic, with the coloured lanterns strung in the trees and the band playing softly from beyond the fountains. He was unusually silent, and then quite suddenly he came out with his proposal.'

'And you had no idea this was in his mind?'

'None! Oh, Gustav has been attentive, and I cannot pretend I did not suspect he felt ... a certain interest in me. But marriage! And so soon!' Her look reproached Victoria for her obvious lack of enthusiasm. 'I know what you are thinking. You feel it is far too early after your poor papa's death. But only reflect a moment, Vicky darling. Would dear James himself have objected? He would want me to find new happiness, I am sure. After all, it is over six months now, and neither Gustav nor I are in the first flush of youth.'

Victoria remained seated before the piano, at a loss how to respond to this astounding news. Her stepmother looked enraptured as she floated across the room to tug the bell handle.

'We must celebrate, Vicky – with champagne! Is there any in the house, I wonder? If not, Hans must go to the hotel for some. Nothing less will do for such an occasion.'

Victoria asked weakly, 'When is the wedding to be? Have you fixed on a date?'

'The dear man will hear of no delay. As soon as arrangements can be made, he insists. He refuses to wait a day longer than is absolutely necessary.' Gerda came to the door and Franziska told her to fetch champagne. Unclasping her cape, she tossed it with her gloves upon the sofa and continued excitedly, 'We shall live at the schloss, Vicky – you as well, of course. And – have you realized yet? – I shall be a baroness. Just imagine! No more plain Mrs for me. Baroness von Kaunitz! I can still scarcely believe it myself.'

Bewildered, Victoria wished above everything that she could speak to Lorenz, to hear his opinion of this amazing development. Did he know about it yet? Perhaps at this very moment his father was informing the family at the schloss. How would they react, she wondered? Would they think that Franziska had schemed her way into Baron Gustav's affection? And what about Baron Heinrich, who had introduced them to each other? Above all, what of Lorenz?

'You might at least show a little pleasure,' Franziska said, her lips curled in a pout. 'You've not even congratulated me yet.'

'I'm sorry, but it came as such a shock – surprise, I mean.' Victoria went on tentatively, 'Why has Baron Gustav done this?'

'What a question! Why does a man usually propose to a woman? Is it so difficult to believe that he has fallen in love with me?'

'But you must admit, the first time he came to call, he seemed ... well, very reluctant and ill-at-ease.'

'That was understandable. Gustav is the younger twin, remember, and he has always been a little in his brother's shadow. Because I was Heinrich's friend, he was naturally cautious about betraying an interest in me. But as soon as he realized that I looked upon him with ... a certain admiration, he felt free to show his true feelings.'

Victoria's unhappy bewilderment made her less than cautious in choosing her words. 'How can Baron Gustav wish to marry you, when in the past you and his brother were ... were ...?'

Franziska shot her a dangerous glance that dared her to continue. Victoria rose to her feet and began to pace the room. She paused before the bust of the poet Grillparzer that stood on its marble pedestal in a corner, and absently smoothed the white stone.

'You said that Baron Gustav has fallen in love with you, but on your

55

side only that you feel a certain admiration for him. Is that sufficient reason for marrying a man?'

Franziska's expression was sorrowing, but indulgent. 'You have so much to learn about the world and its ways, Vicky. A woman needs a man who will protect her, a man who will support her. Love is all very well in its way, but...'

'Did you not love my father, then?'

'Now you are being offensive again! Do not forget, Vicky, that it is in your interest almost as much as my own that I should make this excellent match. From now on, you will be moving in circles of society far above any you have dreamed of hitherto. You will be brought into contact with eligible men of the most superior class.'

'You speak as if I'm to be displayed in a shop window,' Victoria flared. 'Able to command a higher price now, because it's a very superior shop. When I marry, *if* I marry, it will be for love. Nothing else!'

'It is fortunate,' said Franziska coldly, 'that such youthful idealism always gives way to the wisdom of maturity.' She gathered up her cloak and gloves and moved to the door. 'Considering your attitude, Vicky, it would be pointless to open a bottle of champagne. You had better continue with your practising. I shall not let it disturb me.'

Victoria could not settle again at the piano, though, and she soon gave up any serious attempt to practise. She let her hands roam idly over the keys while she brooded about the news that would bring such a dramatic change to her life.

Was it possible that from their very first day in Vienna – or even, perhaps, before leaving England – her stepmother had been scheming a chain of events that would culminate in this highly advantageous marriage? It seemed past belief that Franziska could ever have expected to succeed with such a far-fetched objective. Could it originally have been her hope that, after the passage of so many years, her ex-lover Baron Heinrich von Kaunitz might be a widower; and finding this was not the case, had she redirected her ambitions, making his widowed twin brother her new goal?

Now, with Franziska, she would be taking up residence at the Schloss Kaunitz, the great mansion she had often secretly gazed upon from the shelter of the woods. She would be obliged to meet the others who lived there, become one of them. She would be thrust into the intimacy of family life with Lorenz's wife, his small son, and worse

56

she would actually be related to Lorenz himself. They would have Franziska as their mutual stepmother. The situation would be beyond bearing.

Gerda looked in to say goodnight, but still Victoria sat on. She had moved across to the circular table now, and her fingers toyed restlessly with the fringe of the green chenille cloth. She was hardly aware at first of the distant rumble of thunder in the mountains, but slowly the summer storm moved nearer until it was raging through their own valley.

Franziska appeared suddenly in the doorway. She was in her robe of pale blue silk, her mass of chestnut hair tumbled about her shoulders. In the soft lamplight, the amber eyes looked huge and dark.

'Vicky, I went to your room because of the storm and found you were not yet in bed. What's wrong?'

'I've been thinking about your news.'

Franziska came closer, yet with a faint air of timidity that was quite novel in her. 'Oh, Vicky, I wish you could be happy for me,' she said wistfully.

'I want to be, honestly I do.' Victoria stood up and gave a little shiver, as if the sultry air in the room had suddenly turned chill. 'Tell me, Franziska, please tell me, is it true that Baron Gustav loves you? That *is* his reason for asking you to marry him? I must know.'

Suddenly her stepmother's arms were about her as they had never been before, drawing her close in a warm, maternal embrace.

'My poor dear girl, what have you been thinking? Of course Gustav loves me, and why should he not? Everything is going to be all right – quite, quite wonderful in fact, you will see. Happiness is in store for us both, I promise you. Fate has decided to look kindly upon us.'

Directly overhead the thunder crashed again. The lamp flames flickered and the whole fabric of the little villa trembled as if it were cowering before the anger of the heavens.

6

Outside the window a thrush was singing its sharp sweet song, a soloist to the bird chorus coming from the woods.

Victoria roused herself and peered sleepily around the unfamiliar room that brimmed with amber-gold light from the morning sunshine filtering through the silken drapes. Her new home. So unlike the only other home she had known, her father's three-storey terraced house in Birmingham. A whole world away.

She turned her head to glance at the clock on the rosewood cabinet, its gilded dial cradled between two kneeling alabaster cupids. Ten minutes to eight. She threw aside the covers and stepped out of bed, feeling the carpet's velvet softness between her bare toes, and reached for the quilted satin robe which Franziska had insisted upon as more befitting her new life than her serviceable woollen dressing-gown.

The past fortnight had flashed by in a ferment of activity with the preparations for Franziska's wedding. The two of them had visited Vienna's smartest shops in the Kohlmarkt and the Kärntnerstrasse to ponder over cascades of lovely fabrics, and select gloves and hats and shoes. Dressmakers and needlewomen had come daily to the villa. And now, so quickly, it was all over. The marriage ceremony had taken place yesterday at the pretty twin-towered church in the town square, followed by a grand reception at the schloss. Franziska had made a radiant bride, winning the enthusiastic admiration of all the gentlemen. Baroness Mathilde, though, had been barely gracious to her new sister-in-law, and some of the women guests had taken their cue from her. Now Baron Gustav and his bride had departed on their honeymoon trip to Italy. Victoria, a courtesy member of the von Kaunitz family, faced the first three weeks in her new home without the moral support of her stepmother.

Opening the French windows, Victoria stepped out to the balcony. The view from the schloss was more extensive than from their rented villa lower down the valley's slopes, for here the woodlands of the Wienerwald did not hem them so close around. She looked out across the sparkling lapis lazuli of the lake's clear waters to a distant point between two giant beech trees where the boundary railings glinted. It was there she had stood on many a quiet afternoon, gazing secretly at the great baroque mansion.

Before the day of the wedding Victoria had paid two visits to the Schloss Kaunitz. The first time had been for dinner *en famille*, as an introduction to her stepmother's relations-to-be, a difficult enough occasion which Baroness Mathilde had insisted on making stiffly formal and consequently that much worse. She was a sour-faced woman with thin cheeks and a scrawny neck that ill-matched her curvaceous bosom and hips. 'That all comes off at night, you may take my word for it,' Franziska had whispered maliciously from behind her fan.

However, Victoria's eyes had not been for Baroness Mathilde, but for Lorenz's wife. Baroness Ingeborg von Kaunitz was tall and coolly beautiful. Her eyes were a greenish gold, and she had raven black hair which she wore coiled at the nape of her slender neck. Her gown was of stiff peach-coloured satin with a low *décolletage* and butterfly bows of velvet ribbon. Victoria suspected her of drinking too much wine, for she talked, when she bothered to talk at all, in a bored, overloud voice. She was not in the least interested in Victoria and her stepmother, as she took pains to make clear. And as for the wedding, Ingeborg seemed to view the whole affair with contemptuous amusement.

That evening Lorenz remained remote and aloof. A dozen times Victoria had glanced his way and seen only his unsmiling profile. She learned one thing about him, though, and the realization that he cared little for his wife, that he seemed almost to despise her, brought Victoria a strange feeling of pleasure which made her ashamed.

Of the two elder Barons von Kaunitz, Heinrich, in a benign and jovial mood, was undoubtedly the host, despite the fact that it was his twin brother's betrothal they were celebrating. Gustav seemed content to sit back and take a secondary role, a smile of complacency hovering on his plump face as he quietly watched his affianced bride. Also present for this important family occasion was Heinrich's son, Otto, looking resplendent in his uniform. He was as handsome and dashing as if cast from a mould specially reserved for cavalry officers, even down to the duelling scar blazoned upon his right cheek. Then there was Otto's younger sister, to whom Victoria warmed at once. Liesl von Kaunitz was studying philosophy at Vienna University, and her dark good looks burned with the fire of idealism. She said very little, as though accustomed to the necessity of keeping her views to herself, but Victoria knew that she was going to like Liesl.

The following week she and Franziska were invited to a summer ball at the schloss. 'Just a small affair,' Baroness Mathilde had labelled it. A small affair of only sixty guests or so. The terrace was transformed into a fairyland with coloured lanterns, and a twelve-piece orchestra on a flower-decked dais played for the dancing. By now Baroness Mathilde seemed to have formed a positive hatred for Franziska, no doubt seeing in such a fascinating, beautiful woman someone who could sweep her off her pedestal as the first lady of the Schloss Kaunitz. She had recruited an unlikely ally in Lorenz's wife, and together they missed no opportunity of passing spiteful, if veiled comments. But Franziska was more than equal to them, and with the greatest ease and charm she set about dazzling every male present.

Victoria had spent much of the evening indoors in the grand salon, a spacious apartment in which the ivory-tinted walls were richly embellished with delicate gold ornamentation in the rococo style, and lit by two blazing crystal chandeliers. She found it easier there to avoid the unwanted attentions of Otto and his half-dozen fellow officers who, far from sober, all seemed to have but one thought in their heads – to find a pretty girl they could whisk off into the dark shadows beyond the terrace. Liesl, standing beside her eating a strawberry sorbet from a silver dish, viewed her brother and his friends with disapproving eyes.

'Look at them,' she said scornfully. 'Prancing around in those fancy-dress uniforms without a care in the world.'

'Is it so wrong for them to enjoy themselves at a ball?' Victoria asked mildly.

'But it isn't only at balls and parties. Being in the army is just one larkabout to them. But mark my words, there will be a holocaust soon.' Liesl said this as if it were something she earnestly looked forward to. 'Things cannot go on for much longer as they are. Andrej says—'

She broke off abruptly, and Victoria asked, 'Who is Andrej?'

'Oh, just a friend, a man I happen to know at the University. It . . . it doesn't matter.'

They were joined by a tall blond young man with a neat clipped moustache, whose pallor suggested that he spent little of his time out of doors. Liesl introduced him as her cousin, Pieter Bahr.

'I am most charmed to meet you, Miss Wayland.' As he clicked his heels and raised her hand to his lips, Victoria saw that his eyes were warm with admiration. 'As it happens, I shall be taking up a post in your country in a few weeks' time.'

'Oh, really?'

'As an assistant to the director of the commercial department of our embassy in London. I am greatly looking forward to it.'

'Pieter is one of that vast, un-uniformed army, the Austrian bureaucracy,' Liesl explained scathingly. 'Like all our civil servants, he does what he is told to do and thinks what he is told to think. He slaves away among his dusty files day after day for no other cause than to further his own paltry advancement, and to qualify for the highest possible pension when he retires.'

Outwardly, Pieter remained unruffled, his manners impeccable, but Victoria detected a spark of anger in his pale blue eyes.

'You know, my dear cousin,' he said lightly, 'I might respect you radicals a bit more if you were prepared to forgo some of your privileges, the privileges of wealth and social standing which you affect to despise.'

Liesl coloured violently, but before she could think of a cutting retort Pieter had asked Victoria for a dance.

'Weren't you a trifle hard on Liesl?' she said, as they walked out to the terrace.

'Don't you think she deserved it? Please do not mistake me, Miss Wayland, I am very fond of Liesl. But she is too ready to condemn those of us whose way of life is dictated by circumstances, and who haven't her freedom of choice.'

Pieter turned out to be a better dancer than Victoria had guessed, with a surprising lightness and sense of rhythm. At the end of their polka together she discovered that like her he was very keen on music, and played the violin. For the next twenty minutes or so they happily discussed musical matters over refreshments fetched from the lavish buffet in the dining-salon. Eating goose-liver pâté and asparagus tips, and drinking iced champagne from a crystal goblet, she found herself liking Pieter Bahr more and more. In the end, Franziska came and carried her off on the vague pretext of wanting to introduce her to someone.

'That young man is obviously very taken with you, Vicky. But on no account are you to get too friendly with him.'

'Oh? Why should I not?'

'He hasn't a kreuzer in the world beyond his official salary, and he is something of an embarrassment to Mathilde. It's rather a sordid story.' Franziska drew Victoria into a recess and glanced around to make sure she could not be overheard. 'His mother was Mathilde's younger sister. Their father was Baron Sterneck, who had large interests in the railways. He arranged good marriages for both his daughters, but Sophie had her head turned by a penniless Rumanian artist, and she left her husband and ran off with him. It didn't take long for the wretch to gamble away what her jewellery raised, and he ended up by being killed in a duel by the husband of another woman he'd become involved with. Sophie lived in poverty in Bucharest and finally drank herself to death. When the news reached Mathilde and Heinrich they rescued her baby son and had him fostered and educated.'

Victoria said defiantly, 'I would have thought Pieter deserves to be pitied, rather than shunned.'

'Pity him by all means, Vicky, but you must set your sights higher than a man like that. Mathilde only invites him here because he's a relative, and nobody will be sorry when he goes off to London for a few years.' She interrupted Victoria's further objection with a little warning shake of her finger. 'Now, say no more about it. Here comes Lorenz to introduce you to his grandfather.'

Old Milos Czernin was frail and bent, and leaning heavily on Lorenz's arm. His white hair and untrimmed beard were scant and wispy, and his lips, when he touched them to Victoria's hand, felt paper-thin and cold. His whispered greeting was hardly louder than the rustle of dry leaves.

'My grandson tells me that you have gained entry to the Conservatoire, Miss Wayland. You must be a clever young lady.'

'I was lucky,' she said awkwardly.

'Do not be modest about your talents, my child. I am not, and never was. That was how I came to be so successful at making money. And now, I have to leave it to my grandson to do that for me.'

Lorenz laughed. 'I only continue what you created, Grandfather.'

Their eyes met briefly, the young man and the old, and Victoria was aware of the strong skein of affection and mutual respect that bound them together.

'Have you met my great-grandson, little Emil?' the old man asked her.

'Not yet, Herr Czernin. I am looking forward to doing so.'

His watery old eyes sparked with pride, yet somewhere there was a hazing of sadness, too.

'Emil is a dear, sweet child, the delight of my old age. I am sure you will come to love him. Now, I have had too much excitement for one day, and I must be off to my rooms. Where is my man Josef? Have him sent for, Lorenz, if you please.'

Within a few minutes Lorenz was beside her again, having found her where she had wandered through to the salon.

'You made a good impression on my grandfather, Victoria.'

'I'm glad. I liked him.'

'Perhaps he will now think that much more kindly about the wedding.'

She gave Lorenz a swift glance. 'You mean he disapproves?'

Lorenz said ambiguously, not to offend, 'He was taken by surprise, I suppose, that his son-in-law should decide to marry again after being a widower for so many years. But my father and Franziska appear to be happy together, don't they?'

'Yes, they do,' she agreed, as surprised as Lorenz that this should be so.

His smile at her was kindly, warming. 'I cannot think of two more charming additions to the family than you and your stepmother ... who will,' he added with a grin of amusement, 'become my stepmother, too.'

Victoria confessed nervously, 'I shall feel very embarrassed, living here at the schloss.'

'Why should you? Where else could you go?'

'The lack of an alternative,' she said, 'won't make it any easier for me.'

Lorenz put a hand on her forearm, and the touch of his fingers on her bare skin sent a tremor of emotion through her. 'You mustn't think of it in that way, Victoria. From the moment you move in, this will be as much your home as it is mine.'

She smiled at him gratefully. Then, from beyond his shoulder, she caught the glitter of green-gold eyes. Ingeborg, in a gown of palest ivory silk trimmed with diamanté embroidery and draperies of lace caught at the shoulder and waist, stood beside one of the fluted columns deep in conversation with some unknown man. She kept darting glances their way, and Victoria felt the awful impact of her enmity.

Unaware of his wife – or perhaps uncaring – Lorenz said, 'Come and dance with me.'

Did he notice her hesitation? It was for hardly more than a fraction of a moment. Whirling with him to the *Wiener Blut* waltz she was conscious of nothing beyond his nearness, the hold of his strong hands, the warmth of his breath on her cheeks. Not until the dance was over did her reason return with a swamping sense of panic. Did he know, could he possibly realize, the devastating effect he had on her? They were to live together in this house on terms of family intimacy. How would it be possible, loving him as she did?

On this her first morning, after a breakfast of crisp *semmeln* and honey with a pot of coffee and a dish of thick whipped cream, which had been brought to her room by a young maidservant, Victoria dressed and made her way downstairs, descending the wide central stairway to the entrance hall. There was nobody to be seen. Conscious of her echoing footsteps as she crossed the marble-flagged hall, she passed beneath the gallery into a small octagonal ante-chamber that would lead her to the music room.

It was a day that invited an exploration of the schloss's extensive grounds, and perhaps she would do this later after her piano practice. It would have to be on her own, though, for disappointingly, Liesl was away from home for a few days. She had left immediately after the wedding festivities yesterday to stay with a friend of hers, also a student at the University, at her parents' summer villa in Durnstein, some miles along the Danube.

'I hate the idea of being away just as you are coming to live here,' she had told Victoria. 'But you see, Margarethe invited me ages ago, and I can't very well cancel the arrangement now.'

'No, of course you can't. I wouldn't dream of letting you change your plans on my account. I hope you have a lovely time, Liesl.'

'Oh, I will, I will! The Braumüllers always invite such interesting people ... people whose opinions one can truly respect.'

'Will Andrej be there?' Victoria had teased.

Startled, Liesl said anxiously, 'I wish I'd never mentioned his name to you. Please, Vicky, you won't say anything to my parents, will you? They wouldn't understand.'

'Don't worry, I shall be very discreet.'

'Oh, thank you! He is so wonderful, Vicky, there is no one like Andrej. One day, when he has finished his law studies, we intend to ...' Liesl sighed unhappily at the difficulties she expected to encounter, and finished, 'Until then, it is better that no one knows.'

These ten days Liesl was to be away would not be wasted, Victoria determined. She would put in almost every hour that God sent in practice at the piano. The music room, a large square chamber decorated in soft tones of sepia and eggshell blue and with wall plaques of several famous composers, contained a fine Bechstein concert grand which was hers to play as long and as often as she wanted. No one else in the family, it had emerged, was in any way serious about music. Apart from the few occasions when a professional recital was arranged in aid of some charity, the room was scarcely ever used.

Victoria had been seated at the keyboard for almost an hour when she sensed she was being watched. Turning, she was in time to see a small face disappear behind the partly-opened door, which she knew she had closed behind her when she came in. Smiling to herself, she called, 'Emil, don't run away.'

She had met Lorenz's small son at the wedding yesterday, but there had been little chance to talk to him. She might have suggested taking him for a short walk this morning, but the thought of his mother's antagonism had deterred her. She would do nothing to seek the boy out, but now Emil had come to her.

She called to him again, 'Don't be afraid, Emil. Come along in.'

The face reappeared round the door, slowly, warily. Victoria smiled and beckoned with her finger. One step at a time, Emil began edging forward across the expanse of scroll-patterned oriental carpet until he was standing quite close. He regarded her solemnly with round brown eyes, his fingers plucking at the sleeve of his blue-striped sailor suit.

'Papa told me that I must not dis ... disturb you when you are playing.'

'Did he, Emil?'

'He said ... he said I was not to make a ... a nuisance of myself.'

'Oh well, your papa needn't worry about you disturbing me. I really and truly don't mind you being here, Emil. Would you like to play the piano with me?'

He stepped right up to her, his face serious and rather anxious. 'I don't know how to.'

'Then I shall teach you. Come, sit beside me on the stool. Can you reach? See, this is how you do it ... one, two, three, four, five, six, seven, eight.'

Emil struck a key at random, then another and another, faster and faster, delighting in his achievement. Then he began to bang down both hands with fingers outspread, creating a hideous noise. Victoria made a face, and the boy laughed gleefully. 'But it's not pretty like when you do it,' he acknowledged, puzzled.

'That's because you have to learn which notes to play, Emil. Now, here's a tune you will know. Let me take your hand and I'll guide you.'

Using just one of his fingers, she tapped out the familiar old Viennese melody, and softly sang the words.

> *Ach, du lieber Augustin, Augustin, Augustin*
> *Ach, du lieber Augustin, alles ist hin.*

'Emil! What did I tell you just now?' Lorenz's voice, stern and sharp, cut across the room.

They both turned to see him standing in the doorway. Emil gave a gasp of dismay, then slid off the piano stool and stood with his head hanging down. Victoria rose swiftly to her feet.

'Lorenz, I imagined you must have left for Vienna long ago.'

'No, I had some business to discuss with my grandfather this morning, which delayed me.' He looked at his son. 'Fortunately, as it turns out.'

'Oh, but you mustn't be cross with Emil. I told him it would be all right, that he wasn't disturbing me.'

His father was unrelenting. 'I explained to him very carefully how important it is for you to be free from interruption when you are practising. Emil must learn that I mean what I say.'

She took a few steps toward him, then stopped uncertainly. 'But it was entirely my doing, I assure you. I invited him to join me, in fact I pressed him to. In any case, I was just on the point of breaking off for a rest.'

Lorenz was not deceived, but he gave in, his eyes upon her as he spoke. 'I can see, Emil, that you've already made a loyal friend of Victoria for her to be so ready to spring to your defence. Be careful to treasure her friendship, for I am certain it is not easily won.'

In a fluster, she said, 'I was teaching Emil to play *Augustin*.'

'So I heard. Did you enjoy playing the piano, Emil?' He went to his son and tousled the dark hair with an affectionate hand. The little boy, still not quite recovered from his scare, twisted his neck to gaze up into his father's face. 'Oh yes, Papa! Can Vicky teach me some more tunes?'

Lorenz managed, at one and the same time, to smile at her and frown reprovingly at his son. 'Vicky? Have you Victoria's permission to call her that?'

'He has now,' she said quickly. 'I prefer it.'

'As do I. Alas, though, I cannot claim the privileges of a four-year-old boy.'

Emil looked from one to the other of them. The silence spanned several seconds before Victoria broke it by saying nervously, 'Perhaps I could give Emil some piano lessons – some real lessons, I mean.'

'Do you think he shows any aptitude?'

'That's impossible to say at this stage. He seems eager, at least.'

Emil tugged his father's hand. 'Oh please, please, Papa!'

'He is very young, surely?'

'The younger the better. I could already read music and play several pieces by heart when I was four.'

'Then I gratefully accept your kind offer on Emil's behalf. But I make one stipulation. His lessons must never be allowed to interfere with your own work. Is that understood?'

Emil skipped around in delight. The air of tension in the room had suddenly relaxed, and when he begged his father to come and watch him play the piano, Lorenz fetched a second stool so they could all three sit at the keyboard, Emil in the middle. They picked out a version of the *Augustin* tune with a variety of fingers, and although the result was far from melodious, it hardly mattered.

The curious brisk whipping sound that interrupted them was caused, Victoria discovered when she turned to look, by the impatient slap of Ingeborg's riding crop against her skirts. None of them had heard her enter the room.

'I came to see what the noise was all about,' she said coldly.

Lorenz stood up. His voice was expressionless. 'Victoria has kindly agreed to give Emil some piano lessons.'

'Indeed?' Smiling but hostile eyes fixed upon Victoria. 'This is perhaps a novel teaching method from England?'

'Of course not,' he replied. 'We were just amusing ourselves.'

'I see.' She held out a gloved hand to Emil. 'I think you had better come into the gardens with me now, darling. It is too fine a day to idle your time away indoors.'

'I want to stay with Vicky,' the boy protested.

He glanced up at his father for support, but Lorenz said quietly, 'Do as your mama says, Emil. Run along now.'

Ingeborg dragged the unwilling child across the room, pausing at the door to glance back. 'When the time comes to consider piano lessons for Emil, the best plan will be for us to engage a professional tutor. But he is far too young as yet.'

'Oh, but ...' Victoria checked her protest, knowing how much Ingeborg would resent her interference. It was Lorenz who made the point for her, quietly but with decision.

'Victoria tells me that the earlier he makes a start, the better.'

'Really? Then I must be permitted to differ with her on that score. Two or three years hence will be soon enough.'

Lorenz said dismissively, 'I have already accepted her kind offer to teach Emil.'

Victoria heard the swift catch of Ingeborg's breath. 'I see! You felt it unnecessary to consult me first? Perhaps you thought a mother would have no valid opinion to express on the subject of her son's education?'

He did not trouble to answer. Victoria had to admit, grudgingly, that he had not handled things as tactfully as he might have done, and that Ingeborg had some justification for feeling piqued.

When they were alone together, Lorenz said awkwardly, 'I must apologize for my wife's manner, Victoria.'

'Please don't mention it. I am sure it stemmed from nothing more than being taken by surprise.'

'You are very understanding.' He stood hesitating for a few moments, then drew his watch from the pocket of his checked waist-coat. 'I must go now, or I shall miss the train.' Still he paused, seeming reluctant to leave her. 'I will see you this evening, then.'

Victoria did not resume her playing when he had gone, but sat with her hands in her lap, deep in thought. It had been a mistake, she realized, to offer to teach Emil, but she could not – would not – go back on her promise to the little boy. She must watch her step with Ingeborg, though. If she had not been certain before that Lorenz's wife was her enemy, she knew it now.

7

Victoria leaned out over the balcony of her bedroom, her hands on the wrought-iron balustrade. For ten minutes she had been dressed and ready to go downstairs for dinner, and she was listening intently for the sound of a carriage which would be Liesl returning home in a station fly. Without Liesl there would only be herself and Lorenz at table, and the thought of having to dine alone with him was terrifying.

Her first ten days at the schloss, with Liesl away, had been even lonelier than Victoria had feared. She had virtually no company, apart from the half-hour each morning of Emil's piano lesson. And even that was often cut short. It had become obvious that, whenever she was at home, Ingeborg took a delight in interrupting the lesson. Either she would carry Emil off herself on some flimsy pretext, or send his nursemaid with a message that he was to come at once.

Baroness Mathilde often received callers, or sallied forth herself in the landau to call upon her friends. But Victoria was never once invited to join in these social activities. 'I know you must keep up your piano practice,' Mathilde had said on the first occasion, with a look that defied her to contradict.

Ingeborg lived a life of her own. She went riding a good deal on her magnificent black Arab mare, Klementine, and often she could be heard talking loudly on the telephone, which was housed in a kiosk in an alcove off the entrance hall. Only once in this past week and a half had Ingeborg dined at home, and that was one of the evenings when Lorenz had not returned from Vienna.

Baron Heinrich, until tonight, had always dined at home. He was invariably cordial to Victoria and in his presence the atmosphere became far less strained. But as soon as the meal was over the baron would set out in a trap, looking immaculate in his evening clothes, with silk hat and scarlet-lined cape. Lorenz, if he was at home, would go up to join his grandfather then, and did not reappear. Victoria had the choice of remaining with Baroness Mathilde and listening to her barbed remarks while she sat crocheting endlessly, or retiring early to her room. She was looking forward to Liesl's return as nothing short of salvation.

But she had almost given Liesl up when she heard the clip-clop of hooves and the scrunch of approaching wheels. With a rush of relief she hurried downstairs, in time to greet Liesl as she came in. With servants bustling round bringing in the luggage, the two girls embraced warmly.

'I was so anxious,' Victoria said. 'I'd begun to think you weren't coming this evening.'

'Oh, the wretched train was late, some fault in the signalling.' Liesl glanced around in surprise. 'Where is Mama?'

'Your parents have gone to Vienna. They were invited to a reception in honour of Otto's new commanding officer. So there will only be you and me and Lorenz for dinner.'

'No Ingeborg?'

'She went out over an hour ago.'

'Hooray! We can do without her.' Liesl started bounding up the stairs in her coltish way. 'I won't be two ticks changing, Vicky.'

When she went into the salon, Lorenz was just entering through another door. He gave her a smile that sent secret delight coursing through her.

'Liesl is back,' she told him.

'Yes, I heard the cab just now when I was in the library. I'm glad she's home again, Victoria. Now you will have some company of your own age.' His eyes on her face, he continued, 'I've been concerned that you were lonely here, and wished there was something I could do about it.'

'Don't worry,' she said awkwardly. 'I've kept myself occupied.'

The tall tabernacle clock ticked away the seconds.

'Emil tells me that he is greatly enjoying his piano lessons,' Lorenz said.

'Yes, he has made a splendid beginning. We even played a little duet today – a simplified version of one of Schubert's *marches militaires*.

70

It's always amazing how quickly a child of his age can pick things up. Emil seems to have grasped the idea of musical notation, and he has a nice sense of melody.'

'I'm delighted to hear it, and so will my grandfather be. Any musical flair that Emil possesses comes from his side of the family, not the von Kaunitzes. Grandfather used to play the fiddle in his younger days, and my mother was quite an accomplished pianist – or so I gather. Alas, I never knew her for she died when I was born.'

Into Victoria's mind came a sudden picture of him as a small boy of Emil's age, looking very like Emil, wandering alone and lonely around the great house. And now, though in a different way, Lorenz's son was being deprived of a mother's love. Occasionally, spasmodically, Ingeborg would pet and cuddle the child to an extreme, but Victoria felt sure this was largely done for show, with little genuine affection behind it. Ingeborg was far too concerned with herself and her own pleasures to spare much thought for Emil's needs.

'Were you not given piano lessons as a child?' she asked Lorenz. 'To see if you had inherited your mother's talent.'

'No, never. Perhaps it was because she died giving birth to me that neither my father nor my grandfather felt any inclination to have me taught.'

There was no bitterness in his voice, but perhaps a slight puzzlement. Victoria had heard it said that sometimes when a mother dies in childbirth the husband can never forgive the innocent child for killing the woman he loved. Is that how Baron Gustav felt toward Lorenz? She had never seen any sign of closeness between them, and it was a fact that Gustav had chosen to live all those years as a widower before suddenly remarrying. She was certain, though, that old Milos Czernin had no feelings of resentment against Lorenz. He loved his grandson dearly.

There was the sound of quick, impatient footsteps on the marble floor outside, and Liesl burst into the room. She was dressed well but somewhat severely in a pale beige taffeta gown, her only concession to femininity the green cabochon brooch pinned at her throat.

'Hallo, Lorenz!' she said, and kissed her cousin on the cheek. 'I was as quick as I could be changing. I say, aren't you glad it'll be just the three of us tonight? We won't have to suffer the usual conversational banalities. Come on, let's go through. I'm ravenous.'

In the stately dining salon the mirror-panelled walls reflected a glitter of silver and crystal, but tonight all the grandeur seemed irrelevant. The three of them gathered in a horseshoe around one end of the long table, where they were waited upon unobtrusively by a manservant and a maid in lace cap and apron.

Liesl talked animatedly about her visit to Durnstein.

'I met so many interesting people, and it was thrilling to listen to them discussing the new schools of thought in the arts and sciences which are sweeping away all the stuffy outmoded traditions of the past.' Her dark eyes sparked excitedly. 'I don't expect, Lorenz, that you've heard of a young composer by the name of Arnold Schönberg?'

'Is he the audacious fellow who has put forward a theory that the black notes on the keyboard have a right to equality with the white notes?'

'You can scoff,' Liesl said reproachfully, 'but there is much more to it than that. The ideas Herr Schönberg is developing could change musical attitudes completely. Vicky, you would have been fascinated to hear him talking. And I met another man who is a close friend of Arthur Schnitzler, and several painters of the new Secessionist school. Andrej said that—'

'I might have known the famous Andrej would be among the guests,' Lorenz said, with easygoing affection. 'Doubtless he introduced a political flavour to the proceedings. What would your parents think if they knew?'

Liesl suddenly looked vulnerable. 'You won't mention about Andrej being there, will you? Papa can be so irrational sometimes.'

'It's hardly irrational for your father to be worried about you, considering how impulsive you are, and how easily swayed.' Lorenz's voice took on a gentle, concerned tone. 'Do not become too involved in politics, Liesl. The situation at the moment is highly charged.'

'How can I not be involved?' she flared. 'How can anyone with a conscience not be involved? The Czechs have a right to nationhood and it is being cruelly denied them. A professor from Prague University was saying that there is ferment in Bohemia.'

'There is ferment everywhere in the Austro-Hungarian empire, alas. The Czech problem is just one of many. Think of the Poles, the Rumanians, the Serbs. And what about anti-semitism? Even at your own university, Liesl, a brilliant man like Dr Freud is passed over for a professorship simply because he is a Jew.'

'Yes, I know all about that,' she said with a dismissive gesture. 'But the Czechs—'

'The Czechs! You have thrown yourself headlong into their cause for no better reason than that Andrej von Hroch is Czech. You should take a broader view of the political scene.'

'Don't you *care* any more about the Czechs?' she flung at him accusingly. 'How can you be so indifferent, Lorenz, when Czech blood runs in your own veins?'

'And German blood, too! Perhaps being a hybrid enables me to see both sides of the question, and it isn't as simple as you seem to imagine. You're an intelligent girl, Liesl, and you should ask yourself whether, in the present difficult times, people like you and Andrej, with your single-minded fervour, can hope to achieve any more than cautious, one-step-at-a-time liberals like me.'

Seeing Liesl's hurt expression at her cousin's criticism, Victoria intervened with a question.

'I read in the newspapers that the Emperor has closed Parliament because of violent dissent between the delegates of different nationalities. Is the situation very serious?'

Lorenz gave a wry smile that was tinged with bitterness. 'Serious? Never! The situation may be desperate, Victoria, or even hopeless. But to the Viennese nothing is ever *serious*.'

'Must you always be so flippant?' Liesl burst out mutinously. 'Andrej remarked only yesterday that flippancy has become a disease in Vienna, and—'

Lorenz held up a hand in protest. 'Spare us your beloved's pearls of wisdom. One of these days that young hothead will say a few words too many, and land himself in trouble.' He tossed his napkin on the table. 'Have we all finished?'

They adjourned, not to the grand salon but to a cosy small sitting room with simple Biedermeier furniture and a series of pastoral scenes by Waldmüller beaming down from the primrose-coloured walls. The difference of opinion between the cousins seemed forgotten.

From a drawer in a cherrywood commode Liesl fetched a pack of unusual playing cards, and she and Lorenz taught Victoria the complicated rules of *tarok*. The time passed very happily and Victoria was astonished to discover, when she heard Baron Heinrich and his wife returning home, that it was already well past midnight.

Otto had arrived home soon after breakfast on a short duty visit to his mother. Victoria was giving Emil his lesson when he lounged into the music room and stood watching them, leaning against the piano with

73

his sky-blue dolman slung over his left shoulder in the approved cavalry manner, his hand resting on his sword knot.

'Do you play, Otto?' she asked after a moment, finding his presence unnerving.

His grin was charged with meaning. 'Not the piano!'

Victoria was vexed with herself for giving him such an opening, and her reproof to her pupil was sharper than she intended.

'No, Emil, you've got that timing wrong. Try again.'

'Good advice that, old man,' Otto chortled. 'How does that saying go? . . . *'Tis a lesson you should heed, try, try, try again. If at first you don't succeeed, try, try, try again.* What about me, Victoria, shall *I* try again?'

'Oh, go away,' she said rudely. 'Can't you see we're busy?'

'But I want to stay and listen.'

She knew he enjoyed teasing her and seeing her react. Forcing herself to ignore him, she concentrated on the lesson and Otto soon grew bored. He was strolling toward the door when it was abruptly thrown open and Ingeborg came in. This morning she was not in her riding habit, but wore a white batiste dress with insets of black lace in the yoke and sleeves. Victoria's heart sank. She knew what this meant – another music lesson brought to an abrupt end.

'Otto! What are you doing here?' Ingeborg demanded in disapproving surprise.

He shrugged. 'I just dropped in to see what was going on. I was on the point of leaving.'

'I see!' Flashing a sugar-sweet smile at Victoria that took her permission for granted, she went on in a crisp voice, 'Come along, Emil, I want you.'

The little boy climbed obediently from the piano stool, resigned now to the fact that it was no use pleading to be allowed to finish his lesson. How much did he understand of the situation, Victoria wondered unhappily. Did he realize – even at his tender age – that his mother was using him as a weapon in her personal vendetta?

'Where are you taking him?' Otto asked her.

'For a stroll in the grounds, down by the lake.'

'How about me coming too?' He gave her an odd look that Victoria could not interpret. 'Well, shall I? Would you like me to?'

Ingeborg regarded him coolly, yet there was a challenge in her green-gold eyes. 'As you please. There's no reason why you shouldn't.'

They left by way of the French windows, Emil dragging his feet

74

reluctantly. Victoria watched as they walked the length of the terrace and disappeared down the flight of wide steps that was flanked with tall urns of white Salzburg marble. Then she returned to the piano and viciously crashed out chords that reverberated round the room like the hum of swarming bees.

But it was foolish to allow herself to be so enraged by Ingeborg and her petty spite. Franziska was expected back from her honeymoon today, and things at the schloss would be different once her step-mother was here. Victoria had to admit, too, that she had been enjoying herself since Liesl's return home. Though Liesl was out today visiting friends at Klosterneuberg, they had spent a lot of time together this past week, horse-riding, punting on the lake, and going on various excursions in the neighbourhood. Tomorrow the two of them were planning a trip to Vienna.

'It will be quite different from any other day you've spent there,' Liesl had promised, at the same time swearing Victoria to secrecy because Andrej was to be part of it. Firstly they would visit an exhibition of drawings and paintings by Gustav Klimt at a small gallery near Am Hof owned by the art critic of an *avant garde* journal; then they would take her to a café, to meet some of their university friends who always gathered there at midday, even during the long vacation, to argue and exchange news and discuss the mornings *feuilleton* in the *Neue Freie Presse*. For the afternoon, Andrej had secured invitations to a private piano recital. The programme would be mostly Debussy, the French composer whose daringly anti-melodic music was so despised by the old school.

'You'll see something of the new Vienna,' Liesl had declared with passionate enthusiasm. 'The new Vienna that is emerging from the darkness of hidebound tradition, and striking out for freedom and liberty.'

Would Lorenz approve of this outing, Victoria wondered. She believed he would, remembering their strange conversation that evening on the giant wheel at the Prater when they had seemed cut off from the real world so far below them. What was it he had said? 'An era of history is spinning to an end, and we are too blind to see it.' She let her mind linger on her memories of that bitter-sweet evening, as she had often done before. Still she shrank from the dreadful, shaming moment when she had realized he was intent upon seducing her; yet there were other things she remembered with pleasure, remembered with an aching sense of longing – the warm responses he had awakened in her which in some curious way seemed quite separate from the ugliness of the occasion, and afterwards, the understanding and closeness they had achieved which was now very precious to her.

A summer breeze was teasing the glossy leaves of a magnolia that climbed a trellis against the wall outside, and the soft blue morning sky was flecked with wisps of silver-gilt cloud. Stepping out to the terrace she caught a faint tang of woodsmoke in the air, and saw that it emanated from a blazing bonfire far across the lawns near the apricot orchard, partially concealed by some laurel bushes. A gardener was tending it, and showers of sparks flew high as he tossed on more timber. But that figure, surely, was too small to be a man? Victoria went forward to the stone balustrade and looked more closely, narrowing her eyes against the bright sunlight. It was not a gardener, but little Emil. Where was his mother, she wondered.

Another movement caught her eye – two people strolling under the avenue of balsam poplars at the curving end of the lake. She would not have recognized them at this distance but for the distinctive colours they wore – Otto's blue and scarlet uniform, and Ingeborg's white dress.

Victoria caught her breath in alarm. They were far, far away from the spot where Emil was playing – playing with a huge bonfire!

Anxiously she started forward, hurrying down the shallow steps and across the smooth lawn. Her thin kid slippers, comfortable for the piano, were quite unsuitable for out of doors and she was forced to slow her pace to prevent them falling off. She shouted a warning to Emil, but he took no notice and she guessed that the crackle and hiss of the burning wood deafened him to other sounds.

She was still some way off when she saw the little boy hauling at the end of a springy branch that protruded from the fire, trying to lever it out, presumably to cast it high into the heart of the flames as he must have seen the gardener do. Then, to her horror, the whole blazing pile shifted and a big log slid down and knocked Emil to the ground. She heard him shriek out in terror.

Kicking off her slippers, Victoria raced across the grass in stockinged feet, reaching Emil in moments. The child was still screaming and she saw that he was pinned beneath the smouldering log. Somehow it had to be shifted . . . instantly. Taking a deep quick breath she forced herself to grip the smoking wood with her bare hands and ignore the searing pain as she lifted it off Emil's chest. Heaving it safely aside, she saw that the tunic of his sailor suit had ignited. Feverishly she grasped the burning fabric and ripped it off his body. There had mercifully not been time for his undergarments to catch fire and they were only lightly scorched, but the little boy's screams continued. She cradled him in her arms to soothe him, while she desperately tried to dismiss the pain in her hands that was making her feel sick and faint.

A moment later she heard footsteps pounding, and Otto's voice called breathlessly, 'I say, what the devil's the matter? All this noise . . . '

Hugging the little boy, Victoria stared at Otto mutely, too distraught to speak.

'Good God!' he said. 'The kid's been hurt. How did it happen? Fancy letting him play with fire.'

Victoria gasped out, 'He . . . he was here alone. I saw from the house and I hurried as fast as I could.' She gabbled on with an explanation, not knowing if it made any sense.

Ingeborg had reached the scene by now, and screamed out in horror. 'Oh, my darling Emil, what has happened to him? Here, give him to me.' She snatched her son from Victoria's arms, sobbing hysterically. 'You poor darling little boy, are you dreadfully hurt? We must get a doctor at once.' Her panic conveyed itself to Emil, who began to sob more bitterly as his mother started for the house at a stumbling run.

Otto seemed torn by doubt whether he should run after Ingeborg, or follow behind with Victoria. 'This is a bad business,' he muttered. 'I mean, it was damnably careless of the gardener who left that blaze unattended. Where is the wretched fool?'

Victoria neither knew nor cared. She wanted only to find some salve to bring relief to her searing hands, which she held pressed against her breast.

'It was nobody's fault but Ingeborg's,' she cried furiously. 'She had no right to allow a child of Emil's age to stray so far, completely on his own.'

'But you know what children are like,' Otto blustered. 'They can be the very devil. And she wasn't far away.'

'Yes she was and you were with her, Otto – right over by the lake. I saw you.'

He came to a halt, spinning round on her. 'Now see here, Victoria, we don't want any bad blood over this business, do we? All right,

Ingeborg was a bit remiss and Emil had a little accident. I'm sure she'll be properly grateful that you saved anything worse happening. So can't we just leave it at that? I mean, let's try and keep it between ourselves . . . just Ingeborg, you and me. What do you say?'

She caught her breath in sheer astonishment, appalled that his only concern was to cover up Ingeborg's carelessness and his own involvement in it, heedless of anything else.

'I say, you *are* all right, aren't you?' he asked, looking at her with sudden anxiety. 'Your hands – my God, are they burnt?'

Slowly she lowered her hands and held them out for him to see. Across both palms and on each of the fingers were vicious red weals where she had grasped the hot, smouldering branch, and already ugly blisters were forming. As Victoria stared down at them, the shattering realization of what this injury might mean to her came thrusting past the pain. She felt the ground shift beneath her feet, heaving and swaying, and she knew she was going to faint. Otto caught her just before she slid to the ground unconscious.

8

The familiar perfume of Prater violets hung subtly in the air. Victoria allowed her eyes to open and found it was her stepmother, not the maid, who sat at her bedside now.

'Hallo, Franziska,' she said weakly. 'You're home, then.'

'An hour ago. I came upstairs the moment we arrived and heard what had happened. But you were asleep, and I didn't want to wake you. Oh, my dear child, isn't it dreadful ... those poor hands of yours!'

Her hands! Awareness came rushing back, striking through the morphine haze.

'How badly are they damaged, Herr Doktor?' she had demanded to know when the physician was applying dressings of carron oil to her burns. 'Will I ... will I be able to use them again?'

Dr Waldstein was a family friend, and she had met him at the summer ball and again at the wedding. In appearance he was rather like the Emperor, perhaps intentionally, with a full moustache and bushy side whiskers.

'Good heavens, dear girl, of course you will! You'll have to be patient for a while until the burns heal, that's all.'

'But I go to the Conservatoire in September. I am studying to be a pianist.'

He corked the bottle of oil with deliberation before replying. 'I see no reason,' he said, 'why you should not be able to play the piano again, given time.'

'You mean that I shall regain the full mobility of my hands? There will be no loss of flexion in the fingers?'

He shrugged uneasily. 'Perhaps a slight residual tautness where there is scar tissue. But it will be so trifling as scarcely to notice.'

So trifling – yet sufficient to destroy for ever any hope of a serious career in music. Victoria felt her body go cold and clammy as desolation gripped her. She shivered, and the physician touched his palm to her forehead.

'There is always some degree of shock, of course,' he murmured to Baroness Mathilde, who had put Victoria to bed with the help of a maidservant. 'What I prescribe for the patient, *gnädige Frau*, is a couple of days' rest and a good nourishing diet. You will see to it?'

'But of course, Herr Doktor.'

From that point there had been a period of wavering consciousness, the pain mercifully dulled, until Victoria had roused herself to find her stepmother beside her.

Franziska attempted to take her mind off what had happened by talking quietly about the honeymoon. She and Baron Gustav had done the tourist round – Venice and Florence, Pisa for its leaning tower, the colosseum at Rome. Victoria half-listened, hovering between waking and sleeping. At some stage she was coaxed to take a few sips of egg beaten up in milk, but she soon pushed it away.

Later she became aware of a second person in the room. Liesl had arrived back from visiting her friends and had come upstairs at once to see how Victoria was. She bent and kissed her on the brow, then sat for a few minutes beside the bed offering silent sympathy.

Shortly after Liesl had gone there was another visitor. Lorenz was asking if he might see her for a few minutes.

'He says he wants to thank you for what you did,' Franziska told her. 'Are you sure you feel up to seeing him?'

Victoria nodded her head weakly. Franziska straightened the bedcovers and plumped the pillows, then tidied her hair before admitting him. As Lorenz approached the bed Victoria saw that his eyes were darker than usual, shadowed with concern for her.

'Victoria, I had to come at once – yet what can I possibly say? But for you, my son might easily have . . . ' He shook his head, helpless to express the true depth of his feelings. 'You acted so courageously, at such appalling cost to yourself. This is a terrible thing to have happened.'

'Does Emil know?' Her gaze fluttered from his face, down to the hands lying bandaged and helpless outside the swansdown quilt.

'He knows that you received some burns, but he doesn't yet understand how serious they are.'

'Then there is no reason why he should ever know.'

Lorenz moved a step closer. 'You are generous as well as brave. So far I have no clear picture of what occurred this morning, and I shall be asking you to give me your account. But not now, I think.'

'No, not now!' Franziska echoed. 'Time enough for inquests when Victoria is feeling stronger.'

He stood for a long moment looking down at her, then very gently and tenderly he laid a hand upon her shoulder, and she felt the comforting warmth of his touch through the thin stuff of her nightgown.

'I'll come again tomorrow,' he said huskily. 'Sleep well, my dear Victoria.'

Franziska was quiet when he had gone, moving about the room, straightening things that needed no straightening. From time to time Victoria noticed her stepmother glance at her with a deeply thoughtful look.

Somehow she drifted through the hours of darkness and reached a new day. A new day that held no promise. Dr Waldstein came again and told her she was a fortunate young woman to possess such excellent recuperative powers. In her wretchedness Victoria almost cried out that she might just as well have lost her two hands completely for all the use they would ever be to her again. Hands that would not obey the minutest instruction from her brain, fingertips that had lost their utter sensitivity of touch. But her tormented mind healed faster than her seared flesh, and soon, for all her dark sadness, she could once again take a reasoned view of life and rejoice that at least little Emil was safe and sound.

In the quiet of the second afternoon old Milos Czernin came to see her. His blue-veined hand trembled on the ivory knob of his walking stick as he lowered his sparse frame into the armchair that his valet had pushed forward. For a moment or two he fought for breath, then waved the man away. His whispering voice was so faint that Victoria had to strain to hear him.

'Miss Wayland, I come to offer you my deepest gratitude, and my condolences.'

'Thank you, Herr Czernin.'

'I owe you more than I can ever repay – the life of my beloved great-grandson. I treasure little Emil beyond price.'

Victoria moistened her lips from embarrassment. 'I am only thankful that I was there on the spot to help.'

'No, you were not there on the spot.' His head, large upon his thin neck, shook widely to emphasize the denial. 'I was a witness to it all. Josef had put me to sit in the sunshine on my balcony, and suddenly I caught sight of you hurrying across the lawns. I wondered what it was that prompted such urgency.'

'I was anxious, you see, when I noticed that little Emil was playing by that bonfire. I had a premonition, I suppose, that he was in danger.'

'His mother had no anxiety! His mother had no premonition!' The feeble voice had strengthened, coming now as a sharp hiss. 'She was a long way off. I saw her walking by the lake with Otto, quite heedless of Emil.' His brief flare of spirit died, and he muttered, 'I feel afraid, my dear. I feel afraid.'

The faded eyes held a lost and lonely look. A tear glistened and rolled slowly down the old man's cheek. He looked, Victoria thought, like a bewildered child in need of comfort.

Franziska said gently, 'Herr Czernin, you must not distress yourself. Will you permit me to help you back to your suite?'

His look was uncomprehending, then he nodded slowly. With Franziska's assistance he pushed himself to his feet. Gripping tightly to her arm he sketched a formal bow to Victoria. *'Küss die Hand, gnädiges Fräulein.'*

Five minutes later Franziska was back. She hesitated, fingering the gold band of her wedding ring, before she spoke. 'You realize, don't you, Vicky, what the old gentleman was implying? He's afraid there is something going on between Otto and Ingeborg. If this is true, what fools they are to take such a risk! It only needs Lorenz to find out... '

'Perhaps Lorenz knows already and doesn't care,' said Victoria, surprising herself by the thought.

Franziska gave her a curious look. 'I have it from Gustav that it's a long while since they shared a bedroom. Even so, no man will tolerate being openly mocked by his wife's behaviour. Lorenz may not care about her liaisons as long as she is reasonably discreet... he has his own amours. But on his own doorstep, within the family circle? Never!' She smoothed the skirt of her lavender silk tea-gown, lost in thought. 'He is deeply grateful to you, Vicky.'

Victoria said nothing, her eyes on the huge basket of long-stemmed pink carnations, sent to her by Lorenz's father, which stood on a pedestal by the window.

'This incident with Emil will bring you that much closer,'

Franziska went on. 'Your sacrifice, and his feeling of indebtedness to you. You'll need to be very much on your guard, my dear.'

'On my guard?'

'In such a case, it is always the woman who must find the strength of will. Whatever your feelings, Vicky, you must resist them. Do you understand me?'

Victoria turned her head slowly to meet Franziska's gaze. Never before had she seen such genuine concern in her stepmother's eyes, and she felt strangely moved.

'It was entirely the fault of that cretinous gardener, Zogak,' said Ingeborg, in a voice that carried challenging undertones.

She had not hurried herself about paying a visit, and Victoria was thankful for the delay. She felt better able to cope with Ingeborg now that she was out of bed and fully dressed.

Controlling her anger, she said mildly, 'You can hardly put the blame on him. The man couldn't be expected to know that Emil was running around the gardens with no one close enough to keep an eye on him.'

Ingeborg's eyes gleamed with malice. 'The child wasn't out of my sight above a few moments,' she said with a shrug. 'But the point is this, it's Zogak who always sees to the bonfires, and it was grossly negligent of him to leave a huge blaze like that unattended. I have told my father-in-law and Uncle Heinrich that he should be sent packing at once, but they seem to feel an obligation to keep the fellow on because he has been in their employ since he was a boy, and his mother before him.'

Victoria could see what Ingeborg was about. By laying the blame for the accident on one of the gardeners she hoped to divert it from herself. Perhaps she had even tried to conceal the fact that she had been in Otto's company at the time. But Milos Czernin knew the truth, and probably he had already told his grandson. Lorenz had called to see her several times, but he had not referred again to wanting to hear her account of the accident. To Victoria this had been a considerable relief.

Ingeborg had strolled over to the window and now stood with her back to the room. She sounded slightly aggrieved as she said, 'You seem to have made a quick recovery. I expected to find you still in bed, not up and dressed.'

'It is only my hands that are affected,' Victoria pointed out, 'and

I'm over the shock now. As a matter of fact, I'm waiting for Liesl to come and fetch me. She suggested we might take a short stroll in the gardens for me to get some fresh air.'

Ingeborg nodded without interest. There was a lengthy pause, then she half-turned and said over her shoulder, 'The reason I came, Victoria, was to express my gratitude to you.'

'There's no need. I only did what anyone would have done.'

'No, I must give credit where it's due.' Her tone could scarcely have been more grudging. 'But for you, Emil could have received quite a nasty burn. Still, all's well that ends well, I suppose.'

The sharp sting of pain as Victoria clenched her bandaged fists was a bitter rebuttal of such a facile statement. But Ingeborg still had not finished.

'Do I gather that there will be permanent scarring which could affect your performance at the piano?'

'That seems very likely. In any event, I shall not be able to start at the Conservatoire next month.'

'Ah well, I expect you'll find some other interest to take up that you *can* do.'

Liesl's entry saved the need of finding a reply.

'Am I interrupting a private conversation?' she asked, stopping short at the sight of Ingeborg.

'No, I was just leaving.' She glanced at Victoria as she moved to the door. 'I suppose you'll be down to dinner this evening now that you are up and about?'

'I don't think so, not until I can hold a knife and fork again. I should feel too self-conscious.'

Liesl said, 'For the time being I shall eat up here with Victoria, so that Franziska is free to join Uncle Gustav.'

Fastidiously, Ingeborg rearranged her jabot of white lace, tugging the tiny frills into place.

'So you will be able to have cosy *tête-à-têtes* about the political situation. Ah well, I wish you joy!'

'How I detest that woman,' said Liesl, hardly bothering to wait until Ingeborg had closed the door. 'I simply cannot understand what Lorenz ever saw in her.'

'She is very beautiful.'

'Don't tell me that superficial beauty is all you think is needed in a wife, Vicky. What about intelligence? What about loyalty and tenderness and compassion, the ability to love a man with one's whole heart and soul? Don't these things count for more than beauty in a marriage?'

'I was only saying —' Victoria began, but Liesl cut across her.

'It should never have been allowed to happen! Lorenz was doing his compulsory army service at the time, and he'd been wounded. It must have made him weak in the head.'

'Tell me about it,' Victoria said, trying to sound only moderately interested.

Liesl sat on the edge of the bed and stretched her arms behind her, making props of them. She stared down at the patent leather toes of her walking boots.

'His regiment was stationed in a coal-mining district in Bohemia where there was a lot of unrest. On this occasion the troops had been ordered to break up a demonstration by picking out the ringleaders and shooting them – shooting them down in cold blood!' Restlessly, Liesl jumped to her feet again and began to pace the room. 'As you can imagine, Vicky, the other miners went berserk. In the general fighting one of them struck out at Lorenz with a pickaxe, which pierced his chest and brought him down from his horse. He told me that his colleagues immediately hacked the poor wretch to pieces with their swords.' Liesl's face had grown pale with remembered horror. 'At least that dreadful incident made Lorenz realize the wicked injustice of a system that can treat a whole race of people like the Czechs as ignorant louts – as little better than serfs. He used to talk to me about it when he was convalescing at home after leaving hospital. Being only fourteen at the time, I'd never thought much about such things before, and it truly opened my eyes.'

Liesl had come to a halt behind a tapestry armchair, and her finger absently traced out the shape of the carved scrolls and flowers on its gilded back. After a moment, Victoria prompted, 'And that was when he married Ingeborg?'

'Yes, that's right. He met her at a masked ball at the Sophien-Saal. Ingeborg literally flung herself at him and Lorenz seemed completely bowled over. The strange thing was that the family permitted him to marry her. I mean, at twenty-two he still needed his father's consent, and she was so obviously an unsuitable wife for him. Far from preventing the match, though, everyone was very much in favour. Even at the time I couldn't understand why. So Lorenz and Ingeborg were married all in a rush, and she became pregnant with Emil before he returned to his regiment.'

An image flickered in Victoria's mind of a sensitive young man who had been through butchery and bloodshed and was faced with a return to the same horror, expected to be loyal to a regime he had lost faith in and now despised. No wonder he had been susceptible to the wiles of someone like Ingeborg, beautiful and no doubt softly feminine when she wanted to be. The wonder of it lay in his family's attitude. Why had they not dissuaded him from making such an injudicious marriage?

'Were they happy in the beginning?' she asked.

'Not Lorenz, I'm sure of it. But Ingeborg must have been overjoyed. She'd got what she wanted – money and social position. It was a big step up for her, you see, because her father had only been a fairly minor counsellor at the Hofburg. Oh dear, does that make me sound like a dreadful snob? You know I'm not that, but her mother really was the most awful sort of woman, just a vulgar social climber. Though at least she was able to keep Ingeborg in some sort of check while she was alive. Now there's no one to do it.'

'Except her husband.'

'If only he would! If only Lorenz would put his foot down and stop her carrying on the way she does. But he doesn't seem to care what she gets up to, except . . .'

'Except?' Did Liesl know something about an involvement between her brother and Ingeborg? And *had* Lorenz discovered it?

Liesl shook her head uneasily. 'Oh . . . nothing.'

'You are very fond of Lorenz, aren't you?'

Her lips softened into a smile. 'Oh yes, I always have been, ever since I can remember. He's been like a brother to me – more so than Otto has, and I just hate the thought of him having ruined his life by marrying a woman like Ingeborg. Poor Lorenz! Why couldn't he have waited, Vicky, and married someone nice. Someone like you!'

Five of them were gathered in Milos Czernin's sitting room on Sunday afternoon. Besides the old man himself there was Victoria, Liesl, Lorenz and little Emil. Victoria kept her bandaged hands beneath the level of the marquetry table round which they sat, not wanting to remind the others and bring a note of gloom to the festive atmosphere. Old Milos was brighter today, and in fact seemed less frail than she had ever seen him.

'I have a little gift for you, my dear Victoria,' he said suddenly, and waved an impatient hand at his valet, who was setting out some tiny tulip glasses on a silver tray. 'Bring it here, Josef! It is such a very small thing in comparison with my gratitude to you, dear child, but I thought it might amuse you and give a little pleasure.'

Josef, donning white gloves to lend dignity to the occasion, opened a cupboard and withdrew a mysterious contraption which consisted of various wheels and a large tin horn. Carefully, he laid it on the table before them.

'What is it, Great-grandpa?' asked Emil in solemn curiosity.

The old man's eyes twinkled. 'Do you know what it is, Victoria?'

'It's one of those talking machines, isn't it, Herr Czernin?'

'That's right, you've guessed! The very latest model imported from America. The Berliner Baby-grand Gramophone.'

'But what does it do, Great-grandpa?'

'Aha, we'll see, we'll see! Fetch the plate, Josef. Lorenz, do you know how to make it work?'

Lorenz studied the instrument for a moment. 'I imagine you wind up the clockwork motor with this handle . . .'

'That's the idea!'

'And there must be a needle of some kind that goes in here.'

The old man chuckled. 'The time you spent at the Technical Institute wasn't wasted, was it? Your papa is a very clever man, young Emil. Hurry, Josef, hurry! That's it, start it up. Now then, just you all listen to this.'

At the click of a switch the shining black plate started to spin round and Lorenz carefully lowered the hinged end of the horn into which he had screwed a sharp-pointed needle. There was a loud hiss and a scratch, then suddenly the room was filled with the swelling strains of an orchestra. Emil stared in open-mouthed astonishment.

'Why, it's *An der schönen, blauen Donau*,' said Victoria wonderingly.

'Yes, "On the Beautiful Blue Danube".' Smiling delightedly, old Milos was jigging in his chair, conducting with his hands. They all listened in silence until the performance was over and the machine hissed and scratched again. Lorenz put out his hand to turn it off.

'Well,' his grandfather demanded, 'what do you think of it?'

Lorenz said judiciously, 'It gives better reproduction than one I heard a few weeks ago when I was in Salzburg. That was a cylinder machine, of course. This needs a more effective speed regulator on the motor, I think, and the whole thing would benefit by a sturdier construction.'

Liesl said with shining eyes, 'It's another step forward toward a new world. The day will soon be here when everyone, not just the rich, will have the pleasure of listening to orchestral music right in their own homes.'

Emil had got down from the table and was skipping about the room. 'Make it go again, Papa! Please make it go again.'

Milos Czernin looked at Victoria, suddenly anxious, smiling and frowning at the same time. 'Have I been an old fool, my dear, thinking you would enjoy a contraption like this? It is only a toy, of course, and not at all like the real thing. In no way comparable to being in a concert hall.'

She was deeply touched. Rising to her feet, she went round and kissed him on the cheek. 'It was a lovely thought, Herr Czernin, and I am delighted to have the gramophone. I shall think of your kindness every time I play it, which will be often.' As she returned to her chair she found Lorenz looking at her, his eyes warm with gratitude. 'Do start it again,' she asked him. 'Emil, don't you think it's a nice tune? You will have to learn to play *An der schönen, blauen Donau* on the piano, when we can start our lessons again.'

Three more times the famous Johann Strauss waltz whirled on its way while they sipped apricot brandy from the fragile glasses, with some cordial for Emil. The dominoes were brought out and Emil and Victoria played as partners because she could not pick up the ivory-and-ebony pieces. They were allowed to win, she realized, more often than chance dictated.

Presently, old Milos began to reminisce about his youth in Bohemia. 'There weren't such things as gramophones when I was a boy, young Emil. We lived a very different sort of life, I can tell you. We hadn't even a piano, but my pa was good on the fiddle and he taught me that, and I had an uncle who played the pipes. That's how we used to make music in our home. My pa was the blacksmith in our village, and I was working with him at the forge when I was eight years old. I used to take a good look at the farm implements we had in for repair, and wonder how I could improve them. In the end I made a plough that had a wider share and a curved mould board . . . a digging plough you'd call it now, a funny old thing to look at, but it worked! It worked better than any plough I'd ever seen. I couldn't get anyone interested in it, though. The farming folk around there were far too set in their ways to try anything new. So when I was seventeen I came to Vienna with my wonderful plough in a packing case. Day after day I went round trying to get someone to take notice, until at last I found a rich man who was willing to lend me some money. That's how the Czernin foundry got started.'

'It's a wonder,' Liesl remarked, 'that anyone in Vienna would pay attention to a lad from Bohemia who only spoke Czech. You must have been very persuasive, Herr Czernin.'

He gave her a sly smile. 'Ah well, I was told I had a way with me. You're right, of course, my dear – the whole pack of them from Prince Metternich down to the least important Hofrat in Emperor Ferdinand's service all thought of us Czechs as just ignorant yokels. And their attitude set the pattern. But I made the Viennese see different, myself and a few others like me. My business did well right from those early days, and I was able to send money home to my parents to make life easier for them in their declining years. I was able to marry, too, a lass whose father had come from the same region as myself ten years before, and set himself up as a hat maker. But sadly my poor Selma wasn't with me for long – she died in the cholera outbreak of 1854. That's my wife's portrait, Victoria, on the wall over there. And beneath it, on the writing desk, that photograph in the silver frame is Gustav and Amalie on their wedding day.'

Lorenz's mother. From where she sat Victoria could make out the bride in a white crinoline gown, the fashion of the day. And beside her the groom in a short frock coat, recognizably Baron Gustav though much younger and trimmer about the figure. Another time, when the others were not here, she would ask Herr Czernin if she might look at the photograph more closely, and at the others that crowded on his desk. Many of them would be of Lorenz, she guessed.

The old man, relishing his attentive audience, was saying, 'As time went by I prospered more and more, and the day came when I was ready to double the size of my foundry at Ottakring. I needed to raise more capital, and by then it was a very different story. Even the Rothschilds were willing to listen to me.' He glanced at Liesl. 'It was your father who introduced me to the banking house I eventually chose to finance me. And before long his brother met my daughter and they fell in love.' He shook his grizzled head reminiscently. 'The way life turns out . . . I lost my dear daughter, but in dying she gave me a grandson.'

'That was my papa, wasn't it, Great-grandpa?' piped Emil.

Milos gave him an affectionate prod in the ribs. 'That's it! And then *he* gave me *you*. So my family will go on and on, you see, through you. And with a far grander name, eh? Baron Emil von Kaunitz! But you must never forget that your great-grandpa was the son of a poor Bohemian blacksmith.'

'I'll see that he doesn't,' said Lorenz. 'Now, Grandfather, I think we'd better all be going before we tire you out.'

The old man *was* tired, that was evident. The excitement had been a little too much for him. 'Come and see me again soon,' he said wistfully. 'All of you.'

'Yes, of course.' Lorenz picked up the gramophone. 'I'll carry this to your room for you, Victoria.'

'Thank you.'

Milos kissed Emil on both cheeks, and touched Lorenz's arm in a fond gesture. But he insisted on struggling to his feet to bid the two girls adieu, sketching his feeble bow. As Victoria turned to leave she felt the grip of his clawlike fingers on her arm.

'A word with you, my dear, if you please,' he whispered hoarsely.

So she remained behind a moment while the others filed out of the room. The old man stood looking at her, bent and trembling, then he said, 'My dear sweet girl ... words fail me to express what is in my heart. I feel such a deep affection for you. You have become almost like a beloved grand-daughter to me.' He shook his head sadly. 'If only it could have been possible.'

There could be no doubt as to his meaning, and Victoria was greatly moved. With tears in her eyes she embraced the old man and kissed him upon the cheek, then turned quickly and went to the door.

Lorenz was waiting in the corridor outside her room, and he looked at her with concern.

'You're upset, Victoria. What's wrong?'

'Oh, it's nothing.' Opening the door, she waved him inside. 'Just put the gramophone down anywhere.'

Lorenz carried it across to the blue-japanned bureau and placed it there. Instead of leaving he came and stood before her, his dark smoky eyes studying her face.

'Was it something my grandfather said? I'm sure he didn't wish to cause you any distress. He is very fond of you.'

Lorenz's nearness, only a step away, was more than she could bear. It was impossible to meet the tender challenge of his eyes, yet she could not bring herself to look away from him. She stared at the silk lapels of his coat, at his spotted blue waistcoat and grey foulard necktie, until they blurred into a mist.

Her stepmother had said, *It is always the woman who must find the strength of will. Whatever your feelings, you must resist them.*

A voice she did not recognize as her own said harshly, 'Please go now, Lorenz. I . . . I have things to do. Please go!'

9

A shaft of morning sunlight illumined the gleaming Bechstein piano almost as if it awaited her upon a concert platform. The thought struck chill to Victoria's heart, for that wildly ambitious dream could never now be realized.

This was the first time she had dared set foot in the music room since the day of the accident. Her bandages had been removed for almost a week and each day the scars were looking less angry, the new pink skin feeling less tender. She had been keeping her hands in constant motion, stretching and flexing each finger to its fullest extent and often bringing tears to her eyes. By now, for everyday purposes, the slight loss of suppleness was unimportant. For the piano, though, it was quite another matter. The fear that she would hardly be able to play at all had deterred her from putting herself to the test, but she could postpone the moment no longer.

Still standing, she raised the polished lid and laid it back carefully, then let her fingers ripple an *arpeggio*. The ivory keys felt cold and unrelenting to her touch, and when she tried a few chords the pain of the stretched scar tissue made her wince.

She broke off and massaged her hands, chafing the fingers one by one to make them more flexible. Pulling the stool into position, she sat down and arranged her skirts with great care to delay the start for a few more moments. Then, relaxing her shoulders, she lifted her hands to the keyboard and attempted the opening bars of *Für Elise*.

The effect was that of a modestly competent performer woefully out of practice, acceptable perhaps in the indulgent atmosphere of a family drawing-room. I suppose I could always teach, she thought forlornly. She wished she could weep for her lost ambitions, but her eyes remained dry. Almost vindictively, almost as a punishment to the hands that had failed her, she forced them to play on to the end of the little rondo.

'Bravo! Bravo!' She turned quickly to see Otto in the doorway, grinning at her. 'So you're back to normal, then? That's jolly good.'

'I'm far from back to normal. In fact, I shall never be.'

His face registered disbelief. 'I've heard the others say the same thing, but that piece you just played sounded splendid to me.'

'If you thought my performance was splendid, Otto, it means you have no ear for music.'

He shrugged. 'A chap can't have everything, can he?'

Closing the door, he came over to the piano and leaned against it in a carefully casual pose. He was wearing mufti today, an English jacket and knickerbockers in a fancy tweed. Dressed like this he looked considerably less impressive, and Victoria realized how much his uniform did for him. She touched a few keys at random and their notes quivered softly and died.

'I imagined you would be back on duty this morning,' she said, purely for something to say.

'I wangled an extra day's leave. Mama wanted me home for dinner last evening, and I decided I might just as well spend a day in the country while I'm here.' He gave her a lazy grin. 'As a matter of fact the Divisional General is inspecting the regiment today, and I'm not sorry to skip the old boy's visit – he's a real tartar.' Otto rested his elbows more comfortably on the piano lid. 'I suppose you realized what it was all in aid of, that little family dinner party?'

Victoria looked at him questioningly.

'Ulterior motives, my sweet! There's a plot afoot to make a match between you and my cousin, Pieter Bahr.'

A sense of shock passed through her. 'What on earth are you talking about, Otto?'

'Don't act the little innocent. You must have guessed something was in the wind, the way you were put next to Pieter at table. And then afterwards, given every opportunity in the salon for a cosy little chat *à deux* – something, I noticed, you were by no means averse to.'

'I was merely trying to make myself agreeable, that's all, because it seems to me that poor Pieter gets the cold shoulder in this house. What's all this nonsense about a plot? Who is supposed to be behind it?'

'Oh, everyone.'

'Who do you mean, everyone?'

'Well, Mama . . . if only because Papa has decided upon it. And Uncle Gustav and your gorgeous stepmother.'

'Franziska? Now I know you're making the whole thing up! Not so long ago she actually went out of her way to warn me against Pieter.'

Otto's eyes gleamed satirically. 'So you admit you were discussing the possibility of a match with him?'

Victoria wished she had held her tongue. 'It was only that Franziska advised me not to show any special interest in Pieter. She thought him . . . unsuitable for me.'

'Well, whatever she may have said before, she's certainly changed her tune. Now she's all in favour of the idea.'

' Oh really, you're just trying to vex me, Otto. Be honest, there's not a word of truth in all this, is there?'

'Yes, there is. And I can't see why you're so dead against it. I grant you that Pieter is an insipid sort of chap, but in the circumstances you could do a lot worse.'

'Meaning beggars can't be choosers?' Her feeling of bitterness brought a niggle of shame in its wake, as though she were spurning Pieter to his face for not being good enough for her.

'There's no need to be so damned touchy, Victoria. After all, you're in the best of company. Most of us here at the Schloss Kaunitz are beggars.'

'How so?'

He took her arm and drew her over to the window. 'Once upon a time,' he said, 'everything you can see from here and plenty more besides was the property of the von Kaunitz family. Farms, vineyards, quarries, sawmills – there wasn't a damn thing we didn't own. There have been Kaunitzes living here for centuries, but it was when this present house was built that our troubles started. It was my great-great-grandfather who began selling off chunks of land to pay his debts, and it's a process that's gone on ever since. The schloss and the grounds it stands in are all we've got left now, except the house in Vienna.'

'I don't understand what point you are making, Otto.'

'I'm saying that it was a good day's work when Uncle Gustav married Milos Czernin's daughter. The old boy was so tickled about her catching a noble husband that he was happy to take him and his brother into the business. Not that either of them knew a blind thing about manufacturing farm machinery, but they're able to fix up a few contracts here and there, and one way and another enough lolly floats in their direction to keep things going.' His voice suddenly turned harsh. 'Me, I have to manage with a few odd crumbs that are tossed my way. It's Lorenz who's the lucky one. He'll get the lot when the old man finally snuffs it, every darned thing.'

'Considering that Lorenz is Herr Czernin's grandson,' Victoria said, 'isn't that perfectly just and fair?'

Otto gave a petulant shrug. 'Look at it this way. His father and mine are twin brothers, yet when the time comes I shall be obliged to live on Lorenz's charity. Is that what you call just and fair?'

This argument might have made sense to Otto, but its logic escaped Victoria. In any case, she was too upset about herself and Pieter to care.

'I don't know why you're grumbling,' she said dismissively. 'You seem to get a nice regular allowance to supplement your army pay.'

'But it's nothing to what other fellows in the regiment get from their families. Some of them can really live in style, with their own apartments in Vienna and everything. And there's even one lucky dog who runs an automobile – a Daimler with pneumatic tyres!'

Victoria shrugged and turned back to the window. Two people were strolling along the rose walk below the Chinese pavilion: Franziska and Baron Heinrich. They were deep in conversation, and at one point Heinrich laid a hand on his sister-in-law's arm as if to emphasize something he was saying. Although Franziska looked cool and poised, as always, Victoria received the impression that they were having quite an argument.

Otto jerked his head in their direction. His resentment seemed to have evaporated as quickly as it had arisen.

'What a fantastic creature that stepmother of yours is! If she were just a few years younger, I don't mind telling you I'd be trying my luck with her.'

'Otto! You really are despicable, considering —' Victoria broke off in sudden confusion. She had been about to say considering that Franziska was a member of his family, his aunt by marriage. But to Otto that would be no deterrent. It had not deterred him with Ingeborg, his cousin's wife – *if* that story was true.

Her embarrassment seemed to amuse him. 'A man can't be blamed,' he said, 'for acting like a man and taking what he can get. Just look at my revered pater.'

She felt herself go pale. 'You don't mean . . . you *can't* mean . . .'

'It's clear enough what he's after, and he's not a man to give up easily. He must be wild with envy to think of his brother enjoying the favours of such an entrancing woman.'

Victoria flushed at Otto's crudity. Could he possibly know, she wondered, that his father had once been Franziska's lover? Was Baron Heinrich indeed attempting to renew the old liaison; and if so, would Franziska respond to his advances?

She pulled herself together. 'I can't stay here talking to you, Otto,' she said, going to the piano and closing the lid. 'I've got things to do.'

'Hey, just a minute!' He followed her and laid a hand on her arm. 'What I really came to say was – how would you fancy a spin in my new phaeton?'

Victoria stared at him incredulously, and he went on, 'There's no need to look so staggered. I promise you a comfortable ride. She's as fast as the wind and steady as a rock, is my spider.'

'Thank you, no.'

'No? Give me one good reason why not.'

She pulled herself free of him and went to the door. 'One good reason – a very good reason – is that I don't happen to want to,' she said, and walked out briskly.

She was upstairs in her room, trying in vain to read, when Franziska found her an hour later.

'So this is where you're hiding. I've been searching for you everywhere.'

Victoria gave her stepmother a stony look. 'I wanted to be alone for a while, to consider something Otto has just told me.'

'And what might that be?'

'That there is a plan to push me into marriage with Pieter Bahr.'

'How dare Otto interfere!'

'So it's true?'

Franziska seated herself on the scrolled sofa and fingered the diamond brooch pinned at her throat. 'As a matter of fact,' she said, 'that's the very thing I wanted to speak to you about. The point is, dearest, we have to give serious consideration to your future.'

'Oh yes, of course,' Victoria agreed scathingly, and let the bitterness flood out of her. 'I must be a source of great embarrassment to you, a relic of your previous husband who now has no prospect of making a worthwhile career for herself. No doubt it would suit you very well to get me married off to Pieter and be rid of me once and for all.'

'Vicky! I have done nothing to earn such a cruel attack from you. It is wicked and ungrateful to suggest that I am acting selfishly in this. Have I not always done my best to take the place of the mother you lost?'

'I know I owe you a great deal,' Victoria conceded. 'But that doesn't give you the right to try and push me into a marriage with a man I don't love.'

'No one will force you to do anything against your wishes. I would not permit it. But do try to remember that I ... that we *all*, have your best interests at heart. Pieter Bahr is a fine, reliable young man.'

'So why did you warn me against him?'

'Surely you can see that circumstances have changed completely. When you had the chance of a career in music, marriage could wait a little while. But now, with things as they are, Vicky, it would be madness to forgo this opportunity of making a good match.'

She said coldly, 'If Pieter was a bad match a few weeks ago, why is he suddenly a good one now?'

Franziska allowed her impatience to show. 'Because I didn't appreciate until just recently how things were with Pieter. He may have had a very unfortunate start in life, but he has his uncle behind him. Heinrich has more than once furthered the young man's career by a word or two in the right places, and he's ready to do so again. And if you two were to marry, you could count on there being something very substantial by way of a wedding present.'

'Has Pieter named his lowest price for taking me off your hands?' Victoria inquired sarcastically. 'Or are they still haggling over the deal?'

Franziska gave her a pained look. 'You are using some very ugly expressions today, Vicky.'

'But the subject *has* been discussed with Pieter?'

'Matters of such delicacy are not discussed. But you could say that an understanding has been reached without the need to be explicit. Pieter *will* propose to you, of that I am certain, and I most fervently hope you will accept him. He'll take you back to England – your own country. Wouldn't that be most agreeable?'

'I cannot marry Pieter Bahr,' said Victoria resolutely. 'I do not love him.'

'But you like him?'

'Yes, of course I do. He's very pleasant, but —'

97

'Then that is quite sufficient. The most successful marriages are not based upon love, but upon mutual liking and respect.'

'Including your own?' Victoria immediately wished the words unsaid, but astonishingly her stepmother replied with only the mildest glance of reproof.

'Don't try to change the subject, Vicky. It may well be a long time before anyone as suitable as Pieter shows interest in you. So think it over very carefully.'

With that she swept out of the room and Victoria was left to contemplate a bleak future. How could she marry Pieter, when she did not love him? But if she did not fall in with the family's plan for her, how long would her welcome at the Schloss Kaunitz remain warm? And when she felt obliged to leave here, where could she go, what could she do?

10

Victoria received Pieter's proposal through the post. His letter came with the breakfast tray, and she only had time to scan it before Liesl arrived to join her for the meal. The two girls kissed, then as Liesl drew back she glanced at the opened letter.

'Good news, I hope?'

Victoria hesitated, but she had to talk to someone who would understand her feelings. ' It's a proposal of marriage from your cousin Pieter.'

Liesl, caught in blank astonishment, said nothing for several moments. Then she exploded, 'But you can't marry Pieter! You mustn't dream of accepting him. I mean, he simply isn't right for you.'

'It seems you are alone in that opinion. Your parents, and my stepmother and Baron Gustav ... they are all in favour of a match between us. That has been made very clear to me.'

'I can't believe it! What on earth can they be thinking of?'

'They see it as a neat solution to the problem of what to do with me.' Victoria could not avoid an edge of bitterness in her voice, and Liesl's expression became concerned.

'You mustn't let them bully you, Vicky. You know as well as I do that Pieter is not the right man for you. He's nice enough, but he's too ... ordinary, too orthodox in his opinions. At times he makes me absolutely furious because he's so feeble.'

'Otto called Pieter insipid, but he still thinks I should marry him.'

'Otto? How does he come into it?'

'The subject happened to crop up when he was home the other day.'

Liesl put an urgent hand on Victoria's wrist. 'I beg you, don't allow yourself to become entangled with Otto. He may be my brother, but he's a dangerous man where women are concerned.'

'You needn't worry, I haven't the smallest intention of becoming entangled with Otto.'

'All the same, Vicky, you must beware of him.' Liesl turned away and began fiddling with Victoria's silver-backed hairbrush on the dressing-table. 'I think you should know that a little while ago Otto became involved with Ingeborg.'

Victoria said faintly, 'Yes, I've heard whispers that there's something going on between them.'

'Oh, it's all over now. When Lorenz found out there was the devil of a row. In the normal way he doesn't care two straws what Ingeborg gets up to with her disreputable friends, but obviously he draws the line at his own cousin. Of course, Otto wasn't in the least bit serious – he's never been serious about any woman. I think his main reason was to spite Lorenz.'

But was the *affaire* safely over, as Liesl believed, or had it begun again despite Lorenz's warning? That, surely, was Herr Czernin's fear when he observed them walking by the lake that day, so engrossed in each other that little Emil had been allowed to wander off and start playing with the bonfire. Victoria recalled the odd look exchanged between them in the music room a few minutes earlier, almost as if they were daring one another. And their extreme anxiety to conceal the fact that they had been together when the accident happened was explained now.

Understanding something of the twisted way Otto's mind worked, Victoria could see that he would take special delight in making Lorenz's wife his mistress. But what she found totally inexplicable was why Ingeborg should behave as she did. How could any woman married to Lorenz von Kaunitz not feel that her cup of happiness was overflowing? Yet indignation against Ingeborg was held in check by the hurtful knowledge that Lorenz in his turn was unfaithful to his wife. The image of that beautiful woman in the theatre box constantly returned to torment her.

'I'm hungry, Liesl. Let us have our breakfast,' she said brightly, wanting to drop so distressing a subject.

The two girls stepped out onto the balcony where the maid had placed the tray on a bamboo table. Liesl stood with her hands resting on the iron balustrade, gazing pensively across the gardens to the wooded landscape beyond that was patterned with sunlight and soft cloud shadow.

'There is only one basis for marriage if it is to have any chance of happiness,' she said. 'There must be a genuine meeting of minds, a sharing of beliefs.'

'Like you and Andrej?' asked Victoria.

Liesl turned back slowly to look at her. 'Yes, like me and Andrej. Mama would like to have had me married off by now, of course. She used always to be dropping hints and pushing eligible men my way. But at last she seems to have accepted that before thinking about marriage I intend to complete my studies at the University, even though a woman is not permitted to take a degree. And when the time does come to think about a husband, it will be Andrej or no one. That's how the matter stands for me. But it's you we are talking about, Vicky, you and Pieter. You don't love him, do you? So promise me you will not accept his proposal.'

'I don't love him,' Victoria agreed, and left the rest unanswered. She sat down and broke a crisp *semmel* into small pieces on her plate, but scarcely ate a morsel.

After little more than ten minutes Liesl rose to take her leave, saying she had something important she wanted to get on with this morning. More and more during these past days Liesl had been engaged in mysterious tasks which sometimes kept her shut away in her room, but at other times involved trips into Eisenbad with packages; and once – though whether or not her parents were aware of it was uncertain – a hurried journey into Vienna.

Left alone, Victoria took up Pieter's letter and read it through again. He wrote of his warm admiration for her, his deep respect. He mentioned his future prospects, modestly but with confidence. He spoke of the approval of his aunt, of Baron Heinrich, of Victoria's stepmother – for he had taken the liberty of seeking their opinion prior to making this approach to her. In the most courteous way he begged for a quick decision, for if she did him the honour of accepting his hand, their wedding would need to be arranged before his departure for London in six weeks' time.

It was a carefully phrased, meticulous letter, even down to the final paragraph where he added that there was no necessity to pen her reply as he would come to the schloss in three days' time to receive it in person. Pieter expected, it was clear, that she would be guided in this important, irrevocable decision not by her heart but by her head.

Victoria's head advised her yes, but her heart insisted no. Perhaps if there had been one word of love ... but how could there be, on such a short acquaintance? Pieter did not love her and she did not love him. It would be a sensible, practical marriage, like so many others.

The cupid clock on the cabinet told her it was time for the piano lesson she had promised Emil.

A faint autumnal mist lay across the valley, touched to mellow gold by the rays of the declining sun. Victoria had come walking in the gardens instead of accompanying Emil on a visit to his great-grandfather, as he had begged her to do. She wanted to be alone, needing a quiet time in solitude before taking the decision that would seal her fate.

She took the path that climbed through a grove of oak and ash to the belvedere, a viewpoint constructed from the ruins of the castle where the Kaunitzes had lived in past centuries. The quiet was broken by the song of birds as they chased one another through the trees, dipping and dodging between the mossy branches, and from a little distance she could hear the regular thud of a woodman's axe. A few minutes later she came upon the gardener Zogak, who was attacking the thick trunk of a dying tree, the pale slivers of wood flying from his blade. He broke off to watch her pass by, leaning on the axe's long smooth handle with his hefty shoulders rounded in an apelike posture. Victoria gave him a friendly '*Guten Tag*', but in return she received only a blank stare from those dull, witless eyes. He was of low intelligence, she had been told, and she wondered with a shiver what was passing through his simple mind.

The last few yards of path wound up steeply in sharp bends hemmed in by a tangle of tall bracken that was turning to bronze. Then a final flight of steps led to a flagstone platform which was surrounded on its outer rim by a low parapet wall. Two long rustic benches had been set out for the view.

Victoria was about to sit when she heard a sound behind her. Someone had followed her up the path. She felt a curious, breathless apprehension until she saw that the intruder upon her privacy was Lorenz.

'I was just walking home from the station and I spotted you heading in this direction,' he explained. 'Zogak told me that you'd come up here to the belvedere.'

'I wanted to be alone. I . . . I needed to think.'

'Does that mean you want me to leave you?' he asked quickly.

'Oh no, please don't go!' She checked the betraying eagerness in her voice. 'I mean, there is no necessity for that.'

She wondered why Lorenz had followed her here. In his formal city clothes he looked as elegantly handsome as always, but somewhat incongruous in this sylvan setting. Removing his tall silk hat, he stood fingering the brim and seemed more ill-at-ease than she had ever known him. Suddenly his gaze became challenging.

'I had to talk to you, Victoria. What exactly is the situation between you and Pieter Bahr?'

She glanced away and plucked with her finger at the yellow lichen that encrusted the parapet's ancient stonework, scattering the tiny fragments into space.

'Pieter has done me the honour of asking me to marry him.'

'And you have accepted?' He sounded appalled.

'There has not been time for that. I only received his letter this morning.'

'But you intend to accept?' Laying his hat aside, Lorenz ran his fingers distractedly through his dark, gleaming hair. 'Forgive me,' he said. 'I have no right to try and interfere in your life, no right at all.'

But he had! If Lorenz wanted he could claim the right, and she would grant it. Not willingly, not of her own free choice, but because of a vital, unquenchable force within her.

Keeping her face averted, she said, 'What have you got against Pieter?'

'Nothing. He has much in his favour, and I expect he will make some woman a good husband.'

'Then why should that woman not be me?'

'You know the answer to that, Victoria, you *must* know it. You don't love Pieter.'

'Love!' She snatched at the word. 'Can love be counted as a satisfactory basis for marriage?'

'Can anything else?'

'Perhaps,' she said shakily, 'it is safer to think rather in terms of mutual respect and liking. To marry for love can lead to disaster.'

Their eyes met and in that unguarded moment the truth was revealed. No longer was it possible to pretend, no longer was it possible to ignore the secret bond that tied them together, transcending all other relationships. It was a moment of aching sweetness for Victoria, yet she felt a cold fear in her heart.

Lorenz said, at last, 'If you imagine that *I* married for love, it was not so.'

'For what, then?' she asked, on a thin thread of breath.

There was pain and defeat in his voice. 'A mirage of love, I suppose, arising from my state of mind when I met Ingeborg.'

'Tell me,' she said timidly, sensing in her newfound closeness to Lorenz that this was something she could demand of him.

'It was during my military service,' he explained, 'and I had been wounded and was staying at our house in Vienna on convalescent leave. The prospect of returning to my regiment sickened me. A few short months before I had been so eager and proud to serve as an officer in the Emperor's cavalry, but by that time I was disillusioned. I no longer saw the army as the noble defender of Austria's frontiers, but as a brutal instrument of repression turned against our own peoples. I had seen the bloodiest sort of cruelty and injustice inflicted on poor wretched peasants whose only crime was to demand a little easement of their poverty.' Lorenz paused, searching for the right words. 'Ingeborg, when I met her, seemed to epitomize all feminine beauty and sweetness. The idea of possessing her and of having her beside me always gave new meaning to a life that had become empty and pointless. We were married almost at once.'

Victoria was silent, and after a moment he asked her with a beseeching look, 'Can you understand?'

She replied obliquely, remembering what Liesl had told her about his family seeming eager for the match. 'Were you not very young to marry, Lorenz? Did your father raise no objections?'

'I am not so feeble as to throw the blame on my father's shoulders,' he said, and his voice was terse and angry. 'The responsibility was entirely my own.'

'I'm sorry,' she whispered, feeling crushed.

'I knew my mistake almost at once. I realized to my dismay that Ingeborg and I had nothing in common except on the most superficial level. Our whirlwind courtship was conducted amid the gay abandon of Vienna in the *Fasching*, with a nightly succession of parties and masked balls. I didn't realize then that to Ingeborg the carnival atmosphere was not just an interlude, but the stuff of life itself. When I did, it was too late ... except for regrets.'

A faint breeze rustled the leaves of the creeper that clung to the ancient stonework, like a thousand softly sighing voices.

'Emil must be a great consolation to you,' Victoria said. 'He's such a delightful little boy.'

'A great consolation, yes – and a constant reproach that I have not given my son a better mother. I wish . . . a dozen times a day I wish it were otherwise.'

She hesitated a long while before asking tentatively, 'Could you not have insisted upon your wife behaving more circumspectly, with greater . . . decorum?'

He shook his head in an impatient, dismissive gesture. 'Can you make a leopard change its spots? Besides, I could be held as much to blame as Ingeborg. We are impossibly ill-matched, that is our common misfortune. We have been obliged to settle for a marriage that is really no marriage at all, each of us going our own separate way. Ingeborg's life seems entirely frivolous to me, and I suppose mine must seem abominably dull to her. There are hundreds of men in Vienna who would have made Ingeborg a far more suitable husband than I.'

But not, Victoria thought bitterly, men with wealth and social advantage to equal that of Baron Lorenz von Kaunitz. Doubtless Ingeborg considered she had done exceedingly well, with all the freedom she could desire and the money to indulge it.

Lorenz's wife, though, was not the only barrier that stood between them. Victoria was prodded by jealousy into saying, 'That woman who was with you at the theatre . . . are you in love with her?'

For a fleeting second he looked incredulous; then he gave a faint smile. 'No, Victoria, I am not in love with Leonore. I feel for her, as I believe she feels for me, a deep respect and affection. I am not ashamed of our relationship.'

'She is married, also?'

He nodded. 'Her husband, Count von Taussig, is a great deal older than she is. It was a sordid marriage bargain arranged by her father in cancellation of a business debt when she was only sixteen.' When Victoria exclaimed at that, he smiled grimly. 'Don't tell me that such things never happen in England.'

'I suppose they do.'

'I have no doubt they do! Yet although Leonore was so sadly misused, she has done her best to be the wife her husband expected. They are away in Switzerland at the moment consulting yet another doctor who promises a cure for his gout. She and I are birds of a feather – both of us are married to the wrong person, and Leonore hasn't even the joy of a child to comfort her. I'm sorry if it shocks you, Victoria, but we find solace in each other's company. We meet twice a week except when she is away, as now.'

Her face burning, Victoria asked, 'Is she ... the only one?'

'I am not a rake, if that's what you want to know.'

'And yet ... that evening with me ... '

Lorenz passed a hand across his brow in a weary gesture. 'If I fully understood my own motives, perhaps I could explain so that you too would understand. I said at the time that I was testing you, but it was more than that. I was *hoping* you would refuse me, Victoria. I desired you that evening as much as a man ever desires a woman, and yet if you had shown yourself willing, then I would have desired you no longer. Does such a paradox make sense?'

She hesitated, then said honestly, 'I'm not sure. I have no experience of such matters.'

'No, of course not. But judging from that incident at the Café Radetsky with your stepmother, it seemed to me that you must be a scheming little hussy. So why did you fill my mind in this extraordinary way, as though you were the woman I had been searching for all my life? Was my judgment once more disastrously at fault, as when I married Ingeborg? I had to prove you to be no better than I *believed* you to be, to rid myself of my growing obsession with you.'

In his vehemence he reached for her hand and gripped it so fiercely that against her will Victoria gave a little gasp of pain. At once his hold gentled.

'Oh, my dear sweet girl, I'm sorry! How thoughtless of me.' Lorenz turned her hand in his to look at the scars of the cruel burns across the palm and fingers, fading now but still inflamed. Slowly, he lifted it to his lips in a tender, lingering kiss. As he looked up at her again she saw that his dark eyes were bright and glistening.

'When I think of what you sacrificed for my son—' he said huskily. 'And to know that I can never repay you. I can do nothing for you, nothing!'

'It is enough for me that Emil is safe and unharmed,' she whispered.

In the soft still air the silence hung between them. Then he said, 'I love you, Victoria.'

She felt her heart lurch painfully. 'You should not say that.'

'Yes,' he insisted. 'I would like to give you the whole world, *liebling*, yet all I can offer is those three small words. *Ich liebe dich*. If I never say them again to you they are there between us, and you will remember them.'

Victoria knew that she should leave him, but she could not bring herself to make any move. Through the mist of her tears she heard him say, 'I would give anything to be free. I would give anything if only I could ask you, in honour, to share your life with me.'

Lorenz's hands were on her shoulders, drawing her to him, and Victoria's own fierce longing made her afraid. For a few brief moments she found the will to resist, then she was in his arms, melting against the hardness of his body. Their lips came together in a long breathless kiss that stole away her reason, robbed her of every lingering scruple. She who had never experienced passion before now felt it surging and leaping within her, engulfing her senses. That evening in Vienna, Lorenz had not truly wanted her to give herself to him, but now it was different. Now there was complete honesty between them. Whatever the future might hold for her, Victoria knew with a clear, shining conviction that she could never feel so deeply about any other man.

'I love you too, Lorenz.'

'My darling, my beloved! If only I could give you my name.'

Very softly, frightened by the boldness of what she was proposing yet convinced of its rightness, she murmured against his shoulder, 'Your love will be sufficient for me, Lorenz.'

'No, it would not be sufficient! Do you imagine I am so selfish as to ruin your life?' He thrust her roughly away from him. 'Go to Pieter. Marry him, and try to be happy.'

Victoria stared at him, bewildered, hardly able to believe he could be spurning the love she offered. When he spoke again his voice was coaxing and infinitely gentle.

'Do you not see? With Pieter you will return to England and forget about me.'

'Forget you? No, I shall never forget you.'

'Yes, you will. You must!'

She said, with a leaden weight in every word, 'I will go back to England. I have no option, I can see it now. But marry Pieter? I don't think that would be possible . . . '

She turned from him and hurried blindly to the head of the steps, but he stopped her with an anguished cry.

'No, don't leave me, Victoria. Don't go back to England.'

She felt a stirring of hope, yet hope for what? She waited, not daring to look round.

'I cannot bear to lose you now,' he said. 'Just give me time to think. There must be some way out for us.'

Still she waited. In the silence the leaves all about them whispered in a breath of wind, and there was a soft calling of birds. And then another sound, faint but near at hand. The stealthy scrape of a heavy boot on stone.

Lorenz had heard it too. 'What was that?'

'Someone must be there, I think.'

He ran past her and started down the steps, and Victoria heard the clatter of other footsteps running away, the clang of some metal object dropping. When she reached Lorenz he was holding a long-handled woodman's axe.

'Zogak?' she asked.

He nodded. 'I was worried for a moment, but Zogak . . . it can't matter.'

They began to walk back to the schloss, but where the woods ended they took different paths, not wanting to be seen together. That was the way it would always be, Victoria thought hopelessly, and she knew that the interlude between them on the belvedere had changed nothing.

11

The next day was one of frayed tempers and snapping nerves, a day which, in retrospect, had surely portended disaster from its very dawning. A hot, dry wind blew relentlessly through the valley and the air was harsh and stale.

Soon after breakfast Baroness Mathilde departed on a visit to her elder daughter, to see Brigitte through her third confinement. Victoria had met Liesl's sister at the wedding, disdainful and looking particularly shapeless in the last stages of her pregnancy; her two little girls, Elschen and Kathi, hardly straying a step from her side in their acute shyness. Brigitte's husband, a tall, aloof man of aristocratic bearing, owned large vineyards in the Wachau region.

'*Ach*, this wretched *Föhn*,' exclaimed Mathilde when she was on the point of leaving, surrounded by scurrying servants and a mountain of luggage. 'I hope I shall escape it in Melk. Georg, be careful with those bags, you clumsy fool.' She turned to Franziska who, with Liesl and Victoria, was in the hall to see her off, and said ungraciously, 'I suppose I can rely on you to look after things properly while I'm away?'

Victoria expected a spirited retort from Franziska, but the only response was an indifferent shrug. She had noticed this past week that her stepmother had been curiously withdrawn, as if some problem were weighing on her mind. And as soon as Mathilde had left for the station with Otto, who was home again on a forty-eight-hour pass, Franziska declared that she was going to sit in the pavilion with a book.

This morning Emil was not at home for his piano lesson. He was spending the day with Dr Waldstein's grandson, and the two little boys were going to have a first swimming lesson at the thermal baths in

Eisenbad. Victoria practised desultorily at the piano for an hour, then went up to change for the ride she and Liesl had planned. When Liesl came to fetch her, the gramophone was whirling out the strains of the Beautiful Blue Danube waltz, and Victoria was dreamily fingering the trinket that Lorenz had won for his marksmanship at the Prater fair. Hastily she concealed it in her palm, but she could not prevent herself from flushing.

Liesl gave her an odd look. 'You're always playing your gramophone, aren't you? We'll have to see about getting some more plates, to make a change of tune.'

'Yes, that would be nice.'

'Well, all ready?'

'Just a minute.' Victoria stopped the gramophone, then surreptitiously slipped the tawdry locket back into a satin-lined box in her dressing-table drawer, as though it were made of gold and precious stones instead of tin and coloured glass.

The constant buffeting of the wind was so tiring that the girls let the horses amble at their own pace as they descended to the bridleway beside the tumbling river, where they hoped the air might be freshened a little by the cooling spray of the waterfalls. Presently, at a junction of paths in a silver birch wood, they came upon Ingeborg riding with a group of friends. There was no doubt she had seen them, but she gave no sign of recognition.

'That woman has disgustingly bad manners,' Liesl remarked in a loud, carrying voice.

'Ssh!'

'Oh, I don't care a fig whether she heard me or not!'

Ingeborg had not returned to the schloss by lunchtime. It seemed at first that there would only be three of them – Franziska, Liesl and Victoria – but at the last moment Otto lounged into the dining-salon, yawning with ennui. And then just as they were about to be served the first course of soup with liver dumplings, Baron Heinrich made an appearance.

'I'm sorry to be late, my dear,' he said, bending to kiss Franziska's hand. 'Perhaps I should have telephoned to tell you I would be here.'

Her smooth brow creased in an uncertain little frown. 'I thought Gustav said the meeting with Hofburg officials about those contracts would take all day.'

'They didn't need me,' he said carelessly. 'I oiled the wheels for them, so to speak, and now Gustav and Lorenz can get on with the details. Vienna is unspeakable with this damned wind. Not that it's much better out here.'

Otto was in mufti again today. Sprawling negligently on his chair with the jacket of his striped flannel suit thrown open, he remarked that it was too jolly stuffy for words. 'I think I shall have a snooze this afternoon.'

His father shot him a sour glance through his monocle. 'You look as if you could do with some sleep, Otto. You young lieutenants think you can stay up till all hours, drinking and gambling and womanizing, without having to pay the penalty for it.'

'We must have picked up our bad habits from our elders,' Otto retorted, looking smug.

When the uncomfortable meal was over, they dispersed with relief and the house fell into a state of somnolence. Victoria sat with Liesl in the library, trying to read, but her eyes kept closing. Vaguely she was aware that the telephone was ringing, and a few moments later a manservant appeared to tell Liesl there was a caller on the line for her.

'Who is it?'

'The gentleman did not give his name, Fräulein Baroness.'

Liesl sped away and was gone for almost ten minutes. She returned in a state of considerable agitation.

'What's the matter?' Victoria inquired.

Liesl put on an elaborate performance of unconcern.

'Nothing, nothing at all.' She snatched up her book and held it so that her face was hidden. The pages were turned erratically, sometimes quickly, sometimes after a long interval, and Victoria knew that she was only pretending to read. When almost an hour had gone by, Liesl sprang to her feet and announced that she was going for a walk.

'Shall I come with you?' Victoria asked.

'No!' The word burst out in a shout. Then, 'No, I . . . I just want to clear away the cobwebs. I don't expect I'll be long.'

Alone, Victoria put her book aside. She felt restless, yet she had no urge to do anything. For a while she strolled about taking volumes here and there from the shelves that lined the walls, but she soon grew tired. Though she was now fluent in spoken German, she still found it something of an effort to read.

She opened one of the French windows and stepped out onto the terrace, and at once the wind billowed the soft skirts of her sprigged muslin dress. She wandered down the steps past the urns of pink geraniums, letting her footsteps lead her, and found herself close to the stableyard. At least there were signs of life here. As she stood watching the grooms at work, a horse and rider came through the central archway and clattered to a halt. In one graceful movement Ingeborg slipped to the ground and carelessly tossed the reins to a stable-boy. Noticing Victoria, her green-gold eyes glittered with spite.

'Why so forlorn,' she called, 'when you should be rejoicing in your good fortune?'

'I don't understand you.'

Ingeborg rippled a laugh. 'To know that you are admired and loved, is that not reason enough for felicity? Pieter Bahr has proposed to you, I hear. When is the happy day to be?'

'What makes you think I shall accept Pieter?'

'You would be well advised to!' Lifting the skirts of her riding habit with three fingers, Ingeborg picked her way unhurriedly across the cobbles. 'One may have one's dreams, my dear Victoria, but in this life one must settle for the realities.'

She knows that I am in love with Lorenz, Victoria thought despairingly. A surge of jealous hatred for Lorenz's wife swept through her and she turned and walked quickly away. Without looking back she was painfully aware that Ingeborg had paused before entering the house and was watching her retreat with enjoyment.

As evening approached the gusts of wind lost some of their strength, yet the curious, pervasive feeling of tension still lingered. Victoria remembered that she had not yet visited Herr Czernin today, so she made her way upstairs to his suite. But the valet informed her that the old gentleman was rather indisposed; like everyone else, he found the *Föhn* very trying. Disappointed, she was returning downstairs when she encountered her stepmother on the gallery. Franziska looked unusually pale, the tiny network of lines around her eyes clearly visible.

'Is something wrong?' Victoria asked her.

Franziska gave a ghost of a smile. 'Well, yes, as a matter of fact I do have rather a bad headache.'

'I expect it's this wind.'

'Yes . . . yes, the wind. I think I shall go to my room and rest, Vicky, so I will not be down for dinner. Will you and Liesl see to things for me, if you please?'

'Of course. Shall I have something sent up for you on a tray?'

Franziska hesitated. 'Yes, perhaps I should eat something . . . just an omelette and some fruit, and a glass of wine.'

Downstairs, Victoria rang for a servant and ordered the food for Franziska. A commotion in the hall took her to the door of the salon, but she drew back out of sight when she saw it was Baron Heinrich, his composure ruffled for once, shouting irately at the steward.

'Why the devil is the trap not here by now?'

'It will be directly, *Exzellenz*!'

'When I say I want something now, I mean *now*, by God! If it isn't here within one minute, I'll dismiss that sluggard Gottfried out of hand. Is that understood?'

'Yes, Herr Baron.' The man scuttled away, and within seconds Victoria was relieved to hear the trap at the front entrance.

When Emil arrived home with his nursemaid, he was bursting with pride about his ability to swim four whole strokes. In her present abstracted mood Victoria found a small dose of childish exuberance quite enough, and she was not sorry when Hannchen carried Emil off for his nursery supper.

As the two of them started upstairs Ingeborg was just coming down, dressed to go out for the evening. Aware that Victoria was watching, she stopped to give her son an extravagant display of maternal affection, taking care, though, not to let him crush her black velvet cloak with its domino, or disturb her jewel-studded *coiffure*. Emil, in his excitement, wanted to tell his mother too of his prowess in the water, but she had no time to stay and listen.

'Not now, darling. Tomorrow, perhaps. Mama has a train to catch.'

The boy looked crestfallen. 'Where are you going, Mama?'

She pinched his cheek playfully, but he wriggled away unconsoled. 'To Dommayer's, my sweet, no place for little boys. Off you go with Hannchen, and be good!'

Dommayer's Casino at Hietzing was the dance hall where the young Johann Strauss had made his public debut over fifty years ago, to the fury of his famous father. But it was no longer the fashionable venue it had once been, Franziska had told Victoria – a suitable haunt for Ingeborg and her dubious friends.

The wheels of the carriage carrying Ingeborg to the station had scarcely grated into silence when Lorenz strode into the house. He seemed in a great hurry and looked agitated. Victoria was standing in the shadow of the gallery and she knew that he had not seen her. Calming her emotions, she greeted him in her usual formal manner.

'Good evening, Lorenz.'

'Oh, Victoria . . . hallo!' She had a desolating feeling that he was not pleased to see her at this moment. 'I have to go out again immediately. Something has arisen. Will you tell Franziska that I shall not be in for dinner?'

'Yes, of course, but—'

'I'm sorry, I can't stop now. I barely have time to change.' He smiled fleetingly, distractedly. 'Perhaps I shall see you later, though I have no idea when I shall be back.'

He was gone, taking the stairs two at a time, and Victoria felt an aching sense of emptiness. She realized that all day long she had been eagerly looking forward to his coming home. How could she ever bring herself to leave the schloss and go right away, far away to England, and never set eyes on him again? But what of Lorenz, what did he feel? Tonight he had seemed totally withdrawn from her, almost as though in those few brief hours since yesterday his love for her had faded and died.

From the salon she heard him leave again, in just as much of a rush as he had arrived. She sat there for a while, but the house seemed unbearably oppressive. She glanced at the clock. Just turned five-and-twenty past seven – time for a short stroll by the lake in the gathering twilight before she needed to change for dinner.

She had hardly reached the foot of the terrace steps when Otto's yellow phaeton came dashing round from the stables. Spotting Victoria, he drew to a slithering halt beside her and swept off his bowler hat with an elaborate gesture.

'I say, my love, you look properly dejected. What's the trouble?'

She shrugged. 'It's just the wind, I expect.'

'Why not come for a spin with me? An hour or so of my charming company always works wonders for the fair sex.'

'Thank you, but the idea doesn't appeal to me. Anyway, it's almost time for dinner.'

He leaned down and trickled the end of his whip around her throat.

'How's this for a suggestion? I'll stay in for dinner myself if you'll promise to come out with me afterwards. A pleasant ride together in the gloaming? Pretty thrilling thought, what?'

'You'd be wasting your time with me,' she said, stepping back out of his reach.

114

He laughed heartily, not in the least put out. 'I'll have to find someone who appreciates mè, then. Cheerio!' He whipped the pair of horses into action and was away. The dust of his going took minutes to settle.

So in the end it was only Liesl and Victoria at table that evening. As they took their places, Liesl said feelingly, 'It's a relief that Papa is dining in Eisenbad this evening. He seemed in a shocking bad temper about something or other.'

'Yes, I heard him shouting at Müller.' Victoria gave her a significant look. 'Everyone seems to be in a curious mood today. I don't think the *Föhn* is wholly to blame.'

Liesl stared back defiantly. 'What do you mean by that?'

'Well, you must admit that you have been acting very strangely. And then Lorenz—'

'Lorenz?' she queried quickly. 'What about him?'

'Oh, it was just rather odd the way he arrived home in a great rush, and immediately set out again without saying why, or where he was going.'

Liesl took a clumsy sip of wine. 'He's not obliged to tell anyone if he doesn't want to.'

'No, of course he isn't. But it does seem, well, odd.'

They hardly spoke for the rest of the meal. Liesl seemed to have no more appetite than Victoria and scarcely touched the *Tafelspitz*, excusing herself as soon as she could. Leaving the dining salon, Victoria wandered upstairs to Franziska's boudoir and tapped softly on the door.

'Who is it?' Her stepmother's voice sounded sharp and anxious.

'It's me, Vicky.' Turning the handle to enter, she was surprised to find that the door was locked. 'I was just coming to see how you were feeling now.'

'Oh yes . . . well, I'm about the same. I think I'll stay here for the present.'

Since Franziska made no move to let her in, Victoria went downstairs again and spent a couple of hours in the card room playing solitaire for want of something better to do. The idea of retiring so early to bed seemed unattractive, and she knew that in reality she was waiting for Lorenz's return.

But when she heard a carriage, it was Baron Gustav. He was talking to the steward when she went out to the hall, and he turned to her for further explanation.

'What is wrong with your stepmother? Nothing serious, I hope?'

'No, she's just a little indisposed, Herr Baron, and she is resting in her room.'

'Perhaps I'd better leave her quiet, then,' he said, disgruntled. 'I could do with a drink. Will you have something?'

'No, thank you.'

Telling the steward to bring him cognac, he waved Victoria into the salon. They talked, edgily, about the unseasonable weather until the servant returned bearing a decanter on a chased silver tray. He poured a glass for his master, turned up the gas brackets a little and straightened a cushion, then withdrew. Gustav swallowed thirstily, and after a reflective pause, again.

'I hear that Pieter Bahr has made his proposal to you, Victoria. You must count yourself fortunate.'

'I'm flattered, of course, and honoured, but . . . '

He frowned. 'You are not going to be foolish, I trust? A chance like this may not come your way again. When Pieter calls for your answer, you had better tell him yes without any shilly-shally.'

She said unsteadily, 'I have not finally decided anything yet, Baron.'

That large glass of brandy had obviously not been his first drink this evening. She could hear the slurring of his voice. 'Now you look here, my girl, I may not be your father but I am married to your stepmother and she only wants what's good for you. So just you listen to what we say. My brother and I are not likely to forget our family obligations to that young man or to yourself, and the pair of you would do very nicely by making a match of it.'

'You make everything sound so cold-blooded and calculating,' she said angrily. 'We are talking about my marriage, not some sordid business transaction.'

He lumbered to his feet. 'That's damned impertinent, girl!'

'If you think so, Herr Baron, then I beg your pardon. But I must be allowed to make up my own mind without pressure from other people.'

Unable to contain her temper, she jumped up and ran from the room, almost into the arms of Lorenz who had just arrived home. Behind her, his father had come to the door of the salon while at the same moment Liesl came running down the stairs pell-mell, her skirts flying. Seeing everybody there, she stopped abruptly halfway down,

116

looking anxious and uncertain. Lorenz glanced from one to the other of them, his face as expressionless as a mask.

He said, 'I think I shall go straight up to bed. I've had enough for one day.'

As he passed Victoria, his arm brushed against hers. For a breathless moment she thought it was intentional, a secret little gesture of his love. But his glance just now had looked through her almost without recognition, and she knew it had been a chance contact. There was a weary air about him as he mounted the stairs, pausing briefly to exchange a word with Liesl before he reached the upper gallery and passed out of sight. Liesl hovered as if about to follow him, then took the gallery on the other side which led to her own room.

Victoria became aware that Baron Gustav was watching her. Meeting his eyes, she realized that he knew something of the situation between her and Lorenz. Franziska must have told him.

He cleared his throat. 'What I have just said, Victoria, I said for your own good. Marry Pieter Bahr and go away from here. It is the only sensible thing for you.'

Another sleepless night had brought Victoria no nearer a solution to the questions that tormented her. One thing was clear, she could not remain in Austria. To return to England was the obvious answer, and in some way or another she would have to earn her own living. But she quailed at the thought of the struggle she would have, a girl of only eighteen. Franziska, she knew, would be strenuously opposed to the idea. Should she then, after all, accept the easy path that marriage to Pieter Bahr offered? But was it fair, was it something her conscience could permit, to enter into a loveless marriage for no better reason than to escape from the man she truly loved?

For more than an hour she had been sitting at the open window in her quilted robe, watching the first cold light of dawn warm to a rose-flushed pearl, the wooded slopes across the valley a sombre outline against the paling sky. After the harsh wind of yesterday the air was soft and still, carrying to her the musky scents of a September garden and the wakening chorus of the woodland birds. Surprising her at such an early hour, she heard the muffled ringing of the telephone downstairs, but the servants were up and about by now and it was quickly answered.

Victoria became conscious of unusual activity within the house, of hurrying footsteps and of voices, subdued yet agitated. She tightened the cord of her robe and opened the door to peer out, but the gallery was empty. Turning back, she rang the bell for the maid. There was a longer wait than usual, and when the girl came she was bursting with news, her round face flushed, her blue eyes large with horror.

'Oh Fräulein, it's dreadful. Baroness Ingeborg ... she is dead!'

'Dead!' Victoria's hands went to her throat. She felt dizzy and faint with shock. 'How? How did it happen?'

'Nobody knows, Fräulein, it's a fair mystery. They say her body were found on the railway line this morning, all horribly cut to pieces. She must have fell out of her compartment, and either she were killed right off, or she lay there stunned and helpless till a train come along the other way to run over her.'

12

A tragic accident. That seemed to be the only explanation of Ingeborg's death, since neither money nor jewellery had been stolen from the body.

Yet a question mark hung over the whole dread incident, looming ominously larger when the police inquiries elicited the fact that Lorenz had travelled on the same train as his wife. Was it conceivable that Ingeborg could have fallen accidentally? What possible reason could she have had for opening the compartment door while the train was travelling at speed, or for leaning so far out of the window that she lost her balance? At the burial four days later, a quiet ceremony held at Vienna's great *Zentralfriedhof*, the one thought that filled everyone's mind was not even whispered.

A hasty arrangement had been made for Emil to stay at Dr Waldstein's household five kilometres along the valley, where he would be shielded from the news of his mother's death. Victoria could not guess how it would affect the little boy when he was finally told. Though Ingeborg had never made herself lovable to the child, there must surely be some imperishable tie between a mother and her son.

Victoria was feeling more isolated, with even less sense of belonging at the schloss, than during that first difficult period after her arrival. It seemed impossible to make any contact with her stepmother, whose air of strain and disquiet was swollen to new dimensions. As for Liesl, she had become curiously withdrawn and silent, and it was clear that she had no desire for company. More and more Victoria spent her time with Lorenz's grandfather. The old man was quite ill with anxiety, and although she had no reassurance to offer him, she felt that her presence brought him a certain degree of comfort.

One morning when she made her usual visit to his suite, she sensed that Herr Czernin had something special he wanted to say. Yet for a long time he sat in silence, his trembling fingers fidgeting with the watch in his waistcoat pocket. At last he leaned forward and rasped on a thin breath, 'That Inspector of Police, has he finished with us?'

Victoria hesitated. 'For the present. But I cannot believe that he won't be back.'

'Yes ... yes, I fear you are right. Has he questioned you?'

She nodded, shuddering at the memory. The interview had taken place two days after the discovery of Ingeborg's body, with a uniformed officer stiffly in attendance. The police inspector, whose upright bearing stamped him a military man, had been very correct, very courteous, but Victoria sensed a hint of menace behind his every question. He wanted to know from her the precise movements of each member of the household during the evening of Baroness Ingeborg's death. She had attempted, but knew she had failed, to make Lorenz's strange behaviour appear less suspicious.

'You say that the Herr Baron left again hurriedly within a few moments of arriving home that evening? What was his purpose in doing so, *gnädiges Fräulein*?'

'He is under no obligation to give me a reason for what he does.'

His glance lingered upon her disconcertingly. 'If you say so, Fräulein. But perhaps you could hazard a guess.'

'I presume it was some business matter or other. Have you not asked him?'

The inspector's bland, impassive face gave nothing away. Had he asked Lorenz? And if so, what answer had he been given?

Sitting facing her now, old Milos Czernin tried in vain to clear the huskiness in his voice.

'Lorenz has offered the police no satisfactory reason for being on the same train as Ingeborg that evening,' he said. 'I have tried to make him see that he must. The authorities have to make these exhaustive inquiries, that is the law. They need to have everything documented in an orderly fashion.'

Victoria said quickly, 'I am sure it was a complete coincidence that Lorenz took the seven twenty-eight train. I mean, although he was seen boarding it, I don't believe anyone actually saw him and Ingeborg together in the same compartment.'

But she knew, and the old man must know, how easily Lorenz could have slipped unseen from one compartment to another at

120

some quiet halt along the line. It had been mid-evening, already growing dark, and the train had been uncrowded, indeed almost empty.

'If only,' his grandfather sighed, 'Lorenz could be made to understand how vital it is for him to tell the police what he was doing, where he was going – something they can believe.'

He meant, quite plainly, that Lorenz should invent any fiction that would satisfy the inspector's curiosity. Victoria realized suddenly how deeply Milos had hated his granddaughter-in-law. He shed no tears for Ingeborg, who had met her end so horribly in the lost darkness of the railway tracks. The old man's only concern was for Lorenz; how to protect his beloved grandson from being charged with her death. He cared nothing what lies were told, if only Lorenz could be cleared of suspicion – innocent or guilty.

Deep down, were her own feelings any different?

And yet . . . the words Lorenz had spoken to her on the belvedere kept ringing in her ears. *I cannot bear to lose you now. Just give me time to think. There must be some way out for us.*

If Lorenz *was* guilty, if he had destroyed his wife so that he and she could come together, then it followed as an awful paradox that they would never be able to do so now. In death, Ingeborg would remain as great a barrier as she had ever been in life, unless by some miracle she could feel convinced that Lorenz was completely innocent.

Old Milos whispered painfully, 'Lorenz hinted to the police something about going to Vienna to visit a woman. But he refused to give a name, as if to shield the woman's reputation.'

A confusion of new emotions ripped through Victoria's mind. If in truth it was an assignation with a woman that had caused Lorenz's hurried journey back to Vienna, that fact in itself would be insufficient to clear him, for he had still travelled on the same train as his wife and would have had the opportunity to kill her. But a plausible reason for returning to Vienna would at least make his actions less suspect. If only she *could* believe there was a woman involved – but Lorenz had told her that Leonore von Taussig was away in Switzerland.

Some other woman? Just allow me to believe him innocent of Ingeborg's death, she prayed, and I shall not be jealous.

But there was *no* woman that night. She felt certain of it. And she suspected that when the inspector was questioning her the other day he had already rejected the story of some unnamed woman.

There had been a strained silence while he watched her from across the table, observing her face minutely. At the door the man in uniform shuffled his feet, and the pendulum clock on the wall spaced out the seconds with a slow, steady tick.

The next question caught Victoria unprepared. 'Tell me, if you would be so kind, *gnädiges Fräulein*, what is your personal estimation of the Baron von Kaunitz?'

'I ... I don't understand.' Then, when the inspector remained silent, she faltered on, 'I have the highest regard for him. After all, we are related – in a manner of speaking.'

'Because your stepmother is married to his father? Ah yes, of course. And doubtless the Herr Baron reciprocates your regard for him?'

'I ... I cannot say. I hope so.'

A pause. 'Forgive me for raising so delicate a matter, Fräulein, but I am led to understand that you have received a proposal of marriage from ...' He flicked back a page or two. '... a Herr Pieter Bahr. Am I correctly informed?'

'Yes. Yes, you are.'

'And – again forgive me, I beg you – is it your intention to accept him?'

Pieter had been sensitive enough not to press her for an answer. He had attended the funeral, and afterwards whispered to her that there was no need to speak yet of the matter about which he had written. Victoria knew now that she could never marry Pieter, but she lied to the inspector.

'I have not yet decided.'

'I see! Now let us dispose of the other members of the family. The gentlemen were all out that evening, I believe?'

'Yes. Baron Gustav had not been home all day, ever since he went to Vienna in the morning with his brother and ... and Baron Lorenz, for a business meeting at the Hofburg. Baron Heinrich was back home for lunch, but he went to Eisenbad before dinner.'

'What time would that have been?'

'Oh, about seven o'clock, I should think, or perhaps a little before. And Lieutenant Baron Otto also went out before dinner.'

'The time, if you please?'

'It must have been seven-thirty, within a minute or two. I was taking a stroll before dinner when I met him setting out in his phaeton.'

'Yes, the Herr Baron Otto mentioned this when I questioned him.

122

He tried to persuade you to join him, as I understand it, but you declined?'

Victoria coloured. 'Naturally I declined.'

'*Aber natürlich!*' The inspector's gaze rested upon her with relentless pressure. 'Let us turn now to the ladies. I should be grateful for an indication of your stepmother's movements during the period in question.'

'She spent the evening in her room. She felt rather indisposed.'

'*So!* And Baroness Liesl von Kaunitz?'

'Liesl was at home. We dined together, and afterwards she went to her room. She has a lot of studying to do.'

He nodded, as if the answer satisfied him. With great deliberation he closed his notebook, then slid the silver point-protector over his pencil before putting it away in his breast pocket.

Unable to bear the silence, Victoria stammered out, 'I . . . I'm sorry that I have been able to give you so little assistance, Herr Inspector . . .'

'On the contrary, *gnädiges Fräulein*, I am most obliged for your invaluable help.'

He was smilingly courteous, escorting her to the door and bowing her from the room. Yet she was left with the sensation that he had dissected her mind with a surgeon's precision. Ever since, the memory of those iron-grey eyes had haunted her.

Milos said sharply, with an old man's querulous impatience, 'Victoria! Did you not hear what I said?'

'Oh yes . . . I'm sorry. This woman . . . I agree, if only she would come forward it would certainly be helpful.'

'Could you not persuade Lorenz to give a name?' His faded eyes met hers, then fled away.

'But how . . .?'

He was suddenly urgent, leaning forward and reaching for her hand, his voice entreating. 'My dear, you are the only one he might listen to. Help him, for pity's sake – *if you love him.*'

Those last words had burst out unguardedly. They lay between them in the silence, impossible to ignore.

To break the tension, Victoria rose and went to stand at the window, looking across the sunlit grounds which glowed with the soft beauty of early autumn. It was from this same window, only a few hours prior to her interview with the police inspector, that she had seen his uniformed aide holding a long, earnest conversation with

Zogak. The gardener had gestured wildly, talking with vehemence. Was he relating every detail of her encounter with Lorenz at the belvedere? How much had he seen, how much had he overheard? Enough, it seemed, for the inspector to feel very certain that she and Lorenz loved one another.

Since Ingeborg's death Victoria had often come to the music room, guessing she would be undisturbed here, though she made no attempt to play. Today, though, she tried to escape her tormented thoughts by concentrating on some difficult sight reading. She chose Brahms, finding in the F minor Sonata problems to engage all her attention.

She became aware that she had an audience, and realized it was Lorenz. Her fingers fluttered to a stop and she rose and turned to face him.

'I'm sorry if my playing disturbed you,' she said. 'Perhaps it's not fitting that I should practise at such a time.'

'No, please – play as much as you wish. I came because I wanted to talk to you.' He drew nearer, his dark eyes challenging. 'You have been avoiding me, Victoria.'

It was true, but what else could she have done? She had taken the greatest care, ever since that dreadful day, not to be alone with him. At first, this was merely because she would have felt a hypocrite in offering the conventional phrases of condolence; now, driven to believe what she did of him, there were no words to express her confused emotions – the feelings of love and pity that had somehow survived the horror.

'You seem to have been so busy, what with one thing and another,' she said huskily.

'I have to keep myself occupied somehow, or I should lose my reason.' His fingers raked through his thick, dark hair. 'You know what people are thinking, what they are whispering behind their hands?'

His closeness was mesmerizing her and she tried to step back from him, but the piano stool prevented her. She felt a rising panic, as though she were helpless in a trap.

'The police, too,' he went on in the same toneless voice. 'Their questions all point in the same direction. That I had the opportunity – and the motive – to send my wife to her death. They seek conclusive evidence of some kind to incriminate me. But of course they will never find any.'

'Of course?' she echoed faintly.

'How can they possibly find any?' He studied her face intently. 'Have you any doubts on that score, Victoria?' When she gave him no reply, he repeated the question more sharply. 'Well, have you?'

'You make it so difficult for ... for people.' Remembering old Milos Czernin's appeal she went on, 'Your grandfather says that you claim there was a woman, but that you refuse to name her. Do you not see, Lorenz, if only you could give this unknown woman an identity, one that the police could verify to their satisfaction, it would go a long way toward removing their suspicions about you.'

Seizing her meaning, he responded angrily, 'Put into plain language you suggest that I am to find some woman who will accept money to support my story when the police interrogate her.'

'But I didn't say—'

'I know what you meant, though. Do you believe I am guilty, Victoria, like the rest of them?'

'How can I know? How can anyone know what to believe?'

Still clamouring in her brain were those despairing words of his. *I cannot bear to lose you now. Just give me time to think. There must be some way out for us.* She closed her eyes for a moment, forcing a logical train of thought. 'If you have it in your power to remove the mystery surrounding your movements that evening, Lorenz, why do you refuse to do so? *Of course* there was no woman involved – if I doubted it before, you have made me quite certain now. So what was your purpose in leaving for Vienna again the moment you arrived home?' Lorenz made no response, and her voice became tense. 'For pity's sake, can't you see that you are in dreadful danger unless you can give a convincing explanation of why you took the train to Vienna that night?'

'I have nothing to tell the police,' Lorenz said obstinately. 'Whatever they might suspect, they cannot touch me. They will be unable to find any evidence that I killed my wife.'

'Perhaps not. But the suspicion will still remain. There will always be a stain attached to your name.'

His shoulders lifted in a shrug. 'People will forget, in time.'

'But *will* they?'

He shrugged again. 'If they don't, then I shall have to bear it. As long as I can have you, Victoria, I can bear any tribulation.'

She was silent.

125

'It is too soon, I know,' he said. 'We dare not reveal our love for one another yet, but —'

'Do you imagine it is not known?' she flung at him.

Lorenz seemed stunned. '*Who* knows?'

'Your grandfather and your father, Franziska . . . almost everyone in the family, I think. I am not sure about Pieter, because I've only seen him the once, at Ingeborg's funeral, and we hardly spoke then. But the police know, too.'

'The police? How is that possible? Who can have told them?'

'Perhaps they guessed for themselves, as other people seem to have done. But in any case, they would have heard about it from Zogak.'

'The police have questioned Zogak?'

'Yes, I happened to be looking out of the window and I saw the policeman talking to him. If we had thought to speak to Zogak first and warn him, we might perhaps have prevented him from revealing anything. But now it is too late.'

She heard Lorenz snatch in a breath. 'Oh God, what have I done, to involve you in all this?'

The look of distress in his eyes was genuine, and Victoria knew it was a measure of his love for her. Despite her conviction of his guilt she longed to touch him, longed to feel his arms around her. She said faintly, 'You mustn't worry about me, Lorenz, but only about yourself. I am terribly afraid for you —'

A creaking sound outside the slightly-open door made her break off abruptly. Lorenz strode across the room and threw it wide open. Franziska stood there, shrinking back.

'Oh Lorenz . . . I was just . . .'

'You wanted to speak to Victoria?'

'Not really, no. It . . . it doesn't matter.' Her face was a dreadful colour, very pale with a greyish tinge. She looked old and ill and desperately unhappy. 'I shall go up to my room,' she faltered. 'I am not feeling very well.'

'Is there anything I can do?' Victoria asked, concerned.

'No, nothing. Just . . . just leave me be. I shall rest.'

In silence they watched Franziska pass through the octagonal ante-room to the main hall, and begin to mount the staircase. There was no hint of her usual elegant, graceful poise. She faltered one step at a time, as if the climb daunted her and was almost beyond her strength.

'How much did she overhear?' Lorenz asked.

'I don't know. Everything, perhaps.'

'I sincerely hope not.'

'Does it make any difference? She can have learned nothing she didn't know already.'

Nothing she did not know already? So why, then, had there been that haunted look in Franziska's eyes, the lost, despairing look of someone who was suddenly afraid?

13

The liquid in the bulbous glass bottle gleamed a dull red-brown, a secret Franziska shared only with her personal maid. The label, an elegant scrolled design on cream-laid paper, bore the name of a pharmacy in Birmingham; and printed in red was the added word *Poison*.

Franziska, having fetched the bottle from a locked cupboard of her toilette stand, placed it upon the mother-of-pearl escritoire. She had locked both doors in the room and felt safe for the time being. She could only trust that she would remain undisturbed for long enough.

Sitting at the escritoire, she drew a sheet of crested writing paper from a drawer, but when she picked up a pen she found that her hand shook so much she could scarcely grip it. With her left hand she stilled the trembling, and took several slow deep breaths such as she had taught herself to do years ago when making an entrance from the wings. The old trick still worked, and she felt a little better. But what to write? Never had she known stage-fright to equal this, and she quailed at the ordeal before her. Yet it must be done, there was no other way.

She dipped the pen and began. *I, Franziska von Kaunitz, do hereby make*...

The handwriting was scarcely recognizable as hers, and that would not do at all. She discarded the sheet and took out a fresh one, steeling herself to calmness by sheer force of will. The success of her effort brought a flash of pride, and this time she began, *I, Baroness Franziska von Kaunitz, do hereby make this confession*...

She broke off again and gazed from one of the tall windows, allowing her thoughts to drift like the autumn mist that curled and lingered on the slopes across the valley. Those years with Victoria's

128

father were good years. She had loved James in her fashion – the only man, perhaps, she had ever truly loved. Heinrich? There had been passion in the old days, on her side as well as his. But not love, never love.

As though the only way of getting the words down on paper was to catch herself unaware, Franziska wrote swiftly, *I killed Ingeborg von Kaunitz, my stepson's wife.*

'How did that marriage ever come about?' she had once demanded of her husband in angered perplexity. 'An intelligent man like Lorenz, and such a woman!'

'He was besotted with her, my dear,' Gustav had replied blandly. 'The hot blood of youth and all that, you know.'

'Heavens above, a dashing young cavalry officer with Lorenz's charm and good looks would have found no shortage of eager girls, and he was absurdly young to marry. Why did you and Heinrich not step in and prevent so disastrous a match?'

Gustav shrugged off all responsibility in the matter. 'Lorenz had been severely wounded and was shortly to return to active duty. It seemed a good idea at the time to let him marry, and we had nothing against the girl.'

'You astound me. She is vulgar and mannerless, and as far as I am aware she didn't bring a penny piece with her.'

'But she did do her duty. She gave Lorenz a son.'

A son, yes, that was the vital thing. A great-grandson for old Milos. Ingeborg could be forgiven a lot for having produced little Emil.

Franziska's pen seemed to flow more easily across the paper now. *Ingeborg had discovered something, how I do not know . . .* She hesitated momentarily, then plunged on, *something that was disreputable about my past. I was afraid she would expose me, and I had to silence her before she did.*

Pausing again, Franziska frowned in concentration, trying to focus her recollections of that evening. It was vital to get things right and in the proper order, not to overlook the smallest detail.

While everyone believed I was resting in my room with a headache, I hurried to the station on foot, veiled, and in clothes I had not worn in the locality before, and I was just in time to catch the seven twenty-eight train. My plan was still only half-formed, but when I had the good fortune to find that Ingeborg was alone in her compartment, I knew it was my signal to act. At first I let her think I had come to talk with her, to plead for her silence.

Franziska formed a mental picture of herself and Ingeborg on the

129

train, the younger woman's face glinting with a smile of triumphant power.

But when we had travelled some distance from Eisenbad I pretended to want some fresh air, and made out that the window was stuck. I asked Ingeborg to help me with it, and while she was standing at the door I quickly slipped the catch and sent her pitching into the darkness. It was all over before I quite realized what I had done.

Was it a complete enough reconstruction? Franziska considered for a moment, then added, *I heard her scream out just once as she fell, but as the train rushed on the noise of the wheels deafened me to any other cries.*

Her heart was beating fast and erratically, almost palpitating. What she needed was a glass of cognac, but she had none in her boudoir and she dared not ring for the maid. She rose and went to the window, stepping out to the balcony. The mist was parting and fans of sunlight gleamed down upon the tree-clad slopes of the valley, making a tapestry in soft tones of green. The sheer loveliness of it caught at her throat and brought tears welling to her eyes. She realized now, when it was too late, that she had never truly appreciated nature's beauty. Somehow there had always been so many other things to be done.

She returned unwillingly to her task. Thus far she had explained, but what else must be recorded? The return home.

I alighted at the next station and waited there for a train back to Eisenbad. Unrecognized, I made my way home through unfrequented paths, and before entering the house I removed my outdoor things and left them temporarily in the pavilion by the herb garden. I let myself in by way of the French windows of the small salon, ready to explain to anyone I chanced to meet that I had merely slipped out for a few minutes to take a breath of air. But no one saw me, and I gained my room without being noticed. It was done. I was safe.

Franziska read through what she had written, nodding her head at each point. Yes, everything necessary was there, except *why* ... why she was taking this drastic step of confessing to the crime. It was essential to explain her reason for that.

I am not a good woman, she wrote. *I have done many things in my life of which I am not proud. But I have never knowingly allowed an innocent person to suffer for my wrongdoing, and I shall not do so now. I have clung desperately to the hope, as day has followed day, that interest in Ingeborg's death would fade and the police would cease their inquiries. But now I have to accept the fact that this will not happen. I have decided, therefore, to put an end to myself. It is the only way out. I am not brave enough to stay alive and face the consequences.*

She scanned this last paragraph again, and was surprised to realize that it had spilled straight from the heart. Well, so be it! Better that way than careful, stilted phrases that might not carry the ring of truth.

Franziska blotted the page and placed a paperweight of Bohemian crystal upon the two close-written sheets. She remained seated at the escritoire, gazing into space. No, she was not brave, and this final thing needed more courage than she had ever needed before. It was a mortal sin, but she believed that God in his mercy would understand and forgive her.

The seconds fleeted by, crowding into minutes. She must act. A few moments more, perhaps, to gather herself together . . . but as she sat there, breathing deeply, little cameo scenes of her life came floating back to her.

She saw her father, tall and very handsome – her own striking looks had come from him. But he was a dissolute man, a foul-mouthed, tipsy fiddle-player who scraped a living at Vienna's dingy waterfront taverns – his wife dead of the consumption and his fourteen-year-old daughter already exciting the lecherous interest of swarthy-skinned sailors from the Danube boats. And him not caring a curse, when he had enough drink in him, who laid their coarse hands on her. It had taken several nasty incidents for her to realize that she could expect nothing more from her father; neither affection, which in odd, careless moments he had sometimes shown her as a child, nor any paternal protection. So stealing a few coins from his pocket while he was in a drunken sleep, she had left him and run away, guided by some instinct to the city's great playhouses. Once in the dazzling world she had always dreamed about, starting with various odd jobs backstage, she had not been so fastidious about giving men what they so obviously desired. But she had kept certain standards nonetheless, and she had chosen shrewdly, making sure that each lover represented an upward step in her theatrical career.

So many men in the beginning, but fewer as she climbed the ladder, and far more influential. At first a shabby sofa in one of the theatre dressing-rooms had served, after the performance was over; but later there had been romantic drives in a closed *fiacre* along the Prater's Hauptallee, and intimate champagne suppers in a *chambre privée* at Sacher's.

Heinrich von Kaunitz had been her ultimate conquest in Vienna. Through his influence she had been chosen for roles at the An der Wien that she could never have won by merit alone, and her name had come to mean something in the theatrical world. And with Heinrich, she had not been obliged to pay the usual price of humiliation and self-disgust; with him it had always been a pleasurable experience. Heinrich was a superb lover. Those two brothers were as different in that respect as two brothers could ever be – something of which she was constantly reminded now that she had become Gustav's wife. How strange the way things turn out! Who could have guessed, when she set out on her sentimental return to Vienna with Victoria, that in less than three months she would be a baroness, Baroness von Kaunitz. Baroness *Gustav* von Kaunitz!

There was an amusing side to it all, if one felt inclined to see it. Heinrich had been so angry, even though the marriage had been his own idea in the first place. 'Gustav always seems to come off with the best of everything, damn him!' he had stormed at her the other day. 'And now he's even got you playing the faithful little wife.'

And that was what she had intended to remain, a faithful wife – however great the pressures, however great the temptations. To be a respectable married woman was something she had always yearned for in those far-off early days. She had finally achieved this cherished ambition with James Wayland, and it was a luxury, once tasted, that she would not willingly forsake. She had been prepared to give full value to Gustav as his baroness, as though born and bred to such a lofty position in society. But now, all her manoeuvring, all that she had achieved, was for nought. The terrible wrong she had done in the past had sown the seeds from which the present tragic situation had sprung.

Franziska closed her mind to the shadowy images of yesteryear and focused on the bottle that stood before her upon the escritoire. Its cloudy contents offered a way of atonement. Suddenly, she found the courage she needed, courage that stemmed from her sense of pride. When it came to the point, she had never yet failed in any role she had undertaken, however daunting. Reaching for the bottle, she twisted out the cork and drank deeply. It cost her an enormous effort of will not to scream out.

Mathilde was due to arrive home that morning. Brigitte's baby, yet another girl, had been born on the very day of Ingeborg's funeral, and now mother and child were well enough to be left. In the event, there were only Liesl and Victoria to greet her, and when Mathilde entered the house and saw just the two of them, her narrow eyes pinched in annoyance.

'Where is everyone? Where is my husband?' she demanded sharply, and dragged off her long grey gloves as if preparing herself for battle.

Liesl, looking uneasy, went forward and touched her mother's cheek in a dutiful kiss.

'Papa is in Vienna, Mama.'

'Even though he knew I was coming home? Really, it is too . . .' Mathilde checked herself, and switched her anger to a safer target. 'And that charming sister-in-law of mine, has she perhaps overlooked the fact that I am due back today?'

'Franziska is a little indisposed,' Victoria explained. 'She is resting in her room.'

'I see! So having had charge of the household in my absence, she now feels entitled to slight me.' With a few curt instructions to the hovering servants, Mathilde made for the staircase. 'Come, Liesl, it falls to you to acquaint me with the details of this dreadful Ingeborg business. How we shall ever be able to live it down, I do not know.'

Victoria watched the two of them ascend the stairs. She could hardly blame Mathilde for considering her welcome home was less than her due. Perhaps she should have stressed the extent of her stepmother's indisposition, but she had wanted to avoid making too much of it. She would go up and see if Franziska had improved enough to come down for luncheon. She doubted it, though, for she could never remember seeing her looking so unwell.

She was not unduly surprised to find that the key had been turned in Franziska's door. That seemed to be becoming a habit. Rattling the handle, she called discreetly, 'Franziska, how are you feeling now?'

There was no reply. Listening carefully, Victoria imagined she could hear an odd rasping sound within the room. She called again, more loudly, and began to feel alarmed.

She knew there was another means of entry through Baron Gustav's dressing-room next door. As she slipped inside she was greeted by a lingering aroma of cigar smoke, and felt guilty at intruding into this private sanctum. But at least there was less danger of being overheard here than in the gallery. She crossed the room swiftly and banged on the door.

'Franziska, are you all right? Please answer me.'

There was only silence, then she heard once more that faint rasping sound, like laboured breathing. This door too was locked, and with her two fists she began hammering on the panels – surely making noise enough to rouse Franziska from a deep sleep? She listened intently, and then came another sound, a feeble voice croaking out her name as though in great pain.

'Victoria . . .'

Her alarm gave way to near panic. What to do . . . she must think clearly. She had to get to Franziska without delay, but to ring for a servant would take too long, and then perhaps only a girl would come. A strong man was needed. She thought suddenly of Herr Czernin's valet, who was usually with his master during the day. Hurrying out of the room, she ran wildly round the balustered gallery to the old man's suite in the other wing, and burst in without even knocking. The valet was tucking a plaid rug around Milos Czernin's legs as he sat in his usual straight-backed chair by the window, and they both stared at Victoria in amazement.

She spared no time for apologies but gasped out, 'Josef, please come . . . oh, please come at once. I need your help. Something dreadful has happened to my stepmother.'

The manservant gaped at her stupidly, but old Milos signalled for him to hurry, while he threw aside his rug and levered himself to his feet.

'Go with the young lady, quickly,' he ordered.

Victoria led the way back at a run, going to Baron Gustav's dressing-room since it seemed likely that the inter-communicating door would not be so stoutly constructed as the main one from the gallery.

'My stepmother has been taken ill,' she explained to Josef hastily. 'This door is locked on the inside, so I want you to break it down.'

The valet looked outraged. 'But Fräulein, I cannot do as you ask. It would be more than my place is worth to cause such damage.'

'I will take full responsibility. Please hurry – use anything you must, this heavy chair, anything.'

He still hung back, aghast at the very idea, until a quavering voice behind them commanded, 'Do as Fräulein Wayland says, Josef. Quickly!'

The servant used his shoulder, once, twice – and at the third attempt the door splintered at the lock and burst open. Victoria ran through and found her stepmother lying in a contorted heap on the floor. Crouching down, she saw to her horror that Franziska's lovely face was now looking skeletal, the cheeks sunk into hollows, her skin transparent and a dreadful greyish-mauve.

'What has happened, what's the matter?' she cried, bewildered, hastening to loose the neckband of Franziska's bodice.

Then her eyes took in the glass bottle containing the dregs of a brown liquid, with more spilled on the carpet in a dark spreading stain. Snatching it up, she read the word *Poison* on the label and almost screamed out, 'Have you swallowed this? Tell me, Franziska, for God's sake!'

For a brief moment Franziska's eyes flickered open and she stared unseeingly, then the lids dropped again and she slid into insensibility. In her fear and helplessness, Victoria was thankful that Herr Czernin was taking charge, giving clipped orders in a thin, high-pitched tone.

'Josef, run down and get someone to telephone for Dr Waldstein. Tell him he must come at once – *at once*, do you understand? Tell him it is desperately urgent, a case of poisoning. And send a couple of girls to help Fräulein Wayland. Hurry, man, we mustn't waste a second.'

Victoria felt his bony fingers grip her shoulder. 'Help will be at hand very soon, my dear. Alas, I cannot assist you to make her more comfortable. I am too old, I have no strength in my arms. But it will not be long before someone comes.'

Yet it seemed an eternity, those long-drawn minutes of waiting.

It was Mathilde who found the letter. Plucking it from beneath the glass paperweight, she carried it to the window and read it through, using the pince-nez which dangled on a black ribbon around her neck.

'Extraordinary!' she said. 'Quite extraordinary, though I cannot say I am surprised. I have always suspected there was something disgraceful in Franziska's past.'

'What do you mean?' Victoria asked distractedly. She was bending over her stepmother, whom she and Liesl had just lifted onto the bed.

'Have you not seen this?'

Victoria stared at the sheets of notepaper thrust out at her with something of a triumphant air. When she hesitated about taking them, Mathilde said impatiently, 'You had better read it. There is nothing you can do for your stepmother at the moment. Nor ever will be, if God is merciful!'

Victoria read the letter through with dismay and horror. Oh no!

135

Somehow Franziska had become terribly confused . . . that could be the only explanation. She started to read it a second time, seeking a clue that would make sense to her, but she found her vision blurring with tears.

Liesl intervened. 'May I see, Vicky?'

She hesitated, then handed the letter over. 'But what it says isn't true, Liesl, it can't be true!' Her voice broke on a sob. 'Oh, poor Franziska, why has she done this?'

'*Why?*' echoed Mathilde. 'Because her guilty conscience gave her no peace, that is why. This means, heaven be praised, that Lorenz will now be cleared of suspicion.'

Giving her daughter no chance to finish reading it, she snatched the letter and went to the door. 'I must telephone your father at once, and acquaint him with what has happened. He will take charge of everything.'

Dr Waldstein arrived very soon and examined Franziska with a worried frown. When Victoria showed him the bottle with the dregs of brown liquid, he shook his head unhappily.

'Without doubt it is some form of aniline dye,' he proclaimed, after touching a drop to the tip of his tongue. 'But heaven knows what else it might contain. I will have it analysed without delay, but meantime I must proceed as best I can.'

'A dye!' exclaimed Victoria. 'But why should my stepmother have a bottle of dye? I see from the label she must have brought it with her from England.'

'It is for tinting the hair, Fräulein. Many ladies of a certain age do this in secret.' While talking, he made ready the equipment to flush out the contents of his patient's stomach. 'Now, you two young ladies will remain and assist me, if you please. But I greatly fear that a considerable amount of poison must already have been absorbed into the tissues. And, of course, the lack of will to survive is bound to lessen the chances of recovery. It is so tragic, when the poor lady has been married such a short time and was to all appearances very happy with her husband. Poor Baron Gustav! What could have caused the desperation that drove her to take poison?'

Reluctantly, Victoria told him of Franziska's pathetic letter. It would be public knowledge soon.

Dr Waldstein's eyes widened. 'I see. How very dreadful!' He paused, considering. 'In the circumstances, one almost wonders . . .'

'Wonders what, Herr Doktor?'

'Perhaps it might be better if your stepmother is already beyond my help.'

Victoria felt a cold clench of fear, and perspiration broke out on her brow. 'No, she mustn't die. For pity's sake, you must save her. You *must!*'

'Do not mistake me, *gnädiges Fräulein*. I have done and I shall do everything medically possible for the baroness. But I think you had better send for the priest.'

Heinrich and Gustav arrived home before the physician's second visit, and Lorenz had returned from the foundry with them. The two brothers had acted with what Victoria felt was indecent haste by informing the police about Franziska's confession even before coming up to see her. When they appeared in the sick room they stood gazing down at the insensible figure on the bed with identical frowns that Victoria found difficult to interpret. In Gustav's face she saw no hint of grief that his wife lay dying; she sensed no compassion for his sister-in-law in Heinrich.

'I will leave you for a while,' she murmured.

'No, don't go!' Gustav said quickly. 'Since she is unconscious there is little purpose in our remaining here. I will speak with Dr Waldstein as soon as he returns.'

When the doctor came an hour later he studied Franziska gravely and pronounced that there was little change in her condition, beyond a slight deterioration. Liesl looked in with a sympathetic message from Lorenz asking Victoria if there was anything he could do. But Lorenz was the last person who could help her now. Liesl offered to sit with Franziska to give Victoria respite from her vigil, but Victoria declined. She had to be here when her stepmother regained consciousness – if she ever did again. There were questions to be asked, answers to be given. Secret questions, secret answers.

Once or twice as the afternoon wore on Franziska muttered to herself as if in delirium, but she did not respond when Victoria spoke to her. Then some time later, in the dim light filtering through the drawn curtains, she became aware that her stepmother's eyes were open.

'Why, Franziska?' she asked in a whisper. 'Why did you take that poison? Why have you done such a terrible thing?'

Franziska had heard her. There was understanding in those pain-racked eyes, understanding and evasion. The dry lips parted, and

Victoria bent closer to hear what her stepmother said. But it was no answer, only another question.

'Am I going to die? For God's sake, tell me I shall die.'

'No, Franziska. Not if you have the will to live.'

The hands which lay limply upon the satin quilt made a tiny gesture of denial.

'Have . . . have you found the letter I wrote?'

'Yes – but it is nonsense! I only wish to heaven I had seen it first, and I would have torn it to shreds. Why ever did you write that letter, Franziska?'

'I had to! I had to confess the truth. The Inspector of Police . . . has he seen it?'

'Yes. And of course he believes it.' A look of relief flickered in Franziska's face, until Victoria rushed on, 'But *I* don't believe it. I know that you made the whole thing up.'

'How can you say that? I swear it is true, every word of it.'

'It is not true, because you couldn't possibly have been responsible for Ingeborg's death. You couldn't have been travelling on that train.'

'But I was!' Franziska tried to raise herself, but had not the strength. Her mass of chestnut hair – false in its glorious rich colouring, as Victoria now knew – lay spilled about the pillow. Her eyes filled with tears as she struggled for breath to go on. 'I . . . I explained how it was done.'

Victoria shook her head. 'No, it was all pure invention. You were here in this room at the time when Ingeborg was killed.'

'I slipped out secretly . . . you must believe me.'

'I cannot believe you, Franziska, because I talked to you that evening – don't you remember? It would have been a physical impossibility for you to have been on Ingeborg's train, and to return here by the time I came up directly after dinner to inquire how you were. I knocked on the door and you answered me – you must remember that.'

'I had forgotten!' The words came in a gasp of dismay. 'You were mistaken about the time, Vicky. When you knocked at my door it must have been much later than you thought. I had already been out and returned.'

Victoria shook her head again. 'I made no mistake about the time. Your confession is completely false, Franziska.' Her voice became insistent, urgent. 'Tell me why you wrote that letter. I must know why.'

Franziska lay with her eyes half-closed, unutterably weary, and Victoria began to fear she would drift off once more. She knew she ought to summon the priest who was waiting downstairs, but first it was vitally important that her stepmother should tell her the truth. Wiping Franziska's brow again with a handkerchief sprinkled with eau-de-Cologne, she willed her to remain conscious.

'Please,' she begged, 'I have to know why. You do see that, don't you?'

A deep juddering sigh shook Franziska's body. 'Are we alone?'

'Yes, there is no one else here.'

A long pause, then in a husky whisper Franziska said, 'I did it to protect Lorenz.'

'*To protect Lorenz!* But this is not the way,' Victoria said gently. 'Confessing to something which you could not possibly have done.'

'You are the only one who can destroy the evidence of that letter, Vicky. You must remain silent. You must swear to me that you will remain silent.'

'But Franziska, if you survive—' Hastily, she amended her words. 'You will survive, of course you will. And then I could not stand by and allow you to take the blame for something you didn't do.'

'Have no doubt, Vicky, I shall not recover. Whether I live or whether I die is in my own hands, I am convinced of that. It will not be long.'

Victoria felt hot tears spill from her eyes. 'Please, Franziska, please don't die. I . . . I couldn't bear it if you were to die.'

A tiny smile hovered for a moment on her stepmother's lips. 'I believe you really mean it,' she said wonderingly. 'But you must not grieve over me, my dear. Just consider . . . everything will be solved for you. There will be no need now for you to marry Pieter Bahr. I never wanted that, but it seemed the best thing, the only thing, knowing how you and Lorenz felt about one another. But now, you and Lorenz will be free to marry in due time.'

The knot of misery in Victoria's breast tightened. 'No, that's impossible. I could never marry Lorenz, not now, knowing that—'

'Don't say it! Don't even think it! Whatever Lorenz did, Vicky, he was driven to it by desperation. All his life he has been manipulated by his father and his uncle for their own ends. You love him, and whatever happens you could never bring yourself to destroy him with the knowledge you hold. So forget that you ever came to my room that night, and instead make yourself believe what I wrote in my letter. If I can die knowing that I have brought you and Lorenz together, it will all have been worthwhile.'

'But it's impossible, what you're suggesting . . .'

'I beg you, Vicky, let me go to my grave happy.'

Victoria tried to turn away, but she was held by those wildly staring eyes, the look of pleading in them. Franziska's lips were trembling, and her voice was husky in her throat.

'Lorenz wants you, he needs you. He has been cheated of happiness, cheated in every way . . . so do it for his sake, Vicky. And then everything I have done will be vindicated. The slate will be wiped clean.'

Victoria felt a numbness take hold of her senses. 'What is Lorenz to you, that you are prepared to make such a sacrifice for him?'

The answer was a long time in coming. 'May not I love him, too?'

'You . . . love . . . Lorenz?' Victoria was bewildered. 'But I don't understand. I know how fond you are of him, how well you get on together. But love?'

'I love him with a mother's love.'

'A . . . a mother's love?'

'Because I *am* his mother. Yes, it is true, Lorenz is my son. There, the secret is out.'

In her feverish agitation Franziska had started up from her pillow, but suddenly she sank back and her lids fluttered closed. Victoria feared that she was dead.

14

Afterwards, when it was finally over, Victoria came to believe that her stepmother had clung to life purely by strength of will.

For minutes on end Franziska lay utterly still, her skin that dreadful grey-mauve colour. Then her eyelids fluttered open again and when she spoke there was a new calmness in her voice, as if she were glad that the truth was out at last – the astonishing truth about Lorenz which screamed in Victoria's mind, dazing her senses.

'Give me some water please, Vicky.'

'The Herr Doktor said you were not to have much to drink.'

'Just a sip, to moisten my lips. Ah, thank you.' Her pale, ghostly face twisted into the shape of a smile. 'You are a dear, good girl. I only wish I had been a better stepmother to you.'

On a wave of belated affection, Victoria said, 'You have been all that I could have wished for.'

'Alas, that is far from the truth. I did my best, I suppose ... the best it was in me to give.' She found the strength to catch at Victoria's hand. 'I truly loved your father, though. You must believe that.'

'Yes, I know you loved him. You made him very happy, and I shall always be grateful.' Victoria could contain her burning curiosity no longer. 'Tell me about Lorenz,' she urged.

'Be patient with me. I shall tell you everything before I die. Yes, Lorenz is my child.' The pale mockery of a smile flickered again. 'Is it so incredible that I have a son? You guessed, did you not, that Heinrich and I were lovers in the old days?'

'But Lorenz is Baron Gustav's son.'

'That's what he has always been brought up to believe, and what the world believes. But Heinrich is his father, not Gustav. They were desperate, you see, because Gustav's newborn son was sickly and at death's door, and his wife had already died in childbirth. They faced ruination.'

'I don't understand.'

Franziska's eyes, even dulled with pain, could still register scorn. 'Where are your wits, girl? Whose money is it that keeps the von Kaunitz family going? Whose business enterprise is it that Lorenz manages now, and will ultimately inherit as entirely his own?'

'Herr Czernin, you mean?'

'Of course, old Milos Czernin. Even with his daughter dead, all would have been well as long as there was a grandchild to become his heir. The von Kaunitz future would still have been secure. But with the child dead, too, would Herr Czernin even have continued to make his home at the schloss? If he left, the constant flood of money that kept the place going would dry up, and Gustav could hardly expect his father-in-law to go on paying both himself and Heinrich the handsome salaries they received for doing next to nothing at the Czernin foundry. The situation was critical for them. Then it struck Heinrich that if they could substitute another child for the baby that was dying, with no one any the wiser, it would solve their problem completely. And my baby had just been born.'

Shock and outrage spun in Victoria's mind, rendering her speechless.

'Lorenz – or Ruprecht as I'd had him baptized – was just six days older than Gustav's son,' Franziska went on. 'They told the family physician that his services were no longer needed as the child had turned the corner and was now thriving. And as for Milos Czernin . . . the death of his daughter had brought on a severe attack of his asthma, and he was away being treated at a sanatorium near Ischl. By the time he returned home he was unable to tell the difference between the two babies.'

'But what about Baroness Mathilde . . . she must have known.'

'Oh yes, Mathilde knew. But only that another child had been found for the substitution. She wasn't told whose child it was.'

'Nor even that her husband was the father?'

'Heavens no! That has always been kept from her.'

Victoria felt sickened. She must have shown it in her face, for Franziska flinched and glanced away.

'Try to see it from my point of view,' she muttered. 'When Heinrich came to me with his proposition, he allowed me no time to think. I had

142

to make up my mind at once. It seemed such a dazzling opportunity for my baby . . . to be brought up as the son of a baron – which he rightfully was – and the heir of a wealthy industrialist like Milos Czernin.' She clutched again at Victoria's hand. 'Consider what I had to offer the child in place of that, a young actress alone in the world, with a career to consider. I would not get the support I had been counting on from Heinrich if I did not fall in with his plan – he made that very clear. Could I be blamed, Vicky? The scales were heavily weighted, and I was very young.'

Victoria remained silent. Words of censure seemed out of place.

'I know what you are thinking, and I myself have thought the same a thousand times. Often I have wondered about my son, wondered how he had grown up and whether he was happy. Yet I could do nothing to find out. Heinrich had given me sufficient money to live abroad, and part of the bargain we struck was that I should keep away from Austria.' Her sigh was a dry rattle in her throat. 'I left Vienna the day after the funeral of Gustav's child, which was buried as mine. The little corpse was brought to me in a bundle by the wet nurse when she took my baby away. That nurse was the only other person who knew anything about what had happened. She was the mother of a half-witted infant, and her silence was secured with a promise that Zogak would always be cared for.'

'Zogak, the man who is a gardener here?'

'Yes, that's the one. His mother has been dead for some years, apparently, but Heinrich and Gustav have kept their promise. That was why they wouldn't listen when Ingeborg wanted Zogak dismissed.'

Suddenly so much had become clear to Victoria. With a cold, leaden feeling, she said, 'So this explains why you were so anxious to get in touch with Baron Heinrich when we first arrived in Vienna. And when you did, you saw your opportunity and forced Baron Gustav to marry you in return for your continued silence.'

'No, no! It was not like that at all.' A shudder ran through Franziska's body beneath the bedclothes. 'You make it sound like blackmail, but such a wicked idea never entered my head. When your father died I felt lonely in England, and I thought more and more of Vienna, and of my son. I longed to know what had become of him, longed to see him, and it occurred to me that if I returned to Vienna and made contact with Heinrich I had nothing to lose. And who knew, something good might come of it. The von Kaunitzes had received so much benefit and I so comparatively little from the arrangement we made all those years ago.'

It *was* blackmail all the same, there was no prettier word for it. Perhaps Franziska had never used an open threat to expose the brothers, but it had nevertheless lain unspoken. Victoria felt shame for her own unwitting part in her stepmother's scheming.

'When Gustav proposed to me,' Franziska went on, 'I could scarcely believe my good fortune. It seemed such a remarkably happy twist of fate that the man who had assumed the role of my son's father should now want to make me his wife. This was surely the perfect solution. It provided a secure, comfortable background for us – yes, I was thinking of you too, Vicky. And above all, I would be reunited with the son I had lost. I would be near him always, as his stepmother. In my wildest dreams I could scarcely have wished for more.' Her voice began to crack, and she whispered, 'Water, please.'

'Should you?'

'Does it matter now? Come, let me take a few sips.'

Even the effort of drinking exhausted Franziska, and she lay back on the pillows with her eyes closed. It was very quiet in the room, with only the soft ticking of the French clock on the lacquered cabinet, and a bird rustling in the creeper outside the windows. Then in a breathy whisper she continued, 'Sadly, instead of all the good things I had been hoping for, my coming has only resulted in bringing tragedy to my son.'

'How is it your fault, Franziska?'

'Don't you see . . . but for my returning, bringing you here, Lorenz would have remained resigned to his disastrous marriage – which is something else Heinrich and Gustav must be blamed for! It is no wonder that, as a young soldier home on sick leave, Lorenz should have fallen in love with a girl like Ingeborg, but he would never have rushed headlong into marriage had he not been encouraged by those two. They ignored the fact that she was totally unsuitable for him, and saw her as a God-sent chance to produce a great-grandchild for Milos Czernin without delay. Then if anything should happen to Lorenz during the rest of his army service – or indeed at any other time – they would still have access to the old man's wealth. My son has been no more than a pawn to them all his life. And poor Lorenz endured that impossible marriage, Vicky, until your arrival, until I brought you here for him to meet and fall in love with. After that, he could endure it no longer and the rest followed.'

The rest? Ingeborg's death ... Ingeborg's *murder*. Even in the privacy of her mind, Victoria had avoided that word until now.

Franziska made an effort to rally again, as if she knew the danger of slipping into a realm that was beyond the reach of her willpower.

'My death will solve everything, Vicky. No, do not shake your head, it is true. I must make you understand. Things were becoming impossible here at the schloss. Not only the situation between you and Lorenz, but Heinrich was making outrageous demands on me.'

'Demands? What demands did he make of you?'

Franziska gestured feebly. 'He seemed to imagine that he had the right, because I had once been his mistress. Because it was he who fathered my son, not Gustav.'

'You mean he expected you to ...?'

'Yes. It was not so much, I think, that he desired me for myself – Heinrich has never had any difficulty in finding women to please him. No, it was jealousy, Vicky. In everything they've done, although Heinrich was the initiator of all their schemes, his twin brother always seemed to come off best. Just consider, right back in the days when they first encountered Milos Czernin in their business dealings, it was Gustav who wooed and won the daughter, because Heinrich was already married to Mathilde. As a consequence, it was Gustav who became closer to Milos, and more important in the hierarchy at the foundry. And then, of course, Heinrich has always resented the situation about Lorenz.'

'In what way?'

'It was *his* plan, you see, involving *his* son – yet while it averted disaster for them both, it had the effect of further securing Gustav's privileged position as the father of Milos's heir.'

'Are you telling me that it was also Heinrich's plan that Gustav should marry you?'

'But of course. Though I made no threats or demands, Heinrich saw me as a danger to them. He decided that the most effective way of ensuring my continued silence would be to make me one of the family. Gustav was opposed to the idea at first, I feel sure, but when he actually met me he was attracted at once. I know how to make myself desirable to a man, and he saw in me a wife other men would envy him. You know, Vicky, it could have been a good marriage, despite the circumstances in which it came about, for I was fully prepared to play my part and be all he could ever hope for in a wife. But Heinrich was enraged when he came to realize that yet again his brother had emerged with the advantage.' Her voice was high-pitched now, rasping like a saw. 'He has been badgering me persistently ever since Gustav and I returned from our honeymoon, until I was at my wits' end how to fend him off.'

'But could you not have told your husband?'

'Haven't you grasped that Gustav is a weak man, no match for his brother? Appealing to him would have been useless. Besides . . . it wasn't only Heinrich I had to fight, it was myself too. I was tormented by memories of what Heinrich and I had once been to each other.'

'But you would never have succumbed?'

'Not as long as I had willpower enough to withstand him. But then, you are too young and inexperienced to know of such things between a man and a woman.'

But I do know, Victoria thought with a rush of understanding. If Lorenz were to make similar demands of her, she feared she would never find it in her to refuse him. Whatever he had done . . .

Franziska was saying between laboured breaths, 'That day Ingeborg was killed, that dreadful day when the *Föhn* blew incessantly, Heinrich deliberately returned home early with one intention in his mind. He wouldn't leave me alone, and in the end I was forced to lock myself in my room and remain there all the evening.'

Ghosts of the past seemed all around them, lurking in the shadows. What to say – what even to think? Franziska had been a willing party to many of the dreadful things she had spoken of, yet somehow Victoria felt closer to her stepmother than ever before. Whatever she had done she had suffered for it, more than she deserved to suffer.

With a sudden urgency, Franziska said, 'You do see, don't you, that my death will put everything to rights? You must never tell anyone that my letter is a falsehood.' She caught her breath painfully. 'Swear to me that you never will, Vicky.'

How could she swear to keep silent and allow her stepmother to be unjustly branded a murderess? Yet how could she refuse the entreaties of someone so close to death?

'I beg you, do not let my sacrifice have been in vain,' Franziska protested. 'I am not asking you to lie, but only to remain silent. Let the blame for Ingeborg's death rest upon my shoulders, and Lorenz will be released from the intolerable burden of suspicion. It will be the only thing I have ever done for my son, beyond giving him birth.'

Victoria said brokenly, through tears, 'I promise I will not speak . . . unless I am forced to speak.'

Was it enough? Franziska seemed about to protest again, then closed her eyes in acceptance.

'And when Lorenz asks you to marry him and share his life – as I know he will – I want you to accept him joyfully and give him the happiness he has been denied till now.'

'But I cannot marry Lorenz,' Victoria insisted.

'You must, you must!' In her agitation Franziska pushed her shoulders from the bed, and Victoria hastened to support her. 'Why should you refuse, when you love him? You owe it to each other to take this chance of happiness.'

'But it would be a marriage based upon a lie.'

'It would be based upon love, and nothing matters but that. Believe me, my dear, whatever I may have said to you before, love is the only thing that matters.'

About to protest once more, Victoria saw the agony in her stepmother's eyes. And so she made a promise, a false promise, and hoped to be forgiven for it.

'I will accept him . . . if he asks me.'

Franziska was content. She fell back wearily, and a little smile hovered around her bloodless lips.

'Now, Vicky dear, you had better call the priest. Tell him to hurry.'

Victoria rang the bell and gave instructions to the maid. While waiting for the priest she smoothed the silk sheets, straightened the pillows and arranged Franziska's hair as becomingly as possible. When the tap came at the door she bent and touched her lips to the fevered brow. She knew that she would not see her stepmother alive again, and as she left the room she felt an inexpressible sense of grief.

In the evening Victoria was summoned to Baron Heinrich's study, a room she had never entered before. She found his brother there also, and the two men stood regarding her with curiously veiled expressions.

Baron Heinrich indicated a highbacked chair facing the desk, and said heavily, 'You had better sit down, Victoria. This is a dreadful business.'

The men remained standing. Gustav shifted his weight uneasily from one foot to the other, while Heinrich polished his monocle with a white silk handkerchief before screwing it into his eye. The branched gasolier hissed steadily, shedding a cool, clear light.

Gustav said at last in an edgy voice, 'Such a tragedy, yes indeed! Tell me, Victoria, when your stepmother regained consciousness before she passed away, did she speak at all of her reasons for . . . for committing the crime she had confessed to?'

Victoria sensed that they were exceedingly anxious to know just how much Franziska might have told her, and she made a spur of the moment decision to reveal nothing until she had had a chance to consider the possible implications.

She took a deep breath, and lied. 'She told me nothing about that.'

'I see. But all the same, what could it have been that Franziska was so desperate to conceal about her past? Have you any idea what it was?'

'How could I possibly know, unless she told me herself?'

'Which she did not do?' he persisted.

Victoria said hotly, 'I refuse to believe it could have been anything so very dreadful. Franziska was always a good wife to my father, and a good stepmother to me. What she had done in the past – whatever it was – she more than made up for.'

It seemed to satisfy them. Victoria could detect an easing of their tension.

Heinrich said smoothly, 'This has been very distressing and unsettling for you, my dear, especially after you have had so much else to contend with. How are your hands now, by the way?'

She flexed her fingers for him to see. 'They are much improved – as well as they will ever be, I am told.'

'Good, good! You will have to start thinking of the future, making plans about what you want to do.'

No mention now of marriage to Pieter! They no longer wanted her connected with their family, to be a constant reminder of what had happened.

She said, with dignity, 'I shall be returning to England as soon as . . . as soon as it is practicable.'

'Excellent, my dear! You will not find my brother and myself ungenerous. Let us know when you intend travelling and we will see about your tickets and reservations – will we not, Gustav? And there will be a little something to tide you over until the lawyers have settled your stepmother's affairs.'

148

They could hardly wait to see the back of her, she thought bleakly as she left the room. If only she could talk to Lorenz – but that was impossible. Even if she did not believe that he had killed Ingeborg, how could she tell him that his entire position here at the Schloss Kaunitz, his entire life, was based upon a shameful deception?

Who else could she turn to? Liesl? Pieter? She trusted them and felt sure she could rely on their sympathy. But they were both of them members of the family which had benefited – and still benefited – from that long-distant deception. It would be a desperately unfair burden to lay upon their shoulders.

Passing through the octagonal ante-chamber, Victoria was waylaid by Baroness Mathilde, and suspected she had been hovering purposely in the doorway of her sitting-room. Mathilde's hands shook from the rage she had worked herself into, and it became clear that she was intent upon wounding.

'What a disgrace it all is! To think what we have had to suffer. Ah well, the sooner your stepmother is buried and this whole wretched business can be forgotten, the better. I take it, Victoria, that you will be leaving us once the funeral is over?'

'Have no fear, I shall not be here to trouble you for much longer. I shall be returning to England very soon, just as I was planning before this happened.'

Mathilde's eyes narrowed with suspicion. 'You don't mean, I hope, that you still expect to marry my nephew? In the circumstances that would be intolerable.'

'As it happens, I never did intend to marry Pieter. It was the rest of you who were pushing us together and taking it for granted that I would accept his proposal.'

'So if he asks for your answer now, you will refuse him?'

'The situation is hardly likely to arise,' Victoria responded with a scornful smile. 'I'm sure your nephew can see for himself on which side his bread is buttered.'

'Well really, such rudeness! I —' Mathilde broke off at the sound of footsteps approaching across the marble-flagged hall. Lorenz came through into the ante-chamber and directed a reproving glance at his aunt.

'Victoria and I were just discussing her future plans,' Mathilde said with a shrug.

'I should have thought that was rather premature.'

'I merely wanted to know where we all stood,' she said peevishly, and disappeared into her sitting-room, closing the door with a deliberate thud.

Alone with Lorenz, Victoria could not bring herself to look at him. She had seen him a few minutes after Franziska's death, when he had come to the bedroom with his father and had murmured a few words of condolence.

Now he said in a gentle voice, 'What can I say to you, Victoria? I know how deeply you must be grieving. The events of the past week have been shocking, tragic. But whatever the rights and wrongs of it all, Franziska was a quite remarkable person. A fascinating woman with great charm and warmth.'

'You sound as if you were truly fond of her.'

He nodded. 'It is difficult to put my feelings into words. I felt drawn to Franziska from the beginning, and although I may have made some harsh comments to you about her, and did not approve of her marrying my father, afterwards I was glad – quite apart from the fact that she brought you here with her. As time went by, I found myself increasingly admiring of her, increasingly fond.'

Victoria clenched her hands together, fighting against tears. Lorenz could speak like this about Franziska as though he meant every word, and yet he was allowing her to bear the blame for Ingeborg's death. What was going on in his mind, behind those keen but impenetrable eyes? Did he not find it extraordinary that Franziska should have confessed to killing Ingeborg, when the guilt was his own?

She said quickly, allowing the thought to slip out, 'I suppose you realize that Franziska sacrificed herself for you? She made her confession to save your skin.'

'I am deeply aware of that,' he said soberly, 'and I honour her for such courage. Obviously she overheard our conversation in the music-room, as we feared, and it must have convinced her that I would be arrested and charged with the murder of my wife. The tragic thing is that she was mistaken. I was in no real danger, for the police could have produced no solid evidence against me.' He sighed. 'But better this way, perhaps, than if the truth had somehow come to light and Franziska had faced the ordeal of a public trial, and the inevitable consequences.'

Every moment Victoria remained here talking to Lorenz, her certainty of his guilt was shredding away. He must be guilty, he *must*! And yet from the way he spoke, it seemed beyond belief. Misery engulfed her, clogging her mind, and she knew she must quit his presence. As she turned and took a step toward the archway through to the main hall, Lorenz caught her arm, stopping her.

'Just now you were discussing your plans with my aunt. What are they?'

She said, almost inaudibly, 'I explained to her that I shall leave here as soon as the funeral is over, and return to live in England.'

'Live in England? But you can't! You cannot leave me now.'

'How can I possibly remain here? It is out of the question, you must see that.'

His mouth tightened. 'It is not out of the question. Why should we care what other people might think? You and I are blameless, and we have a right to happiness.'

'It's impossible! There can be no happiness for us now. We must go our separate ways.'

'In God's name,' he demanded suspiciously, 'you aren't planning to marry Pieter Bahr?'

'Of course not. I have never seriously considered it.' Bitterness crept into her voice. 'And now, it seems, the match is no longer thought desirable by your family. The sooner they can be rid of me, the better.'

'Do you mean they have told you so? I won't tolerate any more of that!'

'Whatever they say, whatever they think, it would make no difference. I have made up my mind to go away.'

'But you cannot go, you must not.' His eyes searched her face for some sign of weakening. 'At least promise me one thing, Victoria – that you will not think of leaving at once. Promise to stay until this dreadful situation is a little behind us, and we can see the way ahead more clearly.'

She shuddered, remembering how once before Lorenz had begged her not to go away. If she had strenuously refused to yield to his pleading that other time, if she had made it clear that she was departing at once from the Schloss Kaunitz, perhaps all the horror that had followed would have been averted. Two deaths – a murder and a suicide. Yet even now she could not summon the words to reject him outright. She made no reply, and she knew that he interpreted her silence as the promise he demanded.

At that moment Liesl appeared in the archway, and Victoria became aware that Lorenz's hand was still upon her arm. She pulled away from him quickly, but Liesl noticed the movement and gave them a look of compassion.

'Vicky, I was coming to find you to see if you felt well enough to put in an appearance at dinner.'

The prospect dismayed her. 'No, I don't think I could face everyone. Besides, I'm not hungry.'

'But you must eat, you've hardly had anything all day. You and I will have a tray upstairs.' Liesl glanced at her cousin, and back again to Victoria. 'I know it's a dreadful situation for you both, but you must give it time. Time is a great healer.'

The advice was well intended, but to Victoria it sounded so facile. She felt that an infinity of experience separated them now. Liesl, in loving Andrej, faced certain problems with her family, but she could know nothing of the agony and despair of a love born under an evil star. With a tremulous smile, Victoria hurried toward the stairs while she could still hold back the tears that pressed against her eyelids.

15

Franziska was laid to rest, if such a term were appropriate, in an unconsecrated corner far removed from the noble plot where Ingeborg had been buried. It was a day of fretful wind and sudden showers, and the few people gathered round the graveside were huddled beneath black umbrellas.

Mathilde had chosen to stay away, and her husband had not insisted on her attendance. She scarcely even took the trouble to give credibility to her claimed cold in the head. But Liesl was there, defying her mother's implicit wishes, in order to lend support to Victoria. Also present were Franziska's husband with his brother, and Lorenz, and Otto, wearing full dress uniform, a blaze of colour against the drab funeral attire of the others. Lastly, there was Pieter Bahr, looking pale and nervous, his gaze coming constantly to rest a moment on Victoria, before flitting hurriedly on.

The committal proceedings were conducted with a haste and lack of feeling that shocked Victoria, even though she had expected little better. As the party was moving away she found Pieter at her side.

'Will it be convenient for me to call upon you this evening?' he asked awkwardly. 'I apologize for appearing hasty, but there is so little time now before I must leave for England.'

Taken by surprise, Victoria murmured, 'I have no intention of holding you to your offer, Pieter. The circumstances are altogether different now.'

He lifted his chin, looking affronted. 'Are you questioning my honour, Victoria?'

'I'm sorry, that was not my intention.' Her heart sank at the prospect of an embarrassing interview, but she said, 'Very well, you may come this evening.'

Outside the gates, the carriages stood waiting. There was need, however, for a redistribution of the passengers. In the funeral cortège Victoria had travelled behind the hearse with Liesl and Franziska's husband; but Baron Gustav, instead of returning to the schloss, was remaining in Vienna with his brother, having muttered something about an inescapable business engagement. As the party stood hesitating, everyone ill-at-ease, it was Lorenz who made the first move. Taking Victoria's elbow, he led her to the foremost carriage and helped her to mount the step.

'This has been an ordeal for you,' he said, his voice tender with sympathy. 'Are you all right? Would you like me to accompany you back?'

He was making a clear demonstration to his family that a special relationship existed between them. When Liesl at once approved of his suggestion, saying that she and Otto would travel separately in another carriage, Victoria felt even more dismayed.

'No, no!' she cried out in panic. 'You mustn't come back, Lorenz. I mean, I'm sure you have work awaiting your attention at the foundry.'

'Nothing so pressing that it can't be postponed.'

'But I shall be perfectly well looked after by Liesl and Otto. Thank you all the same.'

For a moment or two he lingered, anxiously scanning her face. Then he stepped back and gave a small bow. 'As you wish, of course. I shall see you this evening, then.'

With the hood of the landau raised against another sudden downpour, it felt hot and steamy inside. The three of them sat uncomfortably in their damp clothes, jogged to and fro as the carriage rattled over the uneven cobblestones of the highway. Otto was in an unusually subdued mood. It was as if he only knew how to be flippant and jolly, and was unequal to the expression of any graver emotion. He sat facing the two girls, stroking his moustache, as he sought for suitable words of condolence. But the best he could manage was, 'I say, Victoria, this is a bad business, and no mistake.'

'Oh, do be quiet,' said his sister irritably.

He looked pained. 'Dash it all, I'm only trying to say the proper thing, you know.'

Victoria gave him a tight little smile. 'You are quite right, Otto, it is indeed a bad business.'

'Still, thank the Lord it's all over and done with now.'

'I wonder if we can say it's all over?'

He stared at her, taken aback. 'What are you getting at?'

Victoria had a sudden urge to pour out all she knew, the shocking things she had learned from Franziska in her dying hours. She was conscious of them both waiting warily for her answer, Otto fiddling with the hilt of his sword and Liesl teasing a loose thread in the finger of one of her gloves.

'I didn't mean anything in particular,' she murmured. 'It's just – well, when dreadful things start to happen, you can't help wondering where they'll end.'

'There will be nothing more,' said Liesl nervously, trying to sound reassuring. 'Why should there be? Otto is quite right, it's all over and we must start picking up the pieces. The future will be what you make it, Vicky – it lies there waiting for you.'

'Mama tells me it's all off as far as you and Pieter are concerned,' Otto remarked, and received a warning glance from his sister. 'Confounded shame!' he added weakly.

'It's a very good thing, in my opinion,' Liesl snapped back. 'Pieter is totally unsuitable for Vicky. The whole idea was preposterous.'

Victoria listened dully as they bandied their opinions, almost as if it were a matter which did not concern her; but when they became aware she was taking no part in the conversation they fell into an uneasy silence.

The route took them past the Imperial palace at Schönbrunn, its ornate yellow façade streaked and darkened by the rain, its myriad serried windows reflecting the leaden sky. Not far from here, Victoria suddenly recalled, was Dommayer's Casino, where Ingeborg had been going on that fateful evening. She shuddered, and closed her eyes in a vain attempt to blot out the nightmare images that loomed before her.

The carriage had turned in at the tall, gilded entrance gates of the schloss when Otto stirred and gave a yawn.

'Well, I suppose it's all been for the best, the way things have turned out. It would have been the very devil if Lorenz had been arrested.'

Liesl jolted upright, and the intensity of her voice took Victoria by surprise. 'If you imagine there was ever any real possibility of Lorenz being charged with murder, Otto, you are quite wrong. That could never have been tolerated, whatever the risks —' She broke off, glanced at each of them in turn, and gave a hasty little shrug. 'I mean, I am sure it would never have come to that.'

Once in the house, Victoria went directly to her room. Liesl insisted on accompanying her, and closed the door carefully.

'I must talk to you, Vicky. I couldn't say anything in front of Otto, but I have a distinct impression you might still be giving Pieter's proposal serious consideration. I hope to goodness that I'm wrong.'

To cover her agitation, Victoria slowly removed her hat and mantle and went to the dressing-table to tidy her hair before the mirror.

'The question of Pieter doesn't arise any more,' she replied. 'It has been made abundantly clear to me that your parents have withdrawn their support. Baron Gustav, too. And Pieter is in no position to flout their wishes.'

'I'm not so sure he wouldn't! I know that cousin of mine. Though he is hopelessly conventional and makes me furious by always trying to ingratiate himself with my parents, he has a curious kind of integrity all the same. He would probably think it dishonourable to try and back out of his proposal, whatever the cost to his career and ambitions.'

'That's more or less what he said to me at the cemetery today,' Victoria admitted.

'There you are, then! So you will have to be steadfast in refusing him, Vicky. You can't marry Pieter – Lorenz is the only man for you.'

'No, not Lorenz. That could never be.'

'How can you be so stupid? Why shouldn't you two marry now that Lorenz is free? Oh, I know it's all been dreadful, his wife being killed by your stepmother, but you mustn't let that deter you, you really mustn't. You and Lorenz can't be held in any way to blame and it isn't fair that you should have to suffer any more than you've done already. It won't be easy for you and people will say unkind things behind your backs, but after a while they'll come to accept the situation. You and Lorenz have a right to be happy, and you simply cannot let the chance slip by.'

'I feel,' said Victoria in a hollow, drained voice, 'that I shall never be happy again. What you suggest is impossible, Liesl.'

'You are talking nonsense!'

Victoria felt helpless. Liesl, like everyone else, accepted Franziska's confession as the truth, so she was quite unable to see the insurmountable obstacles that divided her and Lorenz. How could she ever make Liesl understand the situation without revealing everything, without explaining why Franziska had sacrificed herself by falsely confessing to Ingeborg's murder? How could she possibly

156

admit that she still believed Lorenz was responsible for his wife's death?

Liesl went on with brisk impatience, 'You cannot deny, can you, that you love Lorenz?' Receiving no answer, she said, 'I *know* you do, one has only to watch your face when you look at him. So for heaven's sake, let's have no more of this foolishness. I care about you both very much, and I want to see you happy. I want Lorenz to be happy after those wasted years with Ingeborg.'

'We could never be happy together,' Victoria insisted, feeling desperate.

Liesl caught her breath in exasperation. 'I know of no two people better suited to each other. You think in the same way, you have the same ideals. And Lorenz loves you just as you love him. Besides, there's little Emil. He is devoted to you, and you would make him a marvellous mother.' She came up behind Victoria who still stood at the dressing-table, and spun her round so that they were facing one another. 'Now give me one good reason why you and Lorenz shouldn't marry after a decent interval has elapsed.'

Victoria made a feeble attempt at flippancy. 'One good reason is that he hasn't asked me to marry him.'

'Pff! He will, you know he will when the time is right. So what else?'

Victoria put her hands up to her face, fighting the black waves that threatened to engulf her. How could she hope to counter Liesl's attack with no weapons – none she could use – and no will, either? Her ears, her heart, were only too receptive to Liesl's passionate pleading; and Liesl's unflinching faith in Lorenz was echoed and re-echoed by her own instinctive trust in him. Despite the weight of evidence that condemned Lorenz, it seemed impossible to believe him guilty of such an awful deed. And yet . . .

'If only,' she began wretchedly, 'if only Lorenz would say straight out why he went hurrying back to Vienna that evening.'

Liesl's expression sharpened with surprise. 'For pity's sake, does that matter any longer?'

'It must do! Until that is cleared up —'

'Are you so shocked at the thought that Lorenz was going to visit a woman? This is no time for petty jealousy, Vicky. In Vienna it isn't unusual for men to have mistresses, you know, even when they are contentedly married. For someone in Lorenz's situation it could surely be forgiven?'

'It's not that at all. I know Lorenz has a mistress, he has been frank with me about her. But I know, too, that he was not going to see her that night, nor any other woman.'

'How do you know?' The question was rapped out. 'Did Lorenz tell you?'

'Perhaps not in so many words, but yes, he told me.'

'Did he say anything else?'

'No – though I begged him to. I begged him to tell the police if he had any justifiable reason for taking that train to Vienna. But he stubbornly refused.'

'And so, just like everybody else, you suspected him of committing murder.' Liesl's voice was bitter with reproach. 'I thought you loved him, yet you can believe such a terrible thing of him.'

'I was confused,' Victoria protested, 'and I didn't know what to believe. Why should Lorenz refuse to speak out if he has nothing to hide?'

Liesl said incredulously, 'You *still* believe him guilty, don't you? Yet how is it possible, now that your stepmother has confessed? Vicky, for goodness sake, what is going on in your mind?'

Victoria turned away from the challenge in Liesl's eyes, the bewilderment. A gust of wind spattered rain against the window and she bleakly watched the grey threads of water on the glass. She could think of nothing to say that would make any kind of sense.

The silence in the room seemed to last an eternity, then Liesl's pleading voice reached her through a fog of pain and shame.

'Vicky, can't you see that what Lorenz is so determined to conceal may be something quite unconnected with Ingeborg? Perhaps, by his refusal to speak, he is protecting some other person.'

She turned round slowly and stared at Liesl.

'Are you saying this is what happened? Do you know something?'

Liesl hesitated, then said in a little rush, 'If I tell you, will you be sworn to secrecy?'

'Yes, of course, if that's what you ask.'

'I do, I must! It is imperative that not a word of this leaks out. There could still be the most dreadful consequences.'

'You mean for someone else?'

'For Lorenz, too. But more so for someone else. Perhaps even for me.'

Victoria gasped and her hands went to her throat. 'Oh Liesl, what is this all about? I don't understand – how are you involved?'

Liesl carefully took off her hat and laid it aside, easing the hair at her temples with the fingers of both hands, as if to steady her thoughts.

'It is to do with Andrej,' she said slowly. 'His . . . *our* political activities. Andrej was in great peril. He faced imminent arrest by the secret police, and Lorenz – at a frightful risk to himself – saved the situation.'

Victoria released her pent-up breath. 'And Lorenz is quite safe now? And Andrej? Tell me.'

'Yes, the letter that would have incriminated Andrej has been destroyed. And Lorenz has extracted a solemn promise from him that he will disassociate himself from the radical group he was working with. Lorenz insists that rebellion is not the best way, and I suppose he is right.' She noted Victoria's look of incomprehension, and added quickly, 'I see I must explain it all. But remember, Vicky, you are vowed to secrecy.'

'Yes, yes,' she said impatiently.

But she was forced to wait while Liesl considered how best to begin.

'It is all to do with the Czech problem. Andrej is a Czech, of course, and he is dedicated to winning justice for the Czech people, to end the unfair discrimination in favour of German-speaking Austrians. At long last there is a move toward reform. But it seems likely that even the minor concessions the Prime Minister, Count Badeni, is proposing will be thrown out when the Emperor reconvenes Parliament. If that should happen, then Andrej and his friends want the Czech peoples everywhere to rise up and seize what is rightfully theirs.'

'You mean by force?'

'Is that so wrong? Desperate situations call for desperate remedies, Vicky. But perhaps,' she conceded, 'in his enthusiasm for the cause Andrej has acted too impetuously. Somehow, the secret police learned of a plan to assassinate General Bieberstein, who is a declared enemy of the Czechs.'

'Oh no!' gasped Victoria, deeply shocked.

'Don't worry, there will be no assassination now,' Liesl said with a grim smile. 'Mercifully, Andrej was warned in time that the secret police were waiting for him. A friend in a neighbouring apartment recognized two of their agents who had been making inquiries about what time Andrej would be home, and he sent him word that they were watching the building for his return. So at least Andrej did not fall into their hands. But he knew that sooner or later they would break in and search his room, and there find a letter that would incriminate him utterly – a letter giving full details of the assassination plot. Poor Andrej didn't know what to do, and he made a telephone call to me here. Oh Vicky, it was terrifying. Andrej might have been caught and . . .' She covered her face with her hands, and her whole body shuddered.

Victoria too felt a shiver of fear. 'How did Lorenz come to be involved in this?'

'When Andrej telephoned me, I told him to take the train to Eisenbad. We had the idea that it might be possible for me to hide him somewhere. But we knew it was useless, really, because once the police knew he was avoiding them he would be a hunted man. In desperation I thought of Lorenz, of appealing to him for help. So Andrej and I waylaid him as he was walking home from the station, and I told him what had happened. He was wonderful, Vicky, and he didn't waste any time arguing or casting blame, but immediately made a plan. He said that Andrej was to go to the Alt Rathaus Café in the town square, and wait there until he returned. I had to come back here and act as normally as possible. Meanwhile, Lorenz would return to Vienna and see what he could do.'

'And he came home himself, to change his clothes first? That was when I spoke to him?'

'It must have been. Lorenz said there was just time for him to change, and he thought it would be less conspicuous in that part of Vienna to wear an ordinary suit of clothes rather than a frock coat. He managed to catch the seven twenty-eight train, but he had no idea that Ingeborg was on it too.'

'And then?' Victoria asked faintly.

'He arrived at the Südbahnhof and went to the tenement building where Andrej lives. There were two men stationed in the street outside, but Lorenz was counting on the fact that they wouldn't recognize him, or think he was in any way associated with Andrej. He went up to Andrej's room, entered with the key we'd given him, and found the letter where Andrej had told him it was hidden. Then it only needed a moment to set a match to the wretched thing and destroy the evidence. After that Lorenz walked out of the building, and in order not to appear in the least suspicious, he went to a nearby inn and sat reading a newspaper over a glass of beer.'

'How very brave he was,' Victoria whispered in deepest admiration.

'Yes, my cousin has great courage.' Seeing the glow of pride in

160

Liesl's eyes, Victoria thought: But he is not your cousin, he is your half-brother – a truth that, sadly, can never be told.

'When Lorenz returned to Eisenbad,' Liesl continued, 'he told Andrej it would be safe now to go home. The police agents were still waiting, and they questioned him interminably. But he gave nothing away, and after a thorough search of his room had produced nothing of an incriminating nature, they concluded that they'd been given false information, and left.'

Tense with emotion, Victoria burst out accusingly, 'You had no right to involve Lorenz! He took a terrible risk for your sake.'

'No, I had no right,' Liesl agreed sombrely. 'But I'm afraid I didn't stop to consider that at the time. I was desperate, Vicky. You know that I love Andrej, and my heart was full of fear.'

The realization came to Victoria, with a soaring sense of joy, that at last she could let herself believe in Lorenz's innocence. She had been given what she had been seeking from the start, what she had longed to hear – a reason for Lorenz's hurried return to Vienna that evening, a reason for him keeping silent.

But hastening hard upon the footsteps of her joy was the chilling awareness that if not Lorenz, then someone else had killed Ingeborg. Someone of the family? She was still alone in knowing that it had not been Franziska; alone, apart from one other person. The guilty one.

16

After luncheon Victoria walked on the terrace with little Emil, his hand clasped within hers. It had cleared up since the morning and a pale sun shone fitfully through broken cloud, making the maple hedge glow crimson and gold against the dark pyramids of the yew trees. A skittish breeze sent the first few fallen leaves whirling across the lawns, and there was a heavy scent of new-mown grass.

'Was it nice staying with the Waldsteins?' she asked him.

'Oh yes! Kurt and I went swimming lots of times and I can manage all the way across the baths by myself now.' Emil smiled up at her, his small face full of trust, his eyes achingly reminiscent of his father. 'But I missed being at home. I missed seeing you, Vicky.'

She bit her lip. Had it been a deliberate move on Lorenz's part to bring his son back so abruptly to this house of gloom, making it that much harder for her to go away? Since yesterday afternoon, when Lorenz had fetched him in a pony and trap, Emil had not once mentioned his dead mother. It was as if he had forgotten her already, and Victoria knew how quickly she herself could come to claim a major place in the child's affections, more so perhaps than Ingeborg had ever done. With all her heart she wished it were possible...

Emil let go her hand and scrambled up onto the low stone wall that edged a bed of michaelmas daisies. He giggled as he pretended to lose his balance, wiggling his outspread arms exaggeratedly, the striped collar of his sailor suit flapping around his ears.

'Oh, Vicky, do you remember that day when a log fell out of the bonfire and we got burnt?' he asked, coming to a sudden halt.

Did she remember? To him it was just an incident, scaring at the time, but now something of an adventure marking a colourful day in his young life.

'Yes, I remember.' Smiling, she held out her arms for him to jump down. Emil kept hold of her left hand, and pulled open the fingers to examine the palm, bringing Victoria the familiar tug of stretching scar tissue.

'You couldn't play the piano for a little while afterwards, could you?' he said. 'I'm glad you're better now. Can I have a lesson again tomorrow?'

Victoria blinked back shaming, resented tears, as she crouched down to his level and put her hands lightly on his shoulders.

'Emil dear, I'm afraid I shall not be able to give you many more piano lessons. You see, I have to go away quite soon now.'

He stared at her. 'Where are you going?'

'I'm not quite sure. Probably back to England.'

His face, which had been solemnly attentive, crumpled with distress. 'But that's ever so far away – across the sea. When will you come back?'

It was hard to tell him, when his eyes were so anxious and imploring.

'I ... I don't expect I shall ever come back, dearest.'

Emil flung himself at her, his small body a missile which nearly knocked Victoria off-balance, and buried his face against her shoulder.

'Please don't go away, Vicky,' he sobbed. 'I want you to stay here for ever and ever and ever.'

She let him cling to her for a few self-indulgent moments, then gently pushed him back and stood up. 'Come on,' she said briskly, 'let's go and pay a visit to your great-grandpa. Dry your eyes, we mustn't let him see that you've been crying.'

She mopped up Emil's tears with her handkerchief and smoothed the hair back from his face. Then hand in hand they made their way indoors and up the stairs. She would tell Herr Czernin about her departure, too. The more she committed herself, the less difficult it would be to leave.

In the early evening Pieter duly arrived. Victoria received him in the small salon, with the formal portraits of the Emperor and Empress looking down on them from the silk-hung walls. Brief though the interview was, it lasted longer than need be, owing to Pieter's reluctance to accept her refusal with any appearance of eagerness.

'I think you should know,' she began, 'that everyone is against the idea of our marrying now.'

'I should be sad to go against the wishes of my aunt and her husband, Victoria, but this is a matter between you and me. Naturally I take their wishes into consideration, but I cannot be governed by them.'

'Yet you rely upon their patronage in your career.'

'I rely,' he said with stiff dignity, 'upon my own ability. I don't deny that their support has helped to smooth my path.'

'Support which would be withdrawn,' she pointed out, 'if you married me.'

'So be it then. The decision is yours, Victoria. You would, of course, be marrying a comparatively poor man.'

'That thought would not deter me,' she said hastily, 'if only . . .'

'If only?'

Victoria wished it need not be said. She had always liked Pieter and indeed her feelings for him at this moment were warmer than they had ever been.

'You see, although I respect and admire you greatly – you must believe that – I do not love you, and for me that is essential.'

She could see the relief in his eyes, for all his care to conceal it.

'My proposal still stands, Victoria. But if you are quite certain?'

'I am quite, quite certain, Pieter. Thank you most sincerely for the honour of your proposal, and please try to forgive me for having to refuse you. I wish you every success in life, and every happiness.'

'And I you!'

Pieter declined to stay for dinner, but before leaving the schloss he went upstairs to see Baroness Mathilde. When Victoria heard him emerge from his aunt's boudoir, she could not resist spying through a slit in her door. Pieter's step was positively jaunty as he started down the stairs at a run, and he had the appearance of someone who had shed a burden, a man for whom life held out promise once more. But to be fair, he was not aware that she was watching.

This exhausting day was still far from over, although at the time Victoria had no foreboding of how much still remained to be endured. When, after dinner, Lorenz suggested a stroll together in the gardens, which were silvered now with moonlight, it was a relief that he readily accepted her plea of tiredness.

'I think I shall have an early night,' she told him.

'Yes, perhaps that's a good idea. With today behind you, things will begin to look brighter.'

The family was gathered in the salon having coffee, all except Otto, who had returned to his barracks during the afternoon. For the sake of appearances (and for no other reason, Victoria felt certain) even Heinrich and Gustav seemed resigned to spending an evening at home.

Mathilde was discussing the possibility of arranging a small dinner party for the following week. Just a dozen guests, perhaps. It was time, she declared, with a covertly hostile glance at Victoria, that things were brought back to normal. Now that September was drawing to a close she looked forward to returning to their town house in the Landhausgasse. There were so many interesting things to be done in the forthcoming season – several new plays had been announced, and this man Mahler who had taken over as director of the Opera sounded promising. And after Christmas, the Carnival season looked to be better than ever, with a special programme of court balls, for by then the Emperor's golden jubilee year would have begun. Altogether, it had been a thoroughly unhappy summer, and the sooner they could put it all behind them, the better.

Lorenz, frowning at his aunt's tactlessness, drained his glass and stood up. He was going, he said, to spend the rest of the evening with his grandfather. Ten minutes later Heinrich and Gustav took themselves off, not troubling to conceal their boredom with the domestic scene. Victoria stayed a short while longer, then glanced apologetically at Liesl who would be obliged to remain and keep her mother company.

'I shall go up to bed now, if you don't mind.'

Liesl gave a quick, warm smile. 'Sleep well, Vicky. It will be a better day tomorrow, you'll see.'

Like Lorenz, Liesl was so confident that there was no longer any barrier to her staying, and that tomorrow would mark the beginning of a happier time ahead. But Victoria had made up her mind. Tomorrow she intended to see about making a reservation for the return journey to England. With a strained smile at Liesl, and a curt goodnight to Mathilde, she left the room.

Passing through the pillared archway to the staircase, she saw a footman emerge from the service door bearing a silver tray with decanter and siphon and glasses. He walked along to the billiard-room and as he opened the door Victoria heard a sound from within, a sound that shocked her – a deep guffaw of laughter. How dare those two men enjoy a carefree evening at billiards on the very day of Franziska's funeral!

A wave of bitterness surged through her. Was she to depart leaving Heinrich and Gustav triumphant; creep quietly away and allow the blame for Ingeborg's death to be borne by poor Franziska, who had sacrificed herself so nobly and so needlessly? Even if, for Lorenz's sake, she must not publicly proclaim the truth, at least she could spike their arrogance by informing them that *she* knew it. The truth that Franziska was innocent, the truth about Lorenz's parentage. This would, in some small measure, bring relief to her torment.

She waited until the manservant had returned to the kitchen quarters, then crossed the hall with swift, urgent strides. She allowed herself the temerity of entering without even knocking.

'Victoria! What brings you here?' Heinrich's resentment was in his voice. This was not women's territory and she had committed an offence by intruding. Both men had removed their coats and were playing in waistcoat and shirtsleeves, each smoking a large cigar and with a glass of cognac to hand on the edge of the green baize table.

'There is something I wish to say, Baron Heinrich. Something I want you to know.'

'My dear girl, surely you can see that this is neither the time nor the place,' Heinrich said stiffly.

'But it is very important.'

With plain impatience he laid down his cue and reached for his coat where he had tossed it on a chair, his brother following his example.

'Then I trust you will be brief about it, if what you have to say really cannot wait until tomorrow.'

Victoria stepped nearer the table and faced them squarely. 'What I have to tell you is this – that Franziska was not responsible for Ingeborg's death.'

There was breathless silence and they both stood rigid, as still as carved stone statues. The only movement in the room was the wreaths of blue cigar smoke that curled under the powerful gas lights and drifted up to the shadowed ceiling.

Gustav spoke at last, his voice blustering and nervous. 'Nonsense, child! Your stepmother confessed. That letter she wrote —'

'That letter,' said Victoria, 'was a complete fabrication from first to last. Franziska invented a story which she thought would be believed.'

'For what possible reason?' Heinrich demanded. 'Why should she have done such a thing?'

'To protect Lorenz. Like everyone else, she thought Lorenz the one who was guilty.'

166

Heinrich rested his outspread hands on the polished edge of the table, and leaned forward. His steely eyes bored into her.

'Let me understand this correctly. You are declaring that your stepmother falsely confessed to a heinous crime in order to prevent Lorenz being held responsible?'

'Yes, exactly that.'

He straightened up again, bracing his shoulders. 'It makes no sense, no sense at all. What are you suggesting was her motive for such an extraordinary gesture?'

'The best possible motive, considering what Lorenz was to her.'

She heard a sharply indrawn breath from Gustav, but his brother remained impassive.

'You had better continue, Victoria.'

She did so in a clear, ringing voice. 'You see, when I assured you that Franziska had said nothing to explain her confession after she regained consciousness, I was not being truthful. She told me a great deal that afternoon. In fact, she told me everything.'

'Everything?' This was an appalled exclamation from Gustav.

Heinrich, more coolly, inquired, 'And what, may I inquire, is everything?'

Even now, Victoria realized, he was hoping she did not know the whole unsavoury story. But she would quickly disabuse him. Addressing herself first to his brother, she began, 'I know, Baron Gustav, that your true son died when he was but a few days old, leaving you with no heir as a security for Herr Czernin's continued goodwill toward you, without which the von Kaunitz family would have been in dire financial straits. And I know that you, Baron Heinrich, had just become the father of a child by your mistress. I know that you bullied poor Franziska into parting with her baby, and that an exchange was made of the two infants.' She jerked a breath. 'My stepmother had the strongest motive in the world for trying to save Lorenz – a mother's protective love for her son.'

Gustav slumped down on one of the leather-covered settees that lined the walls of the billiard-room, his face white and trembling.

'Oh my God!' he groaned. 'What are we to do?'

'Be quiet!' Heinrich took a moment to consider the new situation. 'Tell me, Victoria, to whom else have you spoken about this?'

'To no one else.'

'And is it your intention to do so?'

'I don't know.'

'You realize,' he said slowly, measuredly, 'that if you persist in this disclosure, if you repeat it outside this room, you will bring destruction upon Lorenz. He will have to pay the penalty for his wife's death, after all.'

'But Lorenz is not the one who killed Ingeborg,' she retorted.

'You have this very moment told us that he is. You have just declared that Franziska admitted as much to you.'

'I said Franziska *thought* Lorenz was guilty. But I know that he is not.'

'Do you? What makes you so positive? Because it is what Lorenz himself has been telling you?'

'I haven't really discussed the matter with him, but I know because — ' She checked herself in time. She must not say it, must not betray Liesl's confidence. Instead, she said doggedly, 'I just know, that's all.'

'I see!' Heinrich picked up his cue again and chalked the leather tip reflectively before putting the cube of white chalk down on the rim of the table. 'You allege that it was neither Franziska who killed Ingeborg, nor Lorenz. So how, then, do you suggest she met her death?'

'I think you know the answer to that.' A vague suspicion lurking in her mind that it must have been Heinrich or Gustav – or the two brothers acting together – suddenly crystallized. Heinrich made no pretext of misunderstanding her. But he showed neither anger nor fear, merely scorn. As she watched him fix his monocle unhurriedly in his eye, it was she who felt afraid.

'It grieves me, my dear Victoria, that you have such a low opinion of us. But apart from the fact that we surely had no motive for disposing of Ingeborg, just consider this – if we were prepared to stoop to murder, would that not have been the simplest way of dealing with your stepmother when she reappeared in Vienna and made a nuisance of herself to us? But far from that, my brother married her and made her one of the family.'

Gustav stirred to life, and blustered, 'We can account for every moment of that evening. If you must know, I met my brother in Eisenbad when I was returning home for dinner, and he suggested that we should go to —'

Heinrich checked him with a raised hand. 'I think we will spare Victoria the details, Gustav. Suffice it to say, my dear, that, if challenged, both Gustav and myself have a number of witnesses to our movements on the evening of Ingeborg's death. There is no possibility that either of us could have been on that train. If you disbelieve me, you must put the matter to the test by informing the police of your suspicions.'

He was surely too confident to be lying, and besides there was logic in his argument. It would have been a simple exercise for Heinrich's devious mind to contrive some kind of accident for Franziska that would in no way point suspicion at the two brothers.

'Precisely what is it you are hoping to gain, Victoria, by coming to us with these revelations at this stage?' Heinrich's voice was noticeably less aggressive now. 'Can marriage be your aim? Has your stepmother's marriage to my brother given you large ideas? If so, well, I suppose you'd better have Lorenz – eh, Gustav? I'm sure you will find him only too eager, after a suitable interval to observe the decencies.'

'No,' she protested fiercely. 'I could never marry Lorenz.'

'Indeed? He is in love with you, my dear girl. Such matters are beyond my understanding, but my wife insists that he is.'

She said again, wildly, 'I could never marry Lorenz. It's impossible!'

'Perhaps you should, though. Upon reflection, it would seem to be the best solution to our problems. I do most strongly advise you, however, against telling him of his origins. He might take the news badly.'

'Nothing would induce me to tell Lorenz the truth about himself. And that is why marriage between us is out of the question. I could not live a lie for the rest of my life.'

Heinrich came forward and stood before her, quizzing her through his monocle. 'I really believe you mean what you say. How very singular! Your stepmother, in similar circumstances, would not have scrupled for an instant.'

'How dare you attempt to denigrate her!' In her anger against this man who could remain so calm and detached Victoria felt a blind, unreasoning loyalty to Franziska, a burning need to justify her. 'What she did all those years ago – how can she be blamed, considering her plight? You forced her into giving up her baby. She was just a struggling young actress at the time, and she had no chance against you.'

Heinrich's composure remained unshaken. 'Come now, my dear, you are allowing your imagination to run away with you. Franziska, even in those early days, was eminently capable of turning a situation to her advantage. You may take it from me that she was by no means averse to disposing of her . . . her encumbrance so neatly. But in any case, why this talk of blame? None of us did anything so reprehensible, when all is said and done.'

'How can you possibly say that? You deceived poor Herr Czernin into believing his grandchild had survived, and you brought Lorenz up with a false identity.'

'Rather look at it from this point of view, my dear. Who has suffered from our little subterfuge? Lorenz has had a fine upbringing as the scion of a noble family, while Herr Czernin is a proud grandfather, and great-grandfather, too! Which, with only the one daughter, he would never have been but for us. Not a jot of harm has been done to anyone.'

'But two people are dead, as a direct result.'

'Alas, Franziska was too greedy. We rewarded her most generously at the time, but she came back for more. Had it not been for that, all would still have been well.'

'All would have been well! With your son – yes, *your* son, Baron Heinrich – married off disastrously to the first woman he imagined himself in love with, just to ensure that there would be an heir for the Czernin wealth, in case anything should happen to Lorenz himself.'

'I am sure Lorenz would never agree with the suggestion that he was forced to marry Ingeborg. He did so of his own free will.'

'When he was too young to know his own mind, and had just been severely wounded! Any decent, loving parent would have done his best to prevent such an ill-judged marriage.'

Heinrich's tone was odiously smooth. 'I deeply regret, of course, that Lorenz – my son, as you say – felt obliged to bring his marriage to an end in such a violent way when it became intolerable. Or perhaps inconvenient would be a better word.'

'He did not, I tell you, he did not!'

'It is your heart which urges you to protest that. All the evidence, unfortunately, points in a contrary direction now that we know it wasn't Franziska.'

'Lorenz is innocent,' she persisted wretchedly.

'I'm afraid we must differ in that opinion. But in any event, all will be well as long as you remain silent.'

'Yes, you must heed what my brother says,' Gustav broke in agitatedly. 'You mustn't breathe a word of this to anyone – not even

Lorenz himself. Heinrich, should we not come to some kind of financial arrangement with her? Perhaps—'

His brother again cut him short with a brusque gesture. But then Heinrich himself inquired, 'Well, Victoria, what do you say to that suggestion?'

'I want none of your money,' she blazed. Then, on a dismaying thought, she added, 'At least . . .'

'At least?' he echoed, mocking her.

Colour flooded her cheeks. 'At the moment, until my stepmother's affairs are settled, I have almost no money at all. If I am to leave here, I must request help for the immediate future, and the cost of the fare to England.'

'Our offer still stands.' He was serious now, businesslike. 'As I told you the other evening, you will not find us ungenerous.'

Did he expect her to thank him? She said coldly, 'I shall accept no more than is absolutely necessary. And I shall repay every penny later, as soon as ever I can.'

'How punctilious you are.' Heinrich gave a shrug of indifference. 'So be it! And how do you propose to explain your departure to Lorenz?'

'I have already told him I shall be leaving before long.'

'And he accepted that? You surprise me.' Heinrich frowned thoughtfully. 'As Lorenz sees it, Franziska's confession and suicide must be inexplicable – but in view of the police's suspicions about Ingeborg's death, a God-send to him. I presume he has concluded that it would be prudent in the circumstances to let you depart, and to forgo what he'd so set his mind upon. He can always console himself with his mistress, the charming Baroness von Taussig, until he finds some other pretty young woman he fancies to take for a wife.'

Victoria hated the man, loathed him for imputing his own uncaring cynicism to Lorenz. Throughout this interview, although his brother had been severely shaken, with perspiration standing out on his balding forehead, Heinrich had only once lost his composure for the briefest moment. It was little wonder that such a man could have engineered so monstrous a deception and carried it off through all these years. She had an urge to wound him, to leave him scarred.

'My stepmother told me one other thing before she died. She said that even though you had married her off to your brother, you still expected to . . . to possess her for yourself.' She turned to Gustav and rushed on headlong, 'The day Ingeborg was killed, Franziska spent the whole evening locked in her room, pleading an indisposition. But her real reason was to escape from *him*. She couldn't have realized that he had left the house, and I imagine he only did so out of pique because she had outwitted him for the time being. Franziska wanted to be a loyal and faithful wife to you, Baron Gustav, despite the circumstances in which your marriage came about. Yet the entire time, from the day you returned from honeymoon, he badgered poor Franziska, making her life a misery with his persistent demands. So what do you think of your brother now?'

Gustav's plump face went crimson, the colour reaching the lobes of his ears. He said, examining his fingernails, 'It meant nothing, I am sure. Women usually feel flattered when a man professes to admire them, to desire them. Franziska had only to make it clear to my brother that she did not welcome his attentions.'

'Perhaps,' Heinrich suggested ironically, 'the lady in question found that an adamant refusal was beyond her?'

He was so right, and he knew it! Rage and bitterness consuming her, Victoria swung round once more to Gustav, and threw out recklessly, 'Do you know *why* your brother wanted to seduce Franziska? He was jealous, that was the real reason. He has always been jealous of you, because you were the one who always seemed to come off to best advantage in every situation. To persuade your wife to break her marriage vows and become his mistress all over again would have been an exquisite victory over you. Can you not see – that's the vile sort of creature he is.'

Gustav merely shuffled his feet and looked embarrassed, while the smile remained on Heinrich's face. Victoria saw that she had achieved nothing, less than nothing. She had hoped, out of anger, out of revenge, to drive a wedge between the two of them, to show up Heinrich in his true colours, and cause Gustav to rebel. Instead, she had only strengthened Heinrich's arrogance by underlining the fact of his dominance over Gustav. However much Gustav might resent his twin brother's attempts to seduce his wife, he was expected to suffer the humiliation meekly and make no protest.

With a sense of defeat, of desolation and despair, Victoria turned and hurried from the room.

17

Victoria was startled by the soft tapping on her door. It was late, but she had not yet prepared herself for bed. For this past hour and more she had been hovering at the open window, too restless to sit, too wretchedly unhappy to appreciate the cool serenity of the moonlit scene – the dark ridge of hills across the valley skimmed by trails of silvered cloud; the pale shadowy outlines of the little township where the lights had been going out one by one until few now remained.

She crossed the room quickly and asked in a low voice, 'Who is it?'

'Lorenz. I must speak to you, Victoria.'

She opened the door a mere crack. 'It's very late. I think you'd better leave it until tomorrow.'

'No now, if you please. I should not sleep if this were left unresolved.'

'What is it you want?' She drew the door further open.

'I've been hearing a strange tale that you are planning to go away almost at once. Emil mentioned it first when I went to say goodnight to him, and he was very upset. I thought he had misunderstood something you said, and I soothed him. But a few minutes ago I was told the selfsame thing by my grandfather. I have been playing chess with him for the past couple of hours, and he seemed in a curiously abstracted mood. Then just as I was leaving, he came out with it. Like Emil, he was upset. What does this mean, Victoria? You gave me your promise to stay, at least for the time being.'

'I made no promise.'

'I think you did. Unspoken, perhaps, but all the same a promise we both understood. Can you deny it?'

She shook her head helplessly. 'I . . . I meant it at the time. But I should never have agreed to such a thing. There is no place for me here.'

'Of course there is! Your place is with me.' He gripped her arm as he spoke, and his voice was so loud she was afraid someone might hear.

'Lorenz, we cannot discuss it now,' she protested. 'Not here in the corridor.'

'Then let me come in.'

'Come in! But it's almost midnight. It is the merest chance that I have not yet gone to bed.'

'In which case I should have roused you,' he said impatiently. 'We are going to thrash this matter out, Victoria, be in no doubt of that. So where is it to be? Here in the corridor, somewhere downstairs, or in your room? The choice is yours.'

Better in the privacy of her room, she thought with weary despair, and moved aside for him to enter. 'Only for a few minutes, though,' she insisted.

Lorenz closed the door carefully, and stood with his back to it. 'Now perhaps you will answer my question. I assume that Emil and my grandfather were not mistaken? You are really planning to go away?'

'I must. Please do not make things difficult for me, I beg you. The sooner I am gone, out of your life, the sooner you will forget me.'

His face went taut. 'Forget you? Are you deliberately trying to give me pain?'

'No!'

'Then what? Have I upset you, have I offended you in some way?' Victoria shook her head dumbly. His eyes burned into her with a strangely hostile look. 'Is it because of my association with another woman? I thought you understood about Leonore. Naturally, our relationship will end now, but she has a generous nature and will create no difficulties. So you need not make a problem out of it.'

'No, it isn't that.' She was jealous of the woman who had played such an intimate part in his life – she would be jealous of the smallest smile Lorenz awarded to another woman. But surely he could not believe she would want to give him up for such a reason?

He said, 'There are no other women in my life. I do not deny there have been in the past, I'm not a saint. But not now, nor ever again. If you're thinking that the story I suggested to the police is true—'

'I don't, I told you I didn't. I never believed there was a woman that night. Besides, Liesl has explained to me now exactly what it was that took you to Vienna.'

'She did?' Then, after a moment's silence, 'I hope to heaven Liesl has impressed upon you the need for absolute secrecy?'

'Yes, I understand all about that.'

'I wonder if you really do, Victoria. That young hot-head Andrej had joined a group of Czech fanatics who were trying to stir up rebellion. He had even allowed himself to become involved in an assassination plot! Austria is not a tranquil country like England, you know. Because there is so much unrest here, the secret police spies are all around us. If a whisper of this business should leak out, then God help Andrej von Hroch, and even Liesl. Myself, too.'

Victoria shuddered to think what could have happened; what might still happen, even now. 'Believe me, I do appreciate the danger,' she told him earnestly. 'You can be quite certain that no one will ever hear anything from me.'

Lorenz gave her a small, apologetic smile. 'I think Andrej was sufficiently frightened to learn his lesson. I think he appreciates now that there are other ways – safer and more effective ways – of working for social justice.'

'From what Liesl said to me, I'm sure he does. She fully realizes how indebted they are to you for what you did.'

'She must have complete trust in you, Victoria, to reveal so much.'

'Her trust is not misplaced,' she said with dignity.

'No, I am certain it is not. Yet you yourself cannot place trust in other people. You do not trust *me*.'

'I do! Of course I do!'

'Then why can't you leave me to judge whether it is right and fitting for you to remain here?' His mouth tightened at the corners. 'If it were not for your talk of going away, I wouldn't be forcing the issue like this. I would have allowed time to pass following my wife's death and Franziska's suicide, before talking to you of marriage. But as it is . . .'

It needed but a few brief words, Victoria thought desolately, to put an end to all this. If Lorenz were to learn the truth of his birth, the truth of what Franziska had been to him . . . if he knew that his whole position in life was founded upon a gigantic fraud, he would be utterly crushed, his pride savaged. She looked at him with anguished eyes, and remained silent.

'If you are not yet ready to see me in the way I long for,' he persisted, 'you might at least spare a thought for little Emil. Do you realize just how much you upset him by talking of going away?'

A sudden fierce anger swept colour to her cheeks. 'Don't use blackmail against me, Lorenz! You know I've come to love Emil. How could I help but love him? It will break my heart to leave him, and to know that he will miss me when I'm gone.'

His eyes narrowed, acknowledging the reproof. 'Very well then, purely for my sake and not for my son's, I beg you to stay. Surely you understand that in a little while, as the days go by, you will come to see things differently.'

'No,' she said. 'I shall not change my mind.'

He reached out in an imploring gesture and, afraid of herself, Victoria backed away from him. Anger sparked in his eyes and he came forward until he had her pinned against the scrolled end of the sofa. He grasped her by the shoulders and his fingers dug hard into her flesh.

'If you could give me one good reason for your attitude, I would listen to you. But it seems you are incapable of rational discussion. Do I have to persuade you in another way?'

'Another way?' she faltered.

Suddenly his grip became gentle. His hands moved slowly up the curve of her shoulders, stroking the soft skin of her neck, her ear lobes, her throat, and came to rest with his fingertips cupping her chin.

'I love you, Victoria, and I know that you love me. Is that not sufficient to make you feel totally committed to me? I had no intention of pressing you to anticipate our marriage, but if it is the only way I can persuade you to stay, then I must make you mine here and now . . .'

'Oh, no!'

His hands now were at the nape of her neck, caressing her hair, his fingers twining into its silken softness. She was achingly aware of him, of his closeness; aware of the touch of his body, its warmth and supple hardness pressed against her.

'I would wait,' he murmured huskily, 'if I had your solemn promise to stay. But without that, you force me.'

'No, Lorenz, you must not. I should never forgive you.'

'You will, my darling, because you love me. I shall make you see how much you love me, that you cannot do without me.'

Victoria tried to turn her face away, but the grip of his fingers tightened as his warm lips found hers. At first his kiss was tender;

then, as she attempted to draw back, he became more fiercely demanding, his lips forcing hers apart, his arms crushing her brutally until she was helpless against him. Her feeble resistance crumbled and she found herself exulting in his strength. She cared for nothing except that he was holding her, kissing her, loving her. There was no fear, no shyness, no pain even, although his mouth and his hands were bruising her without pity. There was only a sweet, delirious joy.

He said breathlessly, 'Come then, when we have belonged to one another completely, there will be no more wild talk of you leaving me.'

With a single movement he lifted her into his arms and carried her toward the narrow bed with its prim blue quilt. Panic seized her. If she yielded now she would never find the strength to go away; she would be committed to him for ever, just as he said. From somewhere she found a frail thread of resistance.

'No wait – I want to explain.'

He set her down, and she felt the carpet beneath her feet. But still he held her firmly in the circle of his arms.

'What is it you have to say?' he asked.

'Just let go of me, and I will tell you why I cannot stay here.'

His arms left her so abruptly that she stumbled and almost fell. He stood looking down at her, his dark eyes vividly intent, and she could hear the quick irregularity of his breathing. She glanced away, down at the floor, and found she could not summon her voice.

'Victoria, don't play with me,' he warned. 'You said you had something to say. I want to hear it.'

Words came at last, but indistinct, scarcely audible. 'I must go away because – because I do not love you.'

His hands caught her again, gripping her fiercely, shaking her. 'You do! You know you do!'

'But not enough.'

'For God's sake what do you mean – not enough? Loving is loving. There is no half measure.'

Victoria forced herself to meet his challenging gaze. 'Don't you see, you and I are worlds apart. We are of different nationality, different background, of completely different standing in society.'

With an impatient exclamation he dismissed these things as irrelevant. She made herself keep talking, not daring to stop, churning out foolish, meaningless words. 'Think of what we would have to suffer, Lorenz, the gossip, the scandal, the disapproval on all sides. We are both too involved, too interwoven into the dreadful things that have happened. Your wife and my stepmother, both dead! And in such appalling circumstances.'

'That is a matter for us to come to terms with,' he broke in tersely, 'not other people. If I care nothing for the opinions of others, why should you?'

'Perhaps,' she said, on a swift new wing of thought, 'it is more important to a woman than to a man to be accepted and respected.'

'You would be my wife, Victoria. My wife! For God's sake, wouldn't that be enough for you?'

His eyes were alive with anger, offering no hint of compromise, and Victoria felt herself quailing. Unsteadily, she edged away from him until she had put a couple of yards of carpet between them. Only from this distance could she summon up a voice clear and steady enough to carry the false ring of veracity.

'That is just what I am trying to tell you. That's exactly the point. After what has happened, knowing how much disapproval I should have to face, it would *not* be enough to be your wife. I thought I loved you – I still do love you in a way – but I know now that I have no wish to marry you.'

It was as if nothing existed beyond this room with him standing before her, his angular features menacing, his lean body taut with fury. Yet unaccountably, her ears detected tiny sounds from outside – a stealthy wind sighing through the trees, and far off a late train rattling toward Vienna.

When he spoke, his voice was cruel; cold and clipped and cruel.

'How quickly you have become a true woman of Vienna! You award the name of love to the shallowest emotion – an arousal of the senses so frivolous and trivial that it can be discarded the instant it threatens to be inconvenient or embarrassing.'

'You are being unfair,' she whispered, feeling as though she were dying inside.

'You think you are not being unfair? I must be grateful, I suppose, that you didn't snatch me for my money and position, like Ingeborg. I wonder what held you back, Victoria, when I was so eager to make a fool of myself for a second time?'

She clenched her fists, the nails hurting her tender palms as she struggled to keep control. She wanted to fling herself into his arms, to tell him that she had not meant a single word of the things she had said. Instead, she faltered, 'I think you had better go.'

'By all means! I have no wish to stay.' Already Lorenz was at the

178

door but, with his hand on the knob, he turned back. For an instant, through the mist of her tears, she saw a softening of his features. His arm lifted toward her as though he was about to make one final appeal.

The next moment he was gone from the room. He did not slam the door. He closed it very quietly, and somehow that seemed a further measure of his contempt for her.

18

It was a long, slow climb from Eisenbad station as the railway line snaked up out of the valley. Victoria settled back in her seat with relief, thankful to have escaped from the schloss without the need to explain her plans to Liesl and face the inevitable argument. When she returned, it would be a *fait accompli*.

'What are you doing this morning?' Liesl had asked over breakfast.

'I think I'll walk down to the shops. There are a few things I need.'

'Shall I come?'

'Don't bother,' Victoria said, her heart thudding. 'I expect you've got plenty to get on with.'

'That's true, considering I'm due back at University in a couple of weeks' time. What with one thing and another I'm dreadfully behind-hand with my vacation studies.'

She had told Emil that she was going to Vienna, an unfortunate slip of the tongue when explaining why she could not give him a piano lesson that morning. But Emil did not know her purpose, which was to call at the office of Thomas Cook and Son in Stefansplatz and make a reservation for her return journey to England just as soon as possible.

The locomotive chugged round yet another long sweeping bend, pulling hard, then slackened as it finally reached level ground. Another two minutes and they came to a screeching halt at the next station along the line, a pretty village called Kahlstein which was no more than a huddle of houses round a market square, a domed church, a few shops, and a Gasthof with tables and chairs set out in a leafy courtyard. In the slumbrous quietude two waiting bicyclists wearing *Lederhosen* and tyrolean hats handed their machines over to a porter and climbed aboard. An old woman carrying a cat basket alighted. Then, with a sudden commotion, a young woman came hurrying through the arched entrance, her arm upraised for the guard to wait for her.

Victoria stared in astonishment. It was Liesl. The other girl saw her at the same instant and ran along the platform to her compartment.

'I thought I'd missed you,' she panted, as she scrambled up and threw herself into the seat opposite. Then, regaining her breath, Liesl demanded, 'What on earth are you up to, Vicky, going off to Vienna in this mysterious fashion?'

Victoria could only stammer, 'How . . . how did you get here?'

'Emil happened to mention where you were going a few minutes after you'd left the house. I knew it was too late for me to catch the train at Eisenbad station by then, even in a trap, so I told Georg to drive as fast as he could and hoped to get here in time.'

'But it's further than Eisenbad.'

'No, it isn't, or not much further. There's a road that comes straight over the brow of the hill, whereas the railway winds a long way round. But what's this all about, Vicky? I thought you were behaving oddly at breakfast, as if you were being evasive about something.'

How easy to tell Liesl the truth and be done with it! But what arguments did she have – arguments she dared use – to explain why she must go away? So she lied again, putting on a laugh.

'I don't know what you're making such a fuss about, Liesl. If I'd said I was going to Vienna you'd have felt obliged to come with me, and I knew you must have a lot of studying to do.'

'But why are you going, Vicky?'

It seemed logical to say, 'I just wanted to get away from the schloss for a little while, to get things in perspective. That's it, I wanted to be alone, so as to think things over.'

'Think what things over?'

'Oh, everything!'

The train had gathered speed now, and was clattering over a junction. Liesl regarded her unhappily. 'I do wish you wouldn't keep brooding. Things will sort themselves out if only you'll be patient.' Victoria shrugged, afraid to make any comment, and Liesl went on, 'Oh well, now I'm here we might as well make the best of today. That exhibition of Klimt's work is finished now, but we could go to the Albertina – some of the engravings there are well worth looking at.

And I'd like you to meet Andrej – I've told him so much about you.'

At the Südbahnhof the two girls took a cab and went directly to Griechengasse where Andrej had his apartment. It was a crooked, cobbled passageway between tall buildings, not far from the Danube Canal. They turned in at a narrow doorway arched in crumbling stonework. Andrej's room was up two flights of echoing stone steps, the walls flaking plaster. Liesl banged on a door and it opened to reveal a handsome young man with shining black hair and a drooping moustache. He wore a loose white blouse tied at the waist with a sash.

'Liesl, how marvellous, but—'

'I've brought Vicky to see you.'

'Hallo, Vicky!' He lifted her hand, not in the usual token kiss, but pressing it warmly to his lips. 'This is a great pleasure, I've heard so much about you.'

'And I about you!'

They exchanged smiles, liking each other. Then as the girls stepped inside he caught Liesl to him and they clung together in a brief, ecstatic embrace. Victoria felt a stab of envy for their happiness, despite the difficulties she knew they faced.

The room was wildly untidy, books and papers piled on every surface – a chest of drawers, a small table and chair, a horse-hair sofa. Only the bed was uncluttered, and Liesl promptly flopped down on it. With a sudden conviction Victoria knew that she was no stranger to this bed.

They talked for a while, and Andrej was fulsome in his praise of Lorenz. 'Liesl tells me that you two are going to be married,' he said. 'I'm glad.'

'Oh, but—'

'There are no buts about it,' Liesl said firmly. She gave Andrej a secret smile. 'Poor Vicky is feeling rather fragile, and no wonder! But she'll come to see things in perspective, given time.'

Later they adjourned to a quaint little inn a few doors away called the Griechenbeisl. It was a dark and damp-smelling place, panelled in blackened wood, impregnated with the odour of beer and tobacco and the goulash of a thousand yesterdays.

'This is the oldest inn in Vienna,' Andrej remarked. 'Schubert used to come here.'

Was it in this very parlour where they sat crowded together on a hard wooden bench that Lorenz had come to drink a glass of beer, calm and unhurried, when only minutes before he had risked arrest at the hands of the secret police, and the possibility of a lifetime's imprisonment?

A waiter in a none-too-clean apron bustled up. '*Guten Tag*, Herr Graf,' he greeted Andrej. '*Was möchten Sie, bitte?*'

As Andrej ordered tankards of beer for them all, Victoria stared at him wonderingly.

'He called you Herr Graf,' she said. 'Are you really a count?'

Andrej threw back his head and laughed. 'Oh yes, and I have to confess to the full sixteen quarterings of nobility. I think perhaps you should curtsey to me, Miss Victoria!'

Liesl said crossly, 'We have no patience with all that nonsense, Vicky. Possessing a title doesn't make you better than any other person.'

Not *better*, perhaps, Victoria reflected, but it must certainly oil the wheels. She remembered Pieter's sarcastic remarks about the privileges of social standing, which had so upset Liesl. She doubted whether her parents would really be as opposed to a match with Andrej as Liesl seemed to fear. Although they might not care for his politics, a count was a count, and a degree higher than a baron. Well, good luck to the two of them!

To the accompaniment of zither music played by a blind man who'd come in from the street, they enjoyed a simple lunch of rye bread with spicy sausage and Liptauer cheese. Then Victoria suggested that she went off on her own to do some shopping.

'There's no point you dragging round with me, Liesl. Shall I meet you at the Südbahnhof later on – say five o'clock?'

She was not surprised that Liesl readily agreed to this plan, the visit to the Albertina forgotten. A short walk along the Rotenturmstrasse brought her to Stefansplatz, and her business at Thomas Cook's was soon settled. She could travel in three days' time, and the tickets would await her collection the day before. Victoria wished it was not necessary to approach Baron Heinrich for the money.

Wandering aimlessly, Victoria thought she recognized the entrance of the restaurant where Lorenz had taken her that time, but she could not be sure. In daylight it looked so different. She hurried past, wanting to escape from memories that brought an aching sadness. At the Ringstrasse she waited for a tramcar, intending to pass the time in the grounds of the Belvedere Palace just across the way from the

Südbahnhof. But the first tram to come along indicated Ottakring, and on an impulse she boarded it. Ottakring was where the Czernin foundry was situated.

As the horse-drawn tramcar lurched and grated on its way, she saw that the surroundings grew rapidly less elegant, and the passengers who boarded it were of a humbler class. Soon they were travelling through mean streets flanked with dirty tenement houses and evil-looking workshops where women crouched over machines in the feeble flickering lights of gas jets – quite as bad as anything she had seen in the backstreets of Birmingham. The only factory of any size they passed seemed to be a furniture works, and the tram reached its terminus without coming to the Czernin foundry. As she alighted she asked the conductor for directions, and he told her off-handedly to take a dark alleyway on the left-hand side. Victoria did so dubiously, picking her way over slimy cobbles where ill-clad urchins ran barefoot or squatted at their games. She felt ostentatious in her modish clothes and was aware of watchful eyes following her progress. There was the sour smell of close-packed humanity, and the stench from a tannery made her stomach heave. It was with thankfulness that she came at last to a somewhat broader thoroughfare.

To her right there was a large redbrick building with rows of narrow windows, and a tall chimney smoking in the rear. Was this the Czernin foundry? Drawing nearer she saw mounted sentries at the arched entrance, and in the inner courtyard a group of army officers were lounging and chatting. A barracks.

Clearly, she would have to inquire the way again. But the passers-by all seemed so alien, staring at her with undisguised curiosity. A bleary-eyed woman in a tattered shawl muttered something to her in a thick dialect she could not understand, and Victoria shook her head and walked on, to pause when she came to a baker's shop which looked a little cleaner than most. She would ask in here.

Then, astonishingly, a voice called her name.

'Victoria, wait a minute!'

She swung round quickly and saw it was Otto. He was hurrying after her, his spurs jangling, steadying the plumed shako on his head with one hand.

'I say, what the devil are you doing in this part of the world?' he gasped, slightly out of breath. 'I spotted you going past from the guard-room window, and I thought I'd better come after you.'

Victoria felt dreadfully foolish. 'I didn't realize your barracks were anywhere round here. I had a little time to kill before meeting Liesl at the station, so I thought I'd come and look at the foundry.'

Otto stared as though she were mad. 'What on earth for?'

'Well, I've never seen it before.'

'You haven't missed anything! It's not all that far, actually. I'll take you on a conducted tour.'

'Oh no!' The likelihood of encountering Lorenz was alarming. 'I only wanted to see what it looks like from the outside.'

Otto shrugged. 'We'll have to walk. One can never find a *fiacre* round here. Still, I'd a damn sight rather be stationed in the worst slum in Vienna than in some God-forsaken garrison town where there's no life for a fellow.'

They entered a positive rabbit warren of narrow alleyways where Victoria would never have dared venture alone, and after a few minutes they reached a deserted no-man's-land where a number of buildings had been razed to the ground and others stood empty, awaiting demolition. On the far side of this area a huge factory rose up, four stories high, with an arched glass roof. She heard the clanging of steam hammers, and a screeching sound that set her teeth on edge. Two tall chimneys belched smoke.

'That's the foundry,' Otto told her. 'Over a thousand people work there.'

Victoria gazed in silence, memorizing every detail. Then she asked, 'Why has this space here been cleared?'

Otto made a face. 'It's one of Lorenz's do-gooding ideas – rehousing the workers! He's already built two blocks of apartments on the far side – fancy places with gas and water all laid on, if you please, and a bath-house and communal laundry plus a kids' playground! God knows where all the money's supposed to be coming from.'

Victoria looked around her with shining eyes, imagining the fine modern buildings that would spring up from this sea of rubble – decent homes where people could bring up their children in healthy conditions. To the workers of the Czernin foundry it must seem like a dream come true.

And it was all due to the vision and social conscience of one man, a man she would destroy completely if she were to reveal what she knew of his birth.

Otto was regarding her oddly. 'You're very smitten with Lorenz, aren't you? At one time the whisper was going round that he rid himself of Ingeborg for your sake.'

'Otto, please—'

'Then lo and behold your stepmother goes and confesses to the crime.' He paused, then asked, 'Why d'you think she did that, Victoria?'

She averted her face, not answering.

'Mind you,' Otto went on reflectively, 'it's all worked out for the best – Franziska confessing, I mean. Damn funny business, though. That bit about Ingeborg discovering something about her past. Have you any idea what she meant?'

'How could I have?'

'I just thought she might have told you something. What reason did she give you for returning to Vienna after all those years?'

Victoria still kept her face turned away from him. 'Is it so surprising that Franziska had a longing to see her native city again?'

'Things were looking pretty bad for poor old Lorenz, weren't they?' Otto nudged a pile of bricks with the toe of his highly polished boot. 'I was getting really scared that he'd get nailed for doing Ingeborg in.'

'Why pretend, Otto?' she said bitterly. 'Your only concern was that his arrest would have been a threat to you. If anything happened to stop the Czernin money flowing in, it would have put an end to the comfortable, carefree life you lead.'

With her eyes closed against the thrust of her anger, Victoria had a sudden vision that snapped on and off like the opening and closing of a camera shutter: Otto, perched high above her in his yellow phaeton, whipping the horses into action and disappearing in a cloud of dust.

What was it he had just asked her? Not why Franziska had killed Ingeborg, but why she had confessed to the crime. As if he *knew* that she was not guilty . . .

As they walked on, picking their way over the uneven ground, the camera shutter clicked once more. This time she saw Liesl hurrying breathlessly through the arched entrance of the little station at Kahlstein, as if whisked there by some magic carpet. But no magic had been involved. It was done very simply by taking a road from the schloss that led straight over the brow of the hill, while the train wound its way out of the valley on a gradually rising gradient.

She dared not look at Otto, dared not betray the direction her thoughts were taking. The train Ingeborg caught, the seven-twenty-eight, would have reached Kahlstein by seven-forty. But just before seven-thirty Otto had been talking to her at the foot of the terrace steps. It must have been almost precisely on the half-hour when he set off at such a furious pace. He could have got to Kahlstein in ten minutes in his spider phaeton that was 'as fast as the wind'.

Yes, Otto could have caught that train and killed Ingeborg. But why? What would his motive have been?

Walking beside her between the shells of old buildings, Otto asked, 'What are you going to do now, Victoria? Are you going away?'

'Yes, I shall be returning to England quite soon.'

'We shall miss you,' he said, clearly uncaring.

Victoria's anger swelled to bursting point. Otto saw his easygoing life as a dashing young cavalry officer continuing just as if nothing had happened. As if she and Franziska had never come to Vienna; as if Ingeborg had never died.

'You know that my stepmother didn't kill Ingeborg, don't you, Otto?' she said in a choked voice.

'Do I?' His face was bland, handsomely bland, the fencing scar a pretty decoration on his cheek. 'Are you saying it was Lorenz after all?'

'No, not Lorenz either.'

'Then what *do* you mean?'

Victoria glanced around her, suddenly anxious. There was no one in sight, the only sign of life a heavily laden dray drawn by six horses emerging from the foundry gates. It was no place to throw down a challenge.

'Oh, nothing. It doesn't matter.'

'I think it does matter!'

Otto caught at her arm, his fingers like an iron clamp, and the next instant he had pulled her into the narrow, dark entry of a tenement building. It was very dim inside, with a foetid smell, and Victoria stumbled over some loose bricks on the boarded floor.

'Otto, let me go,' she protested. 'What do you think you're doing?'

His grip relaxed, but he stood solidly between her and the doorway. She knew there was no escape, and all at once she did not care. She flung at him recklessly, 'It was you who killed Ingeborg, wasn't it? What I can't understand is *why* you did it. What possible reason did you have?'

There was a long pause, then he blustered, 'You're talking rot! How am I supposed to have been on that train when I was still at the schloss at the time it left Eisenbad?'

'Very easily, though I've only just realized it. You were so sure of yourself that you even stopped to talk to me. You even invited me to go for a drive with you, knowing very well that I'd never accept. How many minutes did it take you to reach Kahlstein, Otto?'

In the shadowed light she saw his eyes glint.

'You'd have a job to prove anything, especially in the face of your stepmother's confession.'

'I could invalidate that confession very easily, if I chose.'

'How?' Otto was clearly shaken, but when she did not answer he went on triumphantly, 'But you wouldn't dare to, would you, Victoria, because it would topple your precious Lorenz from his pedestal. He'd be finished if old man Czernin discovered that he isn't his grandson. I've been wondering if you knew about it.'

'How did *you* find out?' she breathed.

'On the day it all happened, in the afternoon. I went to find myself a cool spot out of that damned wind to have a quiet snooze, and ended up in the little gallery above the pavilion, where I could chuck off most of my clothes. I was asleep and I roused to hear voices down below. I was tickled pink to discover that it was my revered parent trying to seduce your stepmother. Franziska held out gamely, though it was clear she was sorely tempted. As their conversation grew more heated I kept picking up interesting titbits of information. It came as quite a shock to learn that I shouldn't be calling Lorenz "cousin" after all, but "brother". My bastard brother! One of many, I'll wager, but the others didn't have his luck. It's a fascinating story, Victoria. Have you known it all along?'

'Franziska told me when she lay dying.'

'I realized, of course, why she wrote that letter of confession and took poison – to protect her darling son. And I suppose Lorenz really believed it was Franziska who killed Ingeborg. It all seemed to have worked out quite neatly for me ... until this afternoon.'

'Why did you kill Ingeborg?' Victoria asked again.

'It was a pure accident,' he said. 'I suppose I might as well tell you the lot, now that you know so much. My first thought was what a pleasure it would be to watch Lorenz squirm when I flung in his face the truth of his origins. But then it struck me that with his curious sense of morality, he'd be likely to go straight to old man Czernin and spill the beans, and where would we all be then? So I decided on Ingeborg instead. Knowing what I knew would give me a nice weapon to use against her.'

'What do you mean, weapon?'

Otto shrugged his shoulders, and eased the sword at his hip. 'She needed putting in her place, that one! Nobody would guess it from looking at her and the way she carried on, but when it came to the point she was frost-bitten.' He broke off, and shot Victoria a look. 'I suppose you knew that Ingeborg and I—'

'Yes, I knew.'

'Even though she hated Lorenz, she could never resist rubbing it in that he was the one who held the purse strings and that I was living on his charity. I could hardly wait to see her expression when I announced that her highly respected husband was merely my father's by-blow, with no claim to his noble title or to old Czernin's fortune.'

'So you told Ingeborg?'

'Yes. I waylaid her when she arrived home from riding, and said we must have a talk. But she was very jumpy about being seen exchanging more than a few words with me since that last spot of bother over the bonfire. So we made a rendezvous away from the house. She was meeting some friends at Dommayer's that evening, and we arranged that she should hop off the train at Kahlstein where I'd meet her with the phaeton and we'd drive somewhere quiet – in her domino cloak with the hood up she wouldn't be recognized. The plan was that she'd catch the next train on to Hietzing. Only when she heard what I'd got to say, it didn't quite work out like that. Ingeborg was really rattled, you see. She was terrified that I couldn't be relied on to keep my mouth shut about Lorenz.' Caught up in the excitement of his story, Otto's breath came faster. 'Do you know what, Victoria? Ingeborg tried to do me in. She actually tried to kill me!'

'*Ingeborg* tried to kill *you*?'

'She wanted to make damn sure that I'd never be able to reveal what I knew. The cunning bitch thought it would be easy. She got me to drive hell for leather back to the station – so she wouldn't miss the next train, she said – and when we took a sharp bend onto the bridge over the river, she gave me an almighty shove. I was supposed to fall out and crash against the stone parapet, while she snatched the reins. Only unfortunately for her I clung on, and she went flying instead. One of the rear wheels passed right over her.'

Victoria shuddered 'She was dead?'

'As a doornail! I was in quite a state about what to do, I've got to admit, until I realized that as far as anyone knew she'd still be aboard the seven-twenty-eight to Hietzing, so my best plan was to make it look as if Ingeborg had fallen from the train onto the tracks.'

Victoria stared at him in horror. 'You mean you carried her body all the way to where it was found?'

'Quite a problem, that was, in my lightweight phaeton. In the end I managed to prop her up in the seat beside me, and I kept my arm around her while I drove with one hand. It was getting darkish by then, and with the domino hood hiding her face she looked alive enough. When I found a nice deserted spot by the railway, I laid the body across the line. I didn't wait for a train.'

Victoria felt sickened by this macabre story. In a shred of a whisper, she asked, 'How on earth could you do such a thing?'

'It's wonderful what any of us can do when we must, dear girl! I felt pretty terrible by then, I don't mind telling you, and I went to a *Heurigen* inn at Hietzing and got well and truly plastered. I've had a few nightmares since then.'

'No one would have noticed,' Victoria said huskily. 'You've been acting as if you hadn't a care in the world.'

'A fellow's got to keep his pecker up, eh? It came as a real shock when the police started suspecting Lorenz because he'd been on the same train, but there was nothing I could do about it. Then, mercifully, Franziska saved the situation.'

'And you're willing to let an innocent woman take the blame for what *you* did?'

'Well, it wouldn't help Franziska for me to pop up and confess all, would it? Let sleeping dogs lie, that's my motto.'

He broke off. Suddenly the jauntiness was gone and his voice became weighted with menace. 'The trouble is, though, you don't seem to share that opinion, my dear Victoria. And I can't allow you to go around wrecking everything, now can I?'

Terror snatched at her heart as she realized that Otto meant to kill her. Such a man, trained to kill without mercy, would feel few scruples at quenching out her life, and there was small risk to himself. It would be so easy for him here, in this wilderness in the midst of the great bustling city. No one knew she had come to this district, no one knew that Otto was with her. Probably months would pass before the builders uncovered a woman's body beneath the debris, and her disappearance and death would remain an unsolved mystery.

'Believe me, sweet girl, I deplore the necessity,' Otto muttered, sounding genuinely regretful. 'But you leave me with no option. You have forced my hand by all your clever deductions.'

For several long, drawn-out moments they stared intently at one another in the dim, dusty light of this half-demolished tenement building, locked in a silent bond of inevitability. Victoria's limbs were rigid, frozen in panic, but as Otto's hands came slowly to close around her throat, the instinct for self-preservation surged through her. She thrust at him swiftly with all her strength, and as he staggered back she dodged out of his reach. Turning, she saw that an inner doorway led into a passage, and a glimmer of daylight pierced the gloom from somewhere beyond. Another way out? She seized this one desperate hope and went clambering wildly across the piles of bricks and rubble that littered the floor, her skirts clutched up with both hands. Behind her, Otto was cursing as he came in pursuit, and it seemed certain she would be captured within seconds.

But she had broken through into the open now, and was racing with a speed spurred by fear between high brick walls. Ahead she could see the roadway leading to the foundry gates, and surely there, in full view of people, she would be safe. But it still seemed an impossibly distant goal . . .

Above the strained gasping of her breath and the thudding of her heart, she could hear Otto's footsteps pounding, terrifyingly close now and gaining on her every instant. She made a final frenzied effort. Then, as she rounded the corner and reached the metalled roadway, she saw a four-horse mail coach hurtling toward her. Heedless of the danger she flung herself forward into its path, her arms outstretched in frantic appeal. There was a smothered shout of warning and a wild scrabbling of hooves as the coachman veered aside, desperately trying to avoid her. She felt a violent jolt against her hip as she was struck and flung headlong to the ground. In the blurred confusion of sound she heard a man's scream, cut off abruptly, and she closed her eyes. She knew what this meant, without the need to witness it. Otto had suffered the same horrible fate as Ingeborg – crushed beneath the remorseless weight of a carriage wheel.

19

Unlike Ingeborg, though, Otto had not died an instantaneous death.

The minutes following the accident were a blurred nightmare to Victoria. With the help of the mailcoach driver she attempted to struggle to her feet, but giddiness overcame her and she was forced to desist. Otto lay very still, feeble moans escaping from his throat, and Victoria's one coherent thought was that Lorenz must be sent for. She gabbled out an urgent message for him to one of the onlookers who had sprung from nowhere, before her senses reeled from the throbbing pain in her side and she fell back limply.

To her wandering state of mind it seemed that Lorenz was there on the instant, quicker than possible, kneeling at her side and begging for reassurance that she was not seriously hurt. While they awaited the medical help that had been summoned by telephone, she tried to parry his questions about the accident – how it had come about and why she was here in this district, with Otto. But in the end, despairing of finding an evasion that would satisfy him, she blurted out the truth – that Otto had been pursuing her, intent on killing her, because she had discovered it was he who had killed Ingeborg. Nothing seemed to matter any more . . .

Stretcher bearers arrived and took Otto away to the infirmary wing at the barracks. Then, with a doctor in attendance, Lorenz carried Victoria to his office at the foundry, where a careful examination confirmed that there were no injuries beyond a certain bruising. She was given a small glass of cognac as a restorative, and told to rest quietly for the present on a couch hastily improvised from cushions spread across two chairs. Lorenz departed to see how Otto was faring, leaving her meanwhile in the care of his elderly bookkeeper. But before he went, she thought to tell him that Liesl would be waiting for her at the Südbahnhof.

'I'll send someone,' he promised.

He was gone more than an hour, and when he returned he brought the news that Otto was dead. 'There were severe internal injuries,' he said, 'and nothing could be done to save him.'

Victoria nodded, not speaking. Was it the best thing, perhaps – for Otto, for them all? Numbly she was aware that it was wrong to harbour such thoughts, yet how could she avoid them?

'Do you feel able to talk now?' Lorenz asked. 'There is so much still to be explained.'

She nodded again and rose to her feet, glancing away to avoid the penetrating look in his dark eyes.

'It seems that you have been carrying a heavy burden these past days,' he said after a moment. 'The knowledge about me, my origins.'

'Otto told you?'

Lorenz walked to the window overlooking a central courtyard, which was silent and deserted now that the day's work was over. Victoria watched him, fearful of what could no longer be kept secret, of what must now be voiced between them.

'Yes, Otto told me,' he said in a leaden tone. 'Although very weak, he seemed to delight in the telling, as if he were releasing the pent-up hatred of years. Otto had his revenge on me before he died.'

Victoria took an impulsive step toward him. 'Lorenz, you mustn't be—'

He spun round to face her. 'What mustn't I be? Upset? Bitter? Angry? What do any of these small emotions mean to a man who discovers that his entire existence, everything he has ever purported to be, is based upon a deliberate fraud?'

'I believe Franziska thought she was doing it for the best,' she whispered.

Lorenz's eyes hardened, then he made a small, helpless gesture. 'It's not for me to pass judgment. She must have been very young. And she has more than atoned for whatever blame she deserved by her sacrifice for me – her needless sacrifice!' He passed his hands across his face. 'What a terrible waste!'

She sat silent, unable to find adequate words. Lorenz said heavily, 'I only know what little Otto gasped out to me. You must give me the rest of the story, Victoria.'

'Not now!' she protested.

'Yes, here and now! There is nothing more that needs to be done at the moment. Otto's father – *my* father – is at the barracks. And Liesl, too. While we have the chance to be alone I want to hear everything you can tell me.'

And so, haltingly, while twilight gathered outside and the gas brackets hissed their incandescent light over the simple, unpretentious furniture of his office, Victoria related all she knew: what she had learned from Franziska as she lay dying, what had been said in the billiard-room by Baron Heinrich and his brother, and all that Otto had told her about the night of Ingeborg's death. Lorenz listened in silence, and she could sense the rage he felt.

'My God!' he said, when at last she had done. 'Those two have got something to account for – the man who fathered me, and his brother.'

'What will you do?' she faltered. 'Lorenz, you mustn't let this break you. It need not be the end.'

He looked at her wonderingly. 'The end? No, Victoria, it's not the end, not for us. All day today I have been cursing my ineptitude last night. I was determined that this evening I would have the truth from you.'

'The truth?'

'I knew that you loved me, despite all you said. Someone, or something, was making you deny it, and I intended to discover the reason. Now I understand.'

He stretched out his hands to her and she went to him. Lorenz held her gently with her head pressed to his shoulder. For minutes they said nothing, yet she felt his strength and his love flowing through to her. Then a thought darted into her mind which made her shiver. She drew back from him a little.

'What about Herr Czernin?'

'That's the aspect that concerns me most of all. I love the old man, and I can't bear the thought of causing him so much grief.'

'If only it were possible to keep it from him,' she said with a sigh. 'But I suppose he will have to know.'

'Yes, there can be no question about that. And I shall not delay, I'll tell him this evening, as gently as I can.' Lorenz was sombre, then he said with a faint smile, 'You will not be marrying the Czernin heir, Victoria.'

She looked at him gravely. 'Do you think that matters to me?'

'If I did, you would not be the woman I want for my wife. But we shan't starve, my darling. I may not be the man I have always believed myself to be, but I have skills and abilities that cannot be taken from me. I'm a first-class engineer, able to earn a living anywhere – anywhere in the world.'

Victoria felt exalted by the pride that was in him, despite the savage blow he had taken. She let her love shine in her eyes, and Lorenz drew her close again and kissed her on the lips.

'We had better leave now,' he said at last, reluctantly. 'There is so much to be done tonight, so many things to be sorted out.'

Against all their fears, old Milos stood up to the shock of Lorenz's news with great resilience. The following morning he sent a message asking Victoria to go to his suite.

'I suppose Lorenz has told you what my wishes are?' he began.

'Yes, Herr Czernin, and I think it is wonderfully generous of you.'

He held up a trembling hand in protest. 'My reasons, my dearest girl, are entirely selfish. At first, when Lorenz brought me this shocking revelation, I felt a broken man. Then all at once I realized that I had lost very little compared with what I could still have, and what I stood to gain. Lorenz's character is unchanged, he is the same person I have always known. And little Emil – a sweet innocent child – should I suddenly feel nothing for them both after so much love between us?' He blinked his watery old eyes. 'And one of my fondest wishes is to be granted me. I shall have you as my grand-daughter, Victoria. I shall live to see Lorenz truly happy at last. It would give me so much pleasure if only – no, it is too much to ask. I cannot expect it.'

'Tell me, please.'

He said shyly, 'I should feel so proud if Lorenz would consent to adopt my name.'

'I think the pride would be Lorenz's,' she said. 'We will ask him together, this evening.'

As an immediate, temporary measure, Lorenz leased a furnished house in Vienna, near the Peterskirche, where the four of them would live – Lorenz and herself, old Milos and little Emil, together with Josef and Hannchen. Two days before they were due to move, Victoria raised the question of Liesl's future, which had been causing her concern.

'She swears, Lorenz, that once we have left the schloss, she will not continue to live under the same roof as her parents.'

'Then she must come with us,' he said at once. 'After all, Liesl is my sister.'

'Will her father raise any objections?'

'You may safely leave my father to me! I think that he and his brother are only too relieved to know that no action is to be taken against them, though in future they will have to face a very different mode of life. No, there will be no difficulty about Liesl coming with us.' Lorenz smiled at her. 'Until we are married, she can be your chaperon. Ours will be a highly unconventional household, you realize that?'

'Oh, convention!' she said dismissively.

It was a relief to get away from the poisoned atmosphere at the schloss, and they soon settled into the house in Goldschmiedgasse. Andrej von Hroch was a frequent visitor there, and when he came to dine with them he looked strikingly handsome in his student's gala uniform of black velvet cloak and white trousers. He and old Milos struck up an immediate friendship, and they spent hours talking about their common homeland. Now and then, breaking all the rules, Emil was allowed to stay up for dinner with the adults. This he regarded as a supreme treat, though he usually fell asleep before the meal was finished and had to be carried up to bed.

It was a strange interlude, those waiting days when autumn slipped into winter. Victoria was possessed of a new serenity, yet she felt an impatient longing for what was to come.

She and Lorenz were to be married in the week before Christmas.

Victoria frequently took flowers to lay upon her stepmother's grave. One morning in late November she paid a visit to the cemetery with an armful of chrysanthemums, huge, sun-gold blooms that Franziska would have loved, for yellow had been her favourite colour. As she walked the wide gravelled paths, Victoria buried her face in the soft petals to inhale their musky scent.

Turning the corner by a line of cypress trees she saw a man standing at Franziska's grave, and she caught her breath in surprise. Lorenz was bareheaded, his dark hair ruffled by the wind. He heard her footsteps and turned to smile at her.

'I've wondered who else has been putting flowers here,' she said. 'I thought it must be you, but I wasn't sure.'

'She was my mother,' he said simply.

Victoria stooped to gather the withered blooms she had placed there a few days earlier, then laid down the new tribute beside the sheaf of bronze and white chrysanthemums Lorenz had brought. They stood together for a minute or two with their heads bowed, then turned to go.

At the cemetery gates, Lorenz offered her his arm. 'I propose playing truant from the foundry for a little while longer. Will you have lunch with me, Vicky?'

'It sounds a very agreeable suggestion, Herr Czernin.'

He laughed softly. 'I like to be called that. Odd that a name to which I have no birthright should seem to fit me better than the noble one I grew up with. How ordinary you will be, though, just plain Frau Czernin.'

'Ordinary?' she said, giving his arm a squeeze.

They lunched at a small Hungarian restaurant near the Borse, on saddle of venison and Tokay wine, to the background of a Zigeuner trio. Afterwards, in the muted daylight of the winter afternoon, Lorenz summoned a *fiacre*.

'There is something I want to show you,' he said mysteriously. 'I was planning to suggest it for tomorrow, but today seems a better idea.'

They joined the Ringstrasse at Schottentor where the slender spires of the Votivkirche were a delicate tracery against the rose-flushed western sky. Driving past the University, the gothic Rathaus, the white Parliament House which echoed the style of a Grecian temple, they came to the Kaiserforum and the new Hofburg wing. On their other hand rose the magnificent matching buildings of the art and natural history museums. Then on along the wide boulevard, its double avenue of linden trees bare-branched now, to the Opera. In Kärntnerring Victoria glimpsed the Conservatoire, and it caused her scarcely a pang. Lorenz loved to listen to her at the piano, imperfect though she was, and that was sufficient.

With a jingle of harness the cab drew up in a leafy square somewhere behind the Stadtpark, and Lorenz helped her to alight. They stood together on the pavement looking up at an elegant, three-storey house with a central pediment above the pillared portico. At each of the windows was a small balcony with decorative wrought-iron work.

'Will this do for us?' Lorenz asked.

'Oh, it's beautiful!'

Lorenz had the keys, and they went inside. The empty rooms echoed hollowly as they walked around, but Victoria could picture it furnished – a charming, gracious home for them all. Her mind whirled with plans – the salon in cream and gold, the dining-room a soft shade of green with some paintings of the new Secessionist school, a study for Lorenz. Upstairs, a fine suite for Herr Czernin with a view across the park to the spire of St Stephen's Cathedral, a nursery for Emil, a bright, airy bedroom with long windows for Liesl. Then they came to the room which would be their own – a spacious apartment in the shape of a double cube, with a delicately-moulded frieze and silk-panelled walls.

Lorenz unlatched one of the French windows and they stepped onto the balcony. Below them in the quiet street the *Fiaker* puffed contentedly at a long cheroot as he sat waiting for them, a rug tucked around his knees. Opposite in the square an elderly couple strolled arm in arm beneath the trees, and two children were playing hide-and-seek under the watchful eye of their nursemaid. Very faintly, borne on the wind, came the lilting thrum of a waltz, a concert for a winter's afternoon at the Kursalon.

'I remember a snatch of song about Vienna that Franziska once sang to me,' Victoria said. 'How did it go? *The city where my dreams come true.*'

Lorenz slipped his arm round her shoulders and drew her close to him.

'There is no denying that, my darling. For all its faults – its many faults – Vienna does possess a kind of magic.'